CLEO BROWNE

Tank – Devils Rose MC Book Four

First published by Meihana Pinker Ltd 2025

This novel is entirely a work of fiction. The names, characters and incidents portrayed in it are the work of the author's imagination. Any resemblance to actual persons, living or dead, events or localities is entirely coincidental.

Cleo Browne has no responsibility for the persistence or accuracy of URLs for external or third-party Internet Websites referred to in this publication and does not guarantee that any content on such Websites is, or will remain, accurate or appropriate.

First edition

This book was professionally typeset on Reedsy.
Find out more at reedsy.com

Contents

Trigger Warning

This book deals with badassery in all its forms.
Please be aware that in order for these characters to be badass,
this book contains content that some readers may find
disturbing,
such as a dangerous thong, graphic descriptions of violence
and torture, and R18 sex scenes.

Hey Readers!

Thank you for choosing to pick up Tank's story!
I always knew Tank was going to be a sweetheart and a softy, I just never knew how much of a softy he'd be until he met Mira.

Shout out to Stoves who was my inspiration for the big, bubbly ADHD romance author.
I hope she does you proud!

Who the heck is that?

Devil's Rose MC

Marx - Pres

Rhodie - VP and Enforcer + Tuesday Tombs (Chewy) Icer

Rider - SAA

Wire - Secretary/Hacker + Remy Wright

Jovie (Wire and Remy's adopted child)

Tank - Member + Mira (Doll) Campbell

Switch - Medic

Judge - Member

Sniper - Member

Fox - Member

Nitro - Member

Savage - Member (ex Death Rider) + Nat

Dex - Member (Ex Death Rider)

Jimmy - Prospect

Takoda - Prospect

Tav - Prospect + Blanche (Pixie)

Niko, Sage, Cove, Elio (Tav and Blanche's children)

Tombs Security

August (Gus) Tombs + Ana Tombs

Jules Tombs
Tav Tombs + Blanche Landry
Niko, Sage, Cove and Elio (Tav and Blanche's children)
Tuesday (Chewy) Tombs + Rhodie
Sidney (Pops) Tombs + Debs Taylor (Mother of Ana)

Bartashev Bratva

Roman Bartashev + Sasha Bartashev (BFF's of Ana)

Prologue

Tank

I have to hand it to Chewy, when she throws a baby shower, she really goes all out. The pregnant women are all perched in their Game of Thrones-eque chairs, complete with dildos where the swords should be. Chewy is wearing her baby gator Chomper in a damn front pack and Lovely is crying over some baby motorcycle boots. So a pretty standard day at DRMC.

"Ah Pres, you have a visitor," Jimmy calls out to Marx, everyones heads turning to the door.

"Moss? Did Chewy invite you?" Pres asks, shaking hands with Sergeant Davies who seems slightly distracted.

"Are those penis decorations?"

"Yup, and a vag cake," Chewy answers.

Sergeant Davies stares at her and then points, "Is that an alligator?"

"Yup. His name's Chomper. Cute, huh?"

He squints at her before shaking himself. "Sorry, Marx, this isn't a social call. I need to take in one of your men."

What the fuck?

Marx stands straight, larger than ever. The men with Ol Ladies all edge closer to their women, the rest of us closing ranks in case shit goes down.

"Who?" Marx demands.

"Tyson Sword. He's been accused of assault and battery."

What. The. Actual. Fuck?

There's an uproar as the room loses it. My stomach drops into my ass, even though I know I haven't been in a fight for fucking years. I work at Devil's Big Tow, live at the clubhouse, and rarely go out looking for strange. The amount of opportunities I would have to beat someone to pulp is next to nil.

Marx lets out a piercing whistle, calling us to order. "Tank?"

I walk toward Davies and my Pres, coming to a stop in front of my friend and leader. "I didn't do whatever I've been accused of."

"I know, brother. We'll get this sorted out."

Pres turns to glare at Sergeant Davies who raises his hands, placating him. "I know Johnny, the source sounds sketchy, but we have to investigate no matter if it's a nuisance call or not."

"Take care of my man, you hear me? Anything less and I'll be coming for you," Pres says in all seriousness, holding Davies' gaze.

A lesser man would have shit themselves by now. Instead, Davies just smiles. "I know you will."

He turns to leave, indicating I take the lead, not even cuffing me. "Oh Marx?" Davies swings around once more, leaving me to wait for him. "Better call Maxine, so she can have my balls. Again." He rolls his eyes and then gestures to the door.

"Wire?"

"On it already, Pres," Wire replies, the phone held up to his ear presumably on the phone with his Momma.

Davies nods his head at them both and follows me out the door. I get a feeling the man knows this is bullshit, but is just doing his job. That's why I don't give him too much shit and decide to listen like a good little boy and follow all the instructions.

"I'll try to get this sorted as soon as, OK?" he says, coming up alongside me before stopping abruptly.

I know exactly what's stopped him in his tracks.

"What's with the sand and dildos?" He asks, pointing to the area Chewy has cordoned off.

"It's Chewy's 'dongsai' garden."

He stares at me like I'm nuts, so I shrug in reply.

"Wait, Chewy is Rhodes Paxton's Ol Lady, right?" I nod at him, "Sidney Tombs' granddaughter? The one with the gator?" I nod again and realization dawns across his face. "It's all beginning to make sense now."

"Can we-?" I ask, wanting to get this shit over and done with.

"Yeah, of course." We move toward his cruiser, and he indicates the passenger side. "I'll let you ride up front. DRMC is full of good men, no need to sit in the back. Besides, I don't think I got all the vomit out from earlier." He grins at me and gets in. Either he knows this is all shit, or he's the worst sergeant on the face of the earth.

We travel to the station in silence. If I'm honest, I'm not a big talker anyway, but riding shotgun in a police car on my way to being booked for something I have no idea about? Yeah, words ain't coming easy.

We pull into the small station, Davies studying me for a

moment. "Right, let's get you booked."

He doesn't waste much time after that. The easy going Sergeant Davies replaced with a serious professional. Paperwork gets done, I'm given a rundown of how everything is going to work and the next thing I know I'm sitting in a holding cell minus my wallet, my knives and my boots. Staring down at my feet, I decide that I'll purchase new socks when I get outta here.

"Oh, hey, what are ya in for?" A peppy voice to my left asks. "Lemme guess. Hmmm, did you murder someone?"

Letting out a sigh, I don't even look up. "Do you think it'd be a good idea to make small talk with a murderer?"

"So you DID murder someone? I knew it! How did you do it? Gun? Knife? Expanding foam in the rear end?"

My head snaps to the side. "What the fuck?"

"What?" Wide green eyes stare back at me. "People never think to use mundane DIY products in their murders. It's always the same unimaginative carp."

"Did you just –"

"Yes sir, clean mouth here. No cursing, that's what my nana taught me. Well, no cursing out loud. In my books, I curse all the time."

I raise an eyebrow at her, and she raises one back. This woman is probably crazy. Which would make sense because she's the hottest woman I've laid eyes on in a long ass time. She's sitting on the crappy wooden bench in the cell next to me, so I can't tell how tall she is exactly, but from what I can see she's curvy as hell. Big tits, cleavage peeking out from the top of her pinup type dress, thick thighs, soft belly. Blonde curls, big green eyes and pink pouty lips.

"I write romance novels. But not the usual stuff. My ones

have murder in them. Sexy murder romance. Or romantic, murder sex." She frowns at this.

"So, which one is it?"

Her head snaps up as if she forgot I asked her something. She squints at me, then waves a hand dismissively. "All the above. Maybe?" She shrugs and keeps talking. "So, was I right? Did you murder someone?"

The amount of words that keep spilling out of her is a little overwhelming, but I can't imagine she's going to be quiet anytime soon and I have no idea how long I'll be in here for, so I may as well make the best of it.

"I was accused of assaulting someone."

She nods as if that all makes sense. "I mean I get it. Your hands are the size of hams. The ones with the bones in."

"Thanks?"

"You're welcome," she beams at me. "Wow, you're really good looking. Such a sharp jaw. I bet you could grate cheese on that jawline. A total grater face. And your body looks like the muscles are really meaty. Like whole slabs of muscles instead of little piddly individual ones. What size are you exactly? Like how big are you? Height, weight, all that stuff. You'd make a great book character."

"Excuse me?" I gape at her. There is no way in hell I'm going to be a sexy murder romance character. Instead of giving her my stats I decide to distract her. "So, what are you in for? Did you murder someone?"

She snorts as if that's the funniest thing in the world, "Puhlease. I'd never get caught if I did. But no, I'm in for harassment and indecent exposure."

My brows hit my hairline. This somewhat sweet looking, maybe crazy lady went down for harassment and indecent exposure?

She lets out a sigh, her breasts heaving under her pretty dress, "Yeah, I approached a man, big, like yourself. I wanted to know if he'd be strong enough to lift me up and bang me against a wall. With clothes on. It was strictly for research, to see if it could be done. Anyway, I may have gotten a little dog and bone-ish and may have not taken no for an answer. So I followed him a little pleading my case and then, THEN when I finally decided to give up I slipped on an actual banana peel, ramming into him, taking him down landing with my face in his junk."

I try not to laugh at the visual, but she keeps going.

"And to make matters worse this dress was not built for falling and my girls popped clean out of the top."

"Hence the indecent exposure?"

"Bingo." Her shoulders slump a little at this before she brightens. "Hey! So we're both in the same boat! Wrongly accused! This could make a good story."

She pulls a notepad and pen out of that amazing cleavage of hers and starts mumbling to herself, taking notes.

"Tyson? You're up," Sergeant Davies steps up to my cage and unlocks it, looking over at the blonde next door. "Back again, huh, Mira?" He smiles at the bombshell still muttering to herself.

She looks up at him before grinning, "Yeah. You know how it goes." Her eyes flick to me standing outside my cell. "Good luck Biker Man!"

"You too, Writer Lady."

Mira

"Well, there's all your paperwork, and now you're free to go." Officer Robbie says, pushing all my belongings across the desk.

"Thanks, Officer Robbie." I reply, dropping my ladybird ballet flats on the floor and stuffing my feet into them.

"You know you really should call me Officer Graham, Mira."

"Why? You were Robbie when we went to school with each other, and let's face it, I see you more now than I ever did at school." I shrug.

"Yeah, maybe you should think about your life choices," He replies, his pale blonde brow raised.

"It's all in the name of research, good sir."

He shakes his head at me as I hook my handbag over my arm, spin on my cute little flats and flounce out of the station, coming to a stop on the steps when the first drop of rain hits me. Looking up at the threatening sky, I let out a sigh. Of course I'd get kinda arrested and then have to walk home in the rain in my best dress. The one that goes a little see through when it's wet. On the day that I had to wear "laundry panties". The ones with busted elastic. The ones my thick thighs have to keep up.

I let out a growl and shake my fist in the air, a deep voice interrupting my silent cursing.

"What are you doing?"

I don't even turn toward the voice. I know it's the big, sexy, wrongly accused biker. I committed that voice to memory to call upon during private times.

"I'm cursing the weather gods."

"Why?"

"Because I have to walk home in this weather and my dress is a little see-through when it gets wet and I have bad underpants on."

"Um. Right. Is there anyone you can call?"

"Nope. They're all dead. I didn't do it."

He inhales sharply before coughing. "Wow. OK. Do you want a ride?"

I whip around to stare at him. "Like on your bike? You bet your sweet fanny I do!" I shuffle around in excitement, looking for said bike, seeing nothing but a blacked out SUV

His lips tip up when I turn to him with a frown. "Sorry babe, my brother is picking me up. Come on, let's get you home before the rain really comes in and we get an eyeful."

"It's probably two eyes full, but alright. I guess."

He gestures for me to go first and I approve. Not many men these days have such manners, so it's nice to find the giant, blonde biker does. His dark blonde hair is shaved around the sides and the longer top length is pulled back into a small ponytail thing. Not hipster, more utilitarian to keep it out of the way. He also has super kind eyes and hands the size of boxing gloves. I bet he could do loads of damage with those things. He opens the door to the SUV for me and I climb in the back before he pulls his bulk into the front passenger seat.

"Writer Lady, Judge. Judge, Writer Lady,"

"Hi Bald Biker Man," I wave to our driver, give him my address and settle back into the nice leather seats.

I watch as the town whizzes by the window, content to think through the upcoming scenes in the book I'm writing. It doesn't take much for me to fall into my own world, lines of dialogue running through my mind.

"Yo, Writer Lady, this your place?"

Blinking, I realize we're idling outside my grandmother's

cute little cottage. Well, mine now. She left it to me when she passed away and I love it here.

"Whoa, that was fast! I was away with the fairies that whole time. Well, thanks bikers, I'll see you around," I say, unbuckling my belt and hopping down out of the SUV.

I make my way up my cute little path, weaving through the funny garden ornaments dotted around the place.

"Wait!"

I spin around, startled by the big biker shouting at me.

"Your door is open. Did you leave it like that?" He's right next to me and he smells distractingly good. He's also bigger up close than I thought he would be. I'm a tall woman and I only come up to his shoulder. He could most definitely lift me up I decide. "Hey, was that you? That left the door open?"

Oh, yeah, the door. I squint at it and go through my morning routine, trying to remember if I locked it or not.

"I'm gonna be honest with you, I'm not sure. But it'll be fine. This is a quiet neighborhood and all that." I shrug and carry on up the steps when I'm stopped by a massive warm hand wrapping around my chubby upper arm.

"Ah, there's a bleeding box on your doorstep." He points at what does actually appear to be a bleeding box. Biker Man moves me out of the way and steps up to it, flicking one of the flaps open with a penknife he pulled out of who knows where. "Looks like meat. Butcher meat."

"Sounds about right. I'm an author that writes sexy murder. I get sent all sorts of weird and wonderful stuff from my readers," I give him a shrug before peering into the box. "Oh yay! Liver. My cat LOVES liver." I collect up the box and head toward my open door.

"Wait! Wait here. I'll do a quick check of your house, make

sure it's safe."

"Dude, it's fine, trust me." I decline his offer but he doesn't listen, cautiously walking into my home.

I turn toward the SUV and Judge, the man waiting in the idling car. He gives me a questioning look so I give him a shrug and a smile. I would wave but my hands are full with a leaking box of liver.

"Everything looks clear inside. I think you'll be safe." Biker man frowns down at the box in my hands.

"Thanks, mister, although I could have told you that. These types of things happen to me all the time. Leave the door open, the taps running, things on the stove. Busy, mind you see." I can't tap my temple to illustrate, so I just dart my eyes toward my temple a couple of times. He frowns down at me like I'm a crazy person, then turns to walk down the steps.

Once at the bottom, he turns to look up at me. "Hey, if you need anything, just call the Devil's Big Tow and ask for Tank."

"Sure thing. Have a good day. Oh, and thanks for the ride!" I smile huge so he knows I'm grateful. I need to get rid of them both because I've just had the best idea and I need to get it on paper, stat.

"See ya round, Writer Lady." He throws up a wave as he gets into the SUV and they pull away, leaving me to the new book series forming in my mind.

Chapter 1

Tank

I head past the empty reception desk piled high with papers and throw myself down on the leather couch in the break room of Devil's Big Tow.

"You all good, man?" Judge asks, leaning against the door jamb, light bouncing off his bald head.

"Fucking exhausted. When did we get so busy?"

Judge nods sagely, which doesn't answer my question either way. We're a two-man business, one goes out on a job, the other mans the desk until they get back and we swap. Well, that's what's meant to happen. The past few months we've both been out on jobs nonstop and the reception is now a filing desk. At least the papers are in neat piles. All they're waiting for is one of us to catch a break so we can actually file them where they're meant to go.

"On the upside, you've been too busy to be arrested again," Judge mumbles.

"Ain't that the truth," I sigh, resting my head back on the couch.

Rose Grove PD had nothing on me, but they had to go through all the formalities bullshit. They couldn't tell us who laid the complaint, but whoever it was wanted to mess with me. Or us. It's hard to tell, the past year we've had people lining up with hard ons to take us down. It's a total fucking mystery why. We aren't one percenters. Shit, we don't even move anything worth their while, unless they want to get into delivering moonshine to vets.

"The Computa's will figure it out, dude."

"Yeah, I know. It's just messing with me. Like who the hell did I piss off that would want me in prison?" I shake my head. Maybe if I bounce my pea brain around enough it'll give me something, anything that could help me figure it out.

A massive shadow blocks out what little light we have back here in the breakroom. "Come on brother, let's clock out and take a ride."

Closing my eyes and taking a deep breath, I let it out and give my brother a nod. Nothing is better than feeling the wind in your face and now that the weather is getting a little warmer and the days a little longer, it sounds like the perfect form of therapy.

We quickly go about shutting down the office computer, turning off lights and setting the security alarm before mounting our bikes. My matte black softail with chrome detailing has been with me since I got out of the marines; the one constant in my life until I found the DRMC brotherhood. I didn't have it as bad as some of my brothers - Wire, Sniper and Judge lost good men when they were posted overseas, but that doesn't mean I don't struggle sometimes. My bike, Winnie, as I named her, is my solace on a bad day.

The wind flows around me, blowing away all the shit that

fills up my head. By the time we reach the clubhouse my mood is seriously lifted, and continues to lift as soon as I walk in and smell the scent of fresh cookies wafting through the air.

"Don't even think about it." Rider says, stepping in front of me, stopping me getting closer to the heavenly scent.

"Rider, move."

He shakes his head sadly, as if he would love to move, but he can't. "No can do big man. You go in there and those cookies are destroyed. Never to be seen or worshipped again. Mama Debs has only made four dozen. There's not enough."

I raise my brow. There are a dozen members. The Ol Ladies never eat the cookies, or so they say, and the kids often have their own batch that Mama Debs makes.

"That's enough for four each."

"Nope. Sorry."

I try to sidestep him but the lanky bastard is light on his feet, easily gliding from side to side getting in my way.

"How the hell are you so light on your feet?" I grumble, hands on him now, trying to move him aside.

"Years of ballroom dancing. Elderly widows pay well when you're a handsome boy and good on your feet." He grunts, trying to hold me back.

"Tank, think fast!" Judge calls, lobbing three cookies in my direction.

My hand goes up and they land gently in the palm of my hand, still hot.

"You cheating shit!" Rider yells, rushing at Judge before deciding his better move would be to get himself into the kitchen for cookies seeing as all the brothers are making their way in there. "ONE EACH YOU GREEDY FUCKS!"

Chuckling to myself I drop down onto the leather couch that's seen better days, lean my head back and chew on my mouth-watering cookies.

"Yo Tank! Jimmy says there's a woman at the gate for you." Rhodie yells, phone pressed to his chest.

"A woman? I don't know any woman," I answer, staring at him in confusion.

He says something to Jimmy then pulls the phone back, "Her name is Mira," I shake my head at him. It's not ringing any bells. "Tall, blonde. Said she's a friend of the 'wrongly accused big blonde sex machine biker man," His lips twitch and the nosey bastards in the kitchen make their way into the common room, acting as if they weren't listening to Rhodie and my conversation. "She said you were holding cell neighbors."

"A criminal woman! Criminal women are hot," Rider says around a mouthful of cookie.

Letting out a sigh, I explain the situation. "She's not technically a criminal. She wanted help with research but it went wrong and she got taken in for harassment and indecent exposure."

Everyone looks confused, and I don't blame them. She was very confusing. And memorable. Whenever my thoughts aren't filled with work, DRMC and whoever snitched on me, they're filled with a slightly nuts bouncy blonde. Which would explain why the hell I invited her to Christmas.

"Is she going to be a danger?" Marx asks, standing at the mouth of the hall and snapping me out of my runaway thoughts.

"She doesn't have anyone in her life that I could tell, and she's kinda unusual, but not dangerous." I answer my Pres.

He stares at me for a moment then tips his chin up. "Tell Jimmy to let her in, Rhodie. Let's see what she wants with wrongly accused big blonde sex machine biker man," Marx says with a smirk.

I brace myself for what's coming. I know that whatever it is will be a hell of a trip, that's for sure. In mere moments, she walks in, looking every bit as stunning as I remember. Dressed in purple skin-tight pants that highlight her thick thighs and rounded hips, black and white striped oversized shirt thing hanging off one shoulder, pink high heels and blonde curls pulled into a high ponytail with a sequined yellow bow, it's like a rainbow threw up in the clubhouse.

"There you are, prison buddy! How's life been treating ya? I'm sure you'll be happy to know that I was almost arrested, but I got away with a warning at the scene. Phew! Vegas was a total trip! Oh, hi biker people! Oh look! There are ladies and babies here too!"

She makes a beeline for Nat, Ana and Lovely who have just walked in with their babies.

"Well hello there," Nat says, greeting the new woman. "And who might you be?"

"I'm Mira, a friend of the criminal over there. Practically shared a cell, Shawshank style," she says, waving in my direction.

Mira. I had forgotten that's what Davies called her. I've only really called her as Writer Lady, just like she's only ever called me Biker Man. Or some form of that.

"Tank?" Ana says, drawing Mira's attention again.

She turns to look at me, "Oh, I can see how that works. Yeah, Tank. Me and him go way back," she says, throwing me a wink, those green eyes dancing. She stops looking at me long enough to look around the room. "Whoa, this place is magical. I gotta take some notes." She pulls her notebook out of her cleavage along with her little pencil and starts taking notes, to the amusement of my brothers.

"Good luck brother," Judge murmurs, slapping a hand on my shoulder.

"Mira? Writer Lady?" She holds her long, slender finger in the air for a moment before looking at me.

"Yeah?"

"Mind if we talk?"

"Oh yeah, totally. I bet you're wondering why I'm here, huh? Well, after meeting you I had an idea for a new book, an MC book. First, I had to finish my shifter book. Anyway, then I talked about the MC book with my ladies when I was in Vegas and we all agreed it's a great idea, people will love it. So anyway, you said to call if I needed anything but I figured why waste the phone call when I could just come here? And now that I'm here in this wonderful place," there's a snort that's covered by a cough, "Well, now I think I'm in the exact place I'm meant to be. Hey, do you think I could commandeer this table? I'll set up my laptop here, it's perfect!" she beams up at me and my mouth opens and closes, nothing coming out.

Did she just say she was going to work here? In the club-house? Shaking it off I look toward my Pres, who has a weird as hell look on his face. "Um, an MC book sounds cool and all, but you can't work here. I'm sorry but it's for club members. Pres would never allow it."

Her brows pull together over her bright green eyes and her shoulders slump. Fuck, it's like kicking a puppy. She looks around the room for a moment, her gaze zeroing in on Marx. Not only does he have the word "Pres" under his name patch on his cut, but he exudes leadership. Even someone new to MC's like Mira would recognize he's the boss.

Her eyes narrow slightly before her lips twitch. Marx's eyes widen slightly as they stare at each other for a moment.

"Mr. President, I would like a moment of your time," she says, formally.

"Right this way," Marx gestures toward his office and she follows after him, but not before spinning to look at me, and giving me two thumbs up and a wink.

"Well, don't know about you all, but I like her. Nice work, Tank," Nat smirks.

Mira

OK, so maybe it's not the best idea to turn up to a biker compound out of the blue and demand entry, but I'm sure jail biker guy will remember me. I mean, he did stop by my house to invite me to Christmas dinner. If I wasn't booked in to see my writer lady crew, I would have taken him up on the offer. Not just because he is panty meltingly hot, but since Gran died Christmas dinner for one has been decidedly lame.

"So, who are you looking for?" The kid in charge of the gates asks me.

"The Sexy Wrongly Accused Big Blonde Biker. Tell him I'm here. My name is Mira." I tell him. I'm sure Biker Man will remember me. I mean I felt like we really bonded when we were in those holding cells. He was perhaps the most exciting cell neighbor I've ever had. Most of them are drunks.

"He said you could go on through." The guy whose vest has

"Prospect" on it says, opening the gates. "Just follow the drive and you can park your, um, bike just by the door."

"Thanks buddy." I give him a friendly wave and start pedaling my way to what I'm guessing is the clubhouse.

It's some type of brick monstrosity, like in the olden days it could have been a warehouse or a school or something. The Devil's Rose logo is on the side facing the road and as I get closer I see a long row of motorcycles all parked up, glistening in the sunlight. I stare at them in awe as I glide past them on "Freda." My bike also isn't something to be sniffed at. She's baby blue with a large leather seat with springs for my comfort and she has a basket in the front. She also has a carrier at the back for my groceries and the like and just recently I got new flower shaped spoke decals that glint in the sunshine. She's a real beauty.

I park up next to the front door, flicking down Freda's stand. Should I knock? Or should I just walk in? I mean, they know to expect me so I shrug to myself and push in through the front door. Looking around the room I try to find my biker. Well, not mine per se, but the one I know the best. The one I used to get my foot in the door, and there he is. Our eyes meet across the room and if this was one of my books I'm sure we would both be feeling a jolt at that eye connection. I know I did. His bright blue eyes find mine and he looks momentarily shocked.

"There you are, prison buddy!" I walk toward him with full enthusiasm, but then get sidetracked when I see women and babies arriving.

I take a detour and stop to coo over them. The babies, not the women. Although given that I tower over all three that are standing there, I could probably coo over them too.

"Mira? Writer Lady?" Tank, as I have found out is his name,

calls out to me. I was momentarily distracted. I would like to say that doesn't happen a lot but that would make me a liar and Gran didn't love no liars, let me tell you. "Mind if we talk?"

I wander closer to where he's standing near a leather couch that has seen better days. He has a quiet, solid presence about him, the exact opposite to what I've got going on. By the time I stop in front of him I notice that he's so tall he towers over my 5'9" frame, and I find I like the feeling of being petite. He's so pretty up close, all manly but somehow gentle. His face is nice too. Sure he is ruggedly handsome, with a small scar on his top lip, but he has crinkles next to his eyes which makes me think he smiles regularly. His face is so kind and somehow that underlying kindness reminds me of Gran. She had a similar face, a face well lived in, she would say.

Oh pumpernickel! I stopped listening to what he was saying because he's too darn pretty. Maybe I'll just launch into my intentions for being here. So I do. And I let him have it.

"OK, an MC book sounds cool and all but you can't work here. Pres will never allow it," he says, trying to let me down gently.

Well, I'll just have to have a word with this so-called "Pres." Looking around, my eyes fall on the ridiculously large man standing just inside the doorway. A man that looks very familiar to me even though his name tag is a name I don't recognize.

Deciding to use his formal biker title I call out, "Mr. President? I'd like a word please."

His eyes flash before darting to the men and women behind me before he tips his chin. "Follow me," he replies in the gruff voice I most definitely recognize.

I follow "Marx" down the hall that isn't nearly as dingy and gross as I expected it to be. In all honesty, I had expected the clubhouse to be smelly and dank and covered in old bullet holes and smell like sex and lube, but it's actually really airy and clean smelling, even if it does have bachelor decor. I'll have to make the MC clubhouse in my book way grosser than this one.

"Have a seat, Mira or should I call you Melody Baldwin?" He asks, sitting his very large body into an office chair that looks like it doesn't quite have the structural integrity for a man of his size.

"Aha! I knew you recognized me!" I crow.

"Yeah, so look, about that, my men, they don't know that I read." Marx says, picking at the edge of his desk with his blunt fingernail.

"What do you mean they don't know you read? They think you're illiterate?" My brows furrow as I try to figure that one out. "Did you tell them you can't read to make yourself look cooler?"

"What? No. They don't know I read...your books. The genre you write."

"Ohhhhhh, they don't know you read sexy murder books."

His thick dark brow raises, "They're romance books, Mira."

"Are they? Because I kinda just think of them as sexy murder. I mean, yeah the couples or throuples often fall in love, but the main thread is mystery. Murder. The carnal stuff is just window dressing. Apart from the happy ever afters. Oh, and the declarations of love and the epilogues where they have a million children and live happily ever after." He raises a dark brow at me. Again. He seems to do that a lot. "OK, I guess they're pretty romantic."

"Whatever you want to call it, my men don't know. So if we could keep it between us?" Both brows are raised in question, and I'm thinking that this could be my big bargaining chip. I mean, I want access to the clubhouse to be inspired and get the inner workings and all that jazz. I need to be here for the research aspect. I'm probably less likely to be arrested here too.

"Ohhhh, I hear ya," I dramatically wink at John, or Marx as his leather vest thing says. He frowns back at me. "I keep how I know you hush-hush, and you'll let me hang out here and write? I mainly need to do research and stuff, you know, make sure the action in my book is as realistic as possible."

He frowns even deeper. "You want to set up base here?"

"Yeah. Maybe on one of those long tables. I'll clean all the sex fluids off them." I give him a conspiratorial wink. "You won't even notice I'm here! And I won't write about anyone in particular, because I already have my characters sorted out. I just need to see how a working clubhouse, well, works." I shrug. Then give him the big eyes that I think might make me look imploring. Or nuts, either or.

"I'll let you work in the common room for two weeks. No mention of my men or any of our businesses, I want full confidentiality."

I let him sweat and put on my thinking face. Which is me squinting a little and looking at the ceiling. It's how I write my characters' thinking faces. "So, I get two weeks in the common room in exchange for keeping your little secret?"

He nods. "And signed copies of your next three books."

"How about the next four? I have four MC books planned out. I mean, you are one of my biggest fans." I smile at him.

"That stays between us."

"Of course! So, I get two weeks full access in return for keeping my lips sealed and signed book copies. Deal." I beam and thrust my hand in his direction. He takes it and gives it a gentle squeeze which is somewhat disappointing because I was bringing my handshake A game.

"Deal."

I stand, excited to get settled in immediately.

"Mira?" I turn toward Joh- I mean Marx, "Can I just say that action scene in 'Solar Eclipse of the Heart' was fucking edge of your seat type shit."

"Hey, thanks Mr. President! I hope you enjoyed the pegging scene in there too," I grin as he shudders slightly. Men. Wouldn't know a good thing if it lubed up and entered their back passage. "Well, I better go out there and set up. You won't even notice I'm here!" I give him a curt nod and gather up my things. I have a novel to write.

Chapter 2

Tank

I watch Mira's curvy ass follow Marx down the hall and try to ignore all the looks staring my way. Flopping down onto the couch I rest my head against the back. It's been a day and I have no idea why Mira decided now was the perfect time to resurface. Not that I'm complaining. I think about the unusual woman periodically, and I'm not sure why. Yes, she is gorgeous, but there's more to a person than their looks. Unlike my brothers who loved when we had the club whores and parties where townie women would come to walk on the wild side, I never quite joined them in their excitement for strange women. Don't get me wrong, I'm not, nor have I ever been, a monk. I just need more than a pretty face and a fantastic ass or tits to get me interested. And this woman, Mira? Well, there's no denying she's interesting.

By the time I tip my head up, I'm met with three sets of eyes staring at me. Maybe six if you count all the children in front packs staring at me, along with their moms.

"Can I help you ladies?"

"Yes!" Nat says, taking a seat next to me, jostling little Rosie in the process. "Who was that woman? We need details right now."

"Come on Tank, spill! She was gorgeous AND she looked like a lot of fun. We need more fun women around here," Ana adds. Lovely nods emphatically.

"I think you need more boring women around here. You lot are trouble," Savage says, kissing Nat on the top of her head from behind the couch.

"Shush you. Don't cramp our style. Or steal our pink or whatever the hell the saying is when new moms are trying to get their mojo back. It's been Momville since we popped out these precious bundles. We need excitement. And these lovely ladies–" Nat waves toward Ana and Lovely "– need more than just me to hang out with."

"Maybe don't say it like that. It makes it sound like me and Lovely don't have any other friends," Ana says to her.

"You don't," Chewy says, pushing Chomper in his stroller, parking him up next to me and then joining the other ladies in staring at me. "Spill, dude."

I scrub my hand down my face, knowing they'll harass me until I've spilled everything I know. "Fine. I met her the day I was taken into the station. She was in the holding cell next to mine. She writes 'sexy murder books'," I say, using my fingers as quotation marks, "and she was arrested when she persistently asked a big man if he could lift her up, then something happened and she slipped and fell on top of him with her tits out."

"Wait," Chewy asks, head tipped to the side. "How'd her tits fall out?"

"You'll have to ask her for those details," I shrug. I mean,

I'm still not overly sure about the finer details.

"Huh," Chewy says, squinting at me. "I'm sure I can get it out of her."

I stare at her. Chewy is, for want of a better word, disturbed. In the best possible way. Sometimes.

"Don't look at me like that. I won't hurt her. I'll just ask." She frowns.

"I wouldn't get too attached if I were you," Rhodie says, coming up behind his woman, pulling her back into his front. "She wants to set up an office here in the common room to write her MC themed book. Marx ain't gonna let that fly," he says, dropping a kiss onto the top of Chewy's mop of hair.

"Listen up!" Marx calls us to attention. "Mira here will be based here at the clubhouse while she writes her book for the next two weeks. Nobody mess with her. Got it?" Marx's voice booms out, making all us brothers stare wide-eyed in their direction.

"What the actual fuck?" Rhodie whispers, staring at his brother like he has two heads.

Probably in the same way I'm staring. Not just at Marx wondering what the fuck is going on, but also at Mira, Writer Lady, who has a massive grin on her face as she waves back at everyone, including Blanche who walked in just before Marx's announcement. The women speed talk to get her up to date, all hustling in Mira's direction.

"Church!" Marx calls out, surprising us as we never meet midweek. Luckily, we're all here, so we file into the room where all our serious business takes place.

Judging by my brother's faces I can tell we're all a little shell shocked by Marx's announcement. Not just because we don't know Mira, and Wire hasn't vetted her, but also because he never ran it by Rhodie or Rider, his VP enforcer and SAA.

"What the fuck, Marx?" Rhodie barks as soon as his ass hits his seat.

"Brother, watch your tone," Marx growls back, staring him down, and then the rest of us. "I know this seems out of left field, but I think we can all agree that a woman like Mira, a writer and ballsy as fuck, judging by how she met Tank," his eyes flick to mine, "is not the type to discourage easily. As in, if she wants to research our MC for her romance book or whatever, she'll do that with, or without our help. Or permission."

Now that he's pointing it out, I can see where he's coming from. The woman got arrested after harassing a man much larger than her. She's not going to stop coming around here even if we do say no. Although she's more likely to stalk us from afar. This way, we can control how much she learns about us.

"So, you give her access, and we sanitize how much she sees?" Savage asks, as per usual right on the same wavelength as Marx. Makes sense as he was a Pres himself once.

"Exactly, brother. This also means, *brother*," Marx directs to Rhodie, his actual brother, "that we need Chewy on her best behavior."

"Hey! She's been pretty normal lately. Business has been settled and she hasn't maimed anyone for ages."

"Dude, she owns a fucking gator," Dex says.

"Well, aside from Chomper. But he's, like, totally a normal pet. Loads of people have gators as pets," Rhodie answers sounding a little butthurt that someone would want to use Chomper as a reason for Chewy not to be "normal."

"In Texas?" Nitro asks, brow raised. He's fucking with

Rhodie, because I can see his lips twitching.

"Yes, in fucking Texas! Besides, it's not my woman you should worry about. It's the rest of them. You know they're all a little wild. Especially when they get together," Rhodie lays out, the MC brothers all nodding in agreement. We've all had to get involved in wrangling the women at least once during girls' nights, and it's not pretty.

"Shit, yeah you're right. Everyone, try to keep an eye on the women. As much as you can without it being suspicious. The last thing we need is for them to get into trouble. I know things have been kinda settled recently, Tank's arrest aside, so let's try to keep it that way. We're not a fucking 1% club, but shit if it hasn't felt like it at times." Marx runs a hand down his beard, looking more relaxed than he has for a while. Or I guess as relaxed as he can be given that he's just agreed to let a romance author set up base for a couple of weeks.

"On it, Pres. Try to keep the women and their crazy shit away from the nice writer lady," Fox nods.

"Hopefully she'll be busy tapping away on her laptop working on her book, rather than getting drunk and disorderly with the Ol Ladies."

"Famous last words, Pres," Dex says, a glint in his eye.

Flack's shaking his head from side to side knowing that shit could go sideways any moment with this lot involved. Add in a creative type woman with no inner monologue, and well, it could very well be a recipe for disaster.

Marx must recognize this because after a moment he says, "I'll talk to Mama Debs." He nods.

Everyone knows if there is anyone with the power to look chaos in the eye and wrangle it into submission, it's Mama Debs. I mean, shit, being Pops' Ol Lady ain't for the weak.

"Alright, Church over. Behave yourselves."

Mira

Once Marx makes his announcement I march straight over to the table that I think will be the perfect place for me to write and I start unpacking my tote. It has all my writing essentials - laptop, colorful notepads, and pencils with pompoms on the top. Various fidget toys and this fat hippo that wobbles when you pick it up.

"What are you doing?" a small voice asks and I'm jolted out of my setup. Looking around for the voice, my eyes land on a small dark girl with dark blonde curls and large hazel eyes, and her little friend, pale skin with almost black hair and eyes. There's a boy standing with them that looks a lot like the dark-haired girl, but he seems bored with this conversation already.

"Oh, I'm just setting up my writing stuff."

"Why?"

"Because I write?"

"Is that a question?" the boy asks. I think it's aimed at me even if he's looking somewhere else.

"Yes?"

The dark-haired boy frowns down at the floor like I'm an idiot. A beautiful darkly tanned woman with wild hair steps up next to him. She's also not looking directly at me, instead looking somewhere over my shoulder. The boy turns to her, but doesn't look up.

"She's not very good at answering questions," he tells her before walking off.

I would be offended but I don't have time as more women join the one across from me.

"Hi! Tank didn't introduce us before." An equally beautiful woman with black hair says.

Ruh Roh. These women are all stunning. And kinda normal looking. I, on the other hand, am not normal by any stretch of the imagination. Three of them have baby carriers strapped to their fronts, one looks like she may have a slight bump, and the one with wild hair is pushing a stroller. I'm not sure we'll have much in common, but I'll try.

"I'm Nat," the one who spoke first says. "This is Ana," she indicates a woman who has super shiny dark hair and is wearing very fancy clothes for a mom, super classy like. "This is Lovely, and Blanche, they're sisters," That's easy to tell, they look very alike, much like the boy who questioned me and the little girl who is still staring. "Oh, Remy is coming this way now." A blonde woman skids to a stop in front of me, giving me the sweetest smile. "And the woman with the gator is Chewy."

I double blink at this information. "Can you repeat that?"

Nat gives me a sly grin and then says slowly, "The woman with the gator is Chewy."

"Chewy" gives me a megawatt grin, leans into the stroller, fussing for a moment before slowly bringing her hands up. My eyes follow her movements as she slowly reveals a snout, a long scaled body, and then the tail.

"This is Chomper!" she coos over him then cradles him in her arms.

"Huh. Did you ever think of calling him Darth Gator?" I ask her.

Her eyes narrow for a moment and then she shakes her head. "No, not this baby. He's special needs. See his jaw? Severe underbite, we have to cut his food up for him. The name Chomper gives him back some of his mojo. Do gators have mojo?" she asks the room.

"Momma, what's a mojo?" the little girl with the curls asks one of the women in front of me. I'm not sure which as she doesn't seem to resemble any of them strongly.

"It's like his power. His spirit," the blonde woman, Remy, answers.

"Like the kind that sometimes gets left behind when you die and haunts places?" the little girl asks with a frown.

"Not quite, baby. I'm not sure gators can be ghosts."

"Nothing can be ghosts," Chewy answers matter of factly.

There's a lot of tooing and froing and speculation and it's all a little weird and I kinda love it. Apart from the part where I still have no idea who is who. "OK, wait. There's like, a lot of you here and apart from names I'm going to need a fun fact to remember you all by until we know each other better." I look around at them all nodding. "I'll start, I'm Mira, and I write sexy murder books. Oh, and I have a cool collection of gnomes and swords."

"I'll need to see those sometime," Chewy says, stroking Chomper.

"Um, I'm Lovely, and this is Bee," One of the two sisters says as she waves her baby's fat little hand at me. "I'm not really that interesting." She smiles apologetically. What a total sweetheart.

"That is a boldfaced lie!" The one I think is called Ana says. Well, that's what I think she says.

"Wait, what the heck was that noise!? Do you have an

accent?" I exclaim, and point, so she knows I mean her and no one else.

She just smiles and rolls her eyes. "No. You have accents," she says, waving around at everyone, jostling the very chubby dark-haired baby strapped to her front.

"Look, maybe I should have introduced everyone better before. I just wasn't sure how in-depth you wanted to get." Nat shrugs, her black wavy hair bouncing around her shoulders. Why are all these women so hot? And short? "I'm Nat, this is Rosie." She points to a baby wearing a headband with a giant black bow on her head. "I'm Savage's Ol Lady. We're ex Death Riders MC. We transferred here after the Death Riders Pres tried to kidnap Remy." The blonde woman smiles widely and waves at me. This is good shiitake, I should write this stuff down. For inspiration.

"Do you mind if I take notes? Don't worry, I won't use you as characters, just maybe story inspiration," I ask, brows raised.

"Oh, go ahead. You can even use us as characters, as long as character us gets paired with hot men and stuff," Remy giggles.

"Maybe two," Ana crows to a chorus of cackles.

Grinning, I pick up my pencil and notebook and wave Nat on. "OK, Remy is Wire's Ol Lady and Jovie's mom." Nat points to the little girl. "Wire and Remy were childhood pen pals that fell in love. Remy came here from the Death Riders to learn how to hack from Wire, not knowing that he was the pen pal she had been writing for like, 16 years. Anyway, Remy and Jovie were kidnapped..."

"And Wire saved them after tearing the whole world apart?" I ask. I love that kind of storyline. The big bad biker goes mad trying to save his woman, with all his MC brothers at his back.

"Um, no. Remy got Jovie out, she helped us find where they

were keeping Remy, and by the time Wire got there Remy had freed herself and captured her kidnapper."

I turn my wide eyes to the gentle, sweet mom lady in front of me. "Shut the front door!" I whisper as I note that down.

"Next is Ana. She's originally from New Zealand, came for a holiday, discovered a man in the trunk of a car, saved him and is now best friends with him and his husband. The husband is the Pakhan of the Bartashev Bratva."

"No way!" I yell in shock as Ana tips her head back and laughs. "You know the Bratva?"

"I work for them. Well, not at the moment, I'm on leave." She waves to the baby. "This is Junior."

"Wow. And here I was thinking you were going to be normal boring moms!" I shake my head as they all laugh.

Once they calm down, Nat points to the sisters. "Those two grew up in a religious cult. Blanche got out years ago, but was going back to rescue women wanting to leave. She rescued Lovely and little Bee when their Uncle-husband tried to sell Bee."

I stare wide-eyed at the dark-haired little girl in the carrier and can feel my blood boiling.

"Don't worry, Blanche went in and ended the cult. And their Uncle-husband. Oh, it's probably also good to point out that Blanche has a million kids."

"Hey!" Blanche says indignantly at the same time the little starey girl says it.

Nat just laughs and waves at her. "That's Cove. The boy is Elio. The two big ones over there are Niko and Sage. Anyway, Blanche is Chewy's brother's Ol Lady. Ana is married to another brother. There's still one free if you're a fan of tall, dark and handsome." Nat says with a grin.

My eyes flick toward the other side of the room to the door where the men are walking through, landing on the quiet, big blonde biker.

"Fair enough," Ana laughs.

"Last but not least, Chewy is, well Chewy." Nat says, waving in her direction. The woman gives me a goofy wave.

"So, with that intro, I'm guessing you're the normal one?"

This causes the women to burst into hysterical laughter. Well, all of them except Chewy, who shrugs at me.

"Chewy is wonderful and intelligent and fun and just a little scary," another big blonde biker says, coming up to throw his arm around her shoulders.

"This is my bestie Rider," she says, without looking at him.

"And your bestie still doesn't have a friendship bracelet," he glares at her.

"I'm waiting for the perfect time," she shrugs.

"Get your fucking arm off my Ol Lady," a deep voice growls, sending shivers right down to my undercarriage.

This guy is big and looks somewhat familiar, but I know I've never met him before. "This is my Ol Man, Rhodie," Chewy says, beaming up at him, the first time I've seen her make any sort of eye contact.

"He's Marx's biological brother," Remy adds, and it makes sense now. Rhodie is a lighter, leaner version of Marx's dark and huge. "Both Rhodie and Chewy are the DRMC Enforcers."

"Wait, Chewy is an MC member?" I ask. That makes the DRMC way more interesting. I never knew they had female members. I thought that was pretty rare amongst MCs.

"Yes and no," Rhodie answers me. "Not an official member, but Chewy has a certain set of skills that we use." He winks.

Man, I hit the jackpot accidentally assaulting that man that day and getting hauled into RGPD and meeting Tank and then using his name to get my foot in the door. This place is perfect for my research. I watch as they all mix and mingle. The men who have Ol Ladies all come over and introduce themselves before wandering off with their women and children, and I try to commit everything to memory. Well, the stuff that seems helpful. Like the family vibe and how everyone seems to get on like siblings. There are brothers ragging on each other, children running around, women mixing with the men, the children and each other. Although I wonder where the female entertainment is. The club bunnies or whatever you call them. So far everyone is fully dressed, not an areola to be seen. Maybe they come out under the cover of darkness. Once the kids go to bed they sneak out of their rooms in the back of the clubhouse, bringing with them their dancing pole so they can put on a show. Glancing around I try to make a mental note of where naked bodies and fluids may be.

"It's a lot, huh?" a gentle voice says, breaking me out of my thoughts to focus on Lovely smiling softly at me.

"Is Lovely a nickname because you're so lovely?" I ask her, wanting to know more about everyone here.

She giggles softly. "No, it's my birth name. In Eden's Keep we all were given "virtue" names. Blanche's real name is Patience and our brothers are named Wisdom, Victory, and Christian. They run a swamp boating and gator rescue place in Louisiana."

Ah, now I know why there's a disabled gator living in Rose Grove, Texas. This is all just so weird and wonderful and my brain is firing on all cylinders thinking up scenarios and characters and ideas and oh man I need to get this all down.

I drop down at the table and open my laptop, vaguely hearing a soft, sweet giggle moving further and further away from me as I get to work. I have spreadsheets out the wazoo to help with word counts and characters and plans and all manner of things, so I work my way methodically through them. By the time I've finished planning and plotting and brain dumping everything I sit back and realize the common room is quiet and still. There's a plate next to me with a selection of little sandwiches and cakes and the clock on the wall says it's after 10pm.

"Christ on a cracker!" I mutter to myself and set about packing my things up.

"I wondered when you were going to come out of your writing fog," a voice says, scaring the crumbs out of me, this morning's breakfast trying to beat a hasty retreat out of my bowels. "Shit, sorry Mira! It's me, Tank."

"You need a bell! You move far too stealthily for a big man, holy cluck nuggets!"

He chuckles at me, shaking his head. "I saw you come on your push-bike. Can I drop you home? Or you can stay here in one of the guest rooms. Marx offered."

"Oh, can I?! I've never stayed in a clubhouse before, it'll be a good story. When I tell people I bunked here for the night they'll totally think I had a moment of adventure and became a club 'entertainer' for the night. That'll blow their socks off!"

He gives me a puzzled smile then waves his hand in the direction of the hall, "Come on then Miss Adventure, let me show you to your room."

Chapter 3

Tank

I lead Mira down the long hall to the spare rooms. We may not be a large MC, around a dozen members so far, but we're lucky enough that when Marx and Rhodie's dad and his buddies were setting this place up they had the forethought to put in a lot of rooms, with ensuites for a bit of luxury after the military.

"Whoa, this place goes on forever! What's in all these rooms?"

I turn back to look at Mira, her head whipping this way and that, taking it all in.

"Nothing much. The brothers' rooms are further down, there's a couple of larger rooms for the families. A room that Mama Debs has turned into a movie room for the kids." I shrug.

"Who's Mama Debs? Is she like the woman who rules over the club entertainers? Where are the club entertainers? I haven't seen anybody with their boobs and butts hanging out." She stops in the middle of the hall, hands on hips, clearly wanting answers.

"Well, they had a run in with the Ol Ladies. Marx kicked them out and now the brothers have to go to town to pick up women."

"Huh. This place is not what I was expecting." She says, her brows pinch, a little crease forming between them.

"What did you expect?" I ask, curious, as this woman's way of thinking is a little out there.

"Hazy smoke, the place smelling of vagina and baby oil; the slight rubbery smell of condoms, the used ones tossed carelessly on the floor. Poles in the common room with busty women working them. Public shows of debauchery and in the middle of it all an older woman with a permanent cigarette in her mouth and teased bleached hair making sure the women are doing their jobs. The Pres would sit on a throne like chair, with two women on their knees performing fellatio as the brothers brought another sorry soul to him, this guy not being able to make payments for the loan you gave him. With the flick of the wrist Pres would send him to his doom in the dark, damp basement, where he would be held in chains and beaten to a pulp by the enforcer. Then he'd be tortured until he couldn't take it anymore and he'd be put out of his misery with a well-placed bullet to the brain. His body would then be dumped on the front lawn of his home as a warning, with the message 'Don't funk with the DRMC'." She takes a deep breath and looks at me with her large green eyes, chest heaving with the effort of getting her story out and taking as few breaths as possible.

She's magnificent when she voices the world inside her head, her creativity blowing me away. I stare at her, words not coming to me other than to say "Wow. That was a lot."

"Yeah, sorry bout it. I get a little carried away sometimes." She ducks her head and I can see a slight blush on her cheeks, although I doubt it's from embarrassment, more excitement.

"Let's get you to your room so you can write about this MC that is a lot more exciting than ours."

We start moving again and I stop in front of her room for the night. "Well, this is you." I turn the handle and swing the door open for her to peek in. Her shoulders are tense, however, when she sees inside they drop in disappointment.

"Darn it all. I was sure that the room would be a cesspit with filthy sheets from many nights with unknown women."

It's the opposite. For a long time the spare rooms were just that, spare and barely used. Half the time they had no bedding. If we needed them one of the Ol Ladies would make up the room. Tav was charged with getting them set up so the Ol Ladies didn't have to hustle to prepare them, so they sit looking like a hotel room with way too many pillows and cushions. Shit, they even have art on the walls.

"You might have to take that up with Tav. He's the reason the rooms aren't filthy."

She harrumphs at me, then moves inside. "Tav, that's Blanche's Ol Man, right?" I nod in reply, "Yusss. I'll learn the ins and out of biker life before you know it! Maybe I should get a bike? I ride a bike at the moment. An acoustic one, not one like yours, but I do have free will to do whatever I like, so maybe I'll look at getting a bike one day. Perhaps I can see if someone will let me sit on theirs? Get a feel for it, you know?"

I wait a moment or two, not sure if she's finished or is just taking a breath.

"You can talk now. I think that was the end of it. Maybe."

"You use a lot of words, Writer Lady."

"It's a gift," she shrugs one shoulder then eyes the desk that sits under the window in her room for the night. "I have an idea. Thanks Tank!"

With that she shuts the door abruptly and I let out a surprised chuckle as I make my way to my own room. Much like Mira's in size, it's quite different in decor. Tav may have been let loose with flair and soft furnishings in the other rooms, but mine is still almost as stark as the day I first arrived. Everything is put away neatly in its place. The walls are a light gray, the bedding dark and there are two pillows, that's all. There are no real personal belongings here other than my clothing, and I'm fine with that. I bet Mira would be horrified by my room. From what I saw of her house that time we dropped her off, she would have an abundance of belongings. All things that mean something to her.

I toe off my boots, making sure to line them up, toes to the wall, next to the bathroom door. That's where they go, just like my cut that gets hung over the back of the chair that matches the dark wood desk and dresser. Lowering my bulk onto my bed, I lie on top of the covers. My grandfather would think this was pure luxury, how I'm living now. Shit, it is compared to how we lived when I was a kid.

My parents were career Army. Because of their constant deployment I was sent to live with my gramps, a career military man himself. There was no softness about him at all, only rules. Rules to live by, rules to die by, as he would say. It wasn't a bad childhood. I had good food to eat, a roof over my head, and someone who gave a damn, which is more than a lot of kids get. The old man was fair, but tough and he had ideas on how to raise a child, which was to give him a purpose. From a young age I had chores, physical training and the belief that everything had to be earned. When I was around 7 or 8 I discovered a love of reading, but other than reading to pass my subjects, my grandfather thought fiction books were a waste of time. Who has time to daydream when you have practical things to be doing? Because of his mindset I would spend the evenings reading my books in secret with the pen torch I got in a tool set for my tenth birthday. Around my thirteenth birthday I won a writing competition at school. It wasn't anything special, just a certificate presented in front of the entire school, and a pizza voucher. I was embarrassed by the praise and terrified my grandfather would find out. He did, after a few moms stopped us at the supermarket to congratulate me. I braced myself for that car ride home thinking he'd be disappointed that instead of excelling on the football team, I was excelling in English.

"Proud that you're using your brain at school boy, it'll come in handy when you join the military."

"I was thinking about maybe going to college," I said, biting my lip.

Gramps let out a sigh, "Listen kid, that path, the college path, it's not for this family. We're military through and through, and shit, we're good at it. That's your calling son. But writing, that can be your outlet. Trust me, when you're lying on the hard ass ground in a country being torn apart, you'll need your stories to keep you sane."

I shake off the memory. That is the conversation that stopped me from entertaining ideas of going to college. Instead I knuckled down, got good grades and then enlisted as soon as I was able, following my parents and grandfather before me. Now, ten years and a few scars later I'm here, lying on my bed thinking about the scraps of stories I have locked away in a suitcase under my bed.

Letting out a sigh I get myself up, strip off and place my things in the laundry basket before getting into the shower, not even waiting for it to warm up. I need the jolt to my system to stop me from thinking about what ifs and the gorgeous, bubbly blonde down the hall.

Mira

"Ugh" I groan out, flopping over onto my stomach. My eyes are scratchy as all get out from the long hours of writing that I pulled last night. Normally my peak writing time is during the day, then I have a nice early night as I've always been an early riser. Put me into an MC clubhouse and I want to pull an all nighter.

As rough as I feel though, I'm happy with what I got down. The start of a new novel is always the hardest part for me, but that monologue I gave poor Tank last night really had the juices flowing. And not just the brain juices because holy fish sticks could that man be any hotter? I don't think so. He's so big and gentle and has a jawline that could cut glass. He's not super hard looking, more the type of man who is thick from his work, rather than spending hours in the gym building muscles and then going on a two week diet where all he's eating is boiled chicken breast and sweet potato for every meal. OK, I dated a bodybuilder once. Why is it that gym-going muscle men always want the big girls? Anyway, that was a total mistake because it turns out I don't really like spending my days rubbing tanning lotion onto hard muscles until the owner of said muscles looks like a ginormous oompa loompa.

I flop back over to my back and think about getting up for the day. I've never been one to sleep away the day if I could help it. Thank you Nana. "Go out and greet the day, Mira," she would say in her sweet old lady voice, and by heck would I greet the day. Probably a little too hard knowing the child version of me. I always thought I would grow out of being the odd child. The one who loved to wear all the colors of the rainbow and say what she thought and felt. Instead I grew into an odd adult and I'm funking fantastic so it wasn't a total loss.

A clacking noise goes past my room, followed by the sound of little footsteps running, the patter of the owners' feet a fast beat instead of the steady slow thuds I've heard go past. Tossing off the covers I roll out of bed, getting to my feet and putting on yesterday's outfit: my purple pants, black and white top and pink heels. What can I say? The girl loves color. I straighten up the bed and then head out, following the chorus of voices and the heavenly scent coming from the kitchen.

"Hi, Miss Mira!" the little poppet I think is called Jovie calls out waving.

"Good morning!" Her much louder friend Cove, I think her name was, joins in. Her brother sits quietly next to her, pretty much ignoring everyone, eating a dry pancake.

"Well, hey there kiddos! Fancy seeing you here." I smile down at them. The boy, Elio gives me an odd look then goes back to whatever he was doing.

"Well, course you'd see us here. Jovie lives here and Tav is taking all of us to school so we get to have Mama Debs' breakfast while the Bigs get Mom's breakfast." She says very loudly. Just as I'm questioning her volume control she leans forward and tries to whisper, "Mom isn't as good at cooking breakfast as Mama Debs."

When Cove leans back Jovie leans forward and whispers, "She isn't very good at whispering, so maybe don't tell her any secrets."

"I'll try not to," I whisper back, trying not to laugh. These kids are a hoot.

"Well, hello there, *kotiro*. You must be the new girl Marx told me about. I'm Mama Debs, come and have some *kai*." A little woman with curly dark hair takes me by the hand and leads me to the kitchen hatch, dropping said hand and stepping into the kitchen, ready to serve. "What'll you have, sweetheart?"

I'll have you thanks, the words flit through my mind. Her dark hair is in soft curls around her round face, a huge smile stretched across it, her eyes crinkling with joy. My hand goes to my chest as it fills with something I can't quite put my finger on. It feels like happiness and sadness at the same time. The last time I saw a face like this was my Nana's. Not in looks, my nana clearly looks nothing like Mama Debs given we have blonde hair and green eyes, and Mama Debs obviously has dark coloring. So no, not in likeness, but more so intent. The look that no matter what happens this woman will be there for you, always. To nurture you and love you unconditionally.

Looking along the counter at all the offerings my eyes widen. Shirt, I can see why Cove loves eating breakfast here.

"Um, maybe some pancakes and a piece of bacon, please? Oh, and maybe a hug for after?" Cheese and rice, play it cool Mira!

"Of course, *e hoa*. Pancakes, bacon and eggs coming right up, and a hug for after." She grins.

My eyes get wider and wider as I watch her load the plate up with far more than I'll be able to eat, but she smiles so happily while she does it that I keep my mouth shut. Once she's done she sets it on the counter and then hustles around from behind the hatch. As soon as I'm within arm's reach she pulls me into her, tugging my head gently so it rests on her much shorter shoulder. My larger frame is curled around the little plump woman and I don't care. It's the best feeling in the world. All too soon she pulls away, rubs my cheek and softly smiles up at me.

"Welcome to the family, dear."

"Oh, my name's Mira. Sorry, I didn't introduce myself."

She grins up at me, her eyes squinting because of her cheeks pushing them up, "Welcome to the family, Mira."

She bustles off quickly to serve some of the brothers and I take my overloaded plate to an empty seat at the table the women are sitting at. I figure it would be a good chance to get to know them a little better. Not to base any characters on them, but more to get the inner workings of what it's like being an Ol Lady. People think writing romance is easy, but there is a buttload of research that goes into this stuff. Although there are equal amounts of imagination as well. I don't know any aliens, but that didn't stop me writing a successful little series of novellas. "The Guys of Galaxis" is one series that I won't be recommending to Marx. I snort to myself, imagining the big, bearded burly man reading it. Then laugh harder when I imagine him reading about the Galaxis' penises and their hidden features, like the little tongue that sits at the base of their peens.

"You OK there, new girl?" Nat asks, a bemused smile on her face.

"Oh, yeah, sorry. I was just imagining these guys reading some of my alien romances." I wipe a tear from my eye and contemplate the best way to tackle the mountain of food Mama

Debs served me.

"Wait, I thought you wrote murder romance?" Remy asks, peeling an orange for her daughter.

"Oh, I do. But I have a little side series, where the alien men are tall, broody and have an extra tongue at the base of their junk."

Remy's eyes grow wide. "The Guys of Galaxis? Is that you?" she gasps out. I smile and nod, Remy letting out a little squeal and clapping her hands. "Oh my gosh I love that series! Mannox is one of my many book boyfriends!"

I get a little flutter in my belly, excited at knowing someone has not only read my book but also enjoyed it.

"Wait, is that the one with the alien convict guy?" Nat asks, brow furrowed.

"Yes! That's the one!" Remy yells, then turns to me. "Holy crap I can't believe it's you. That's so cool!"

I take a bite of my eggs and try not to beam too wide. I don't want these people to think that I think I'm too cool or something.

"Chewy, Mira wrote that book I gave you, the one where the heroine tortured the bad guy by infecting him with a tapeworm," Remy says to Chewy.

"Oh, I didn't read it, but that did sound cool. I've filed that away for future use." She takes a sip of her smoothie. "What other good ideas have you got? I've done the spray foam, and an S&M style one."

She must mean she's thought about it already, rather than used it on people. Devil's Rose MC is not a 1% club, they're good guys who do charity runs and donate toys and things like that. Maybe her and Rhodie come up with ideas for torture and things. I mean, I can't imagine charity run bikers need to torture a lot.

"Well, the tapeworm was one of my favorites. I also like to write about psychological torture rather than physical torture."

Chewy's eyes narrow slightly, "Physical torture yields results quicker."

"That's true," I agree, taking a bite of eggs. "Hmm, well, what about burning?"

Nat and Remy are looking between the two of us, clearly intrigued.

"Chinese drip torture with acid instead of water. However, that type of burning isn't widespread so maybe deliberate but widespread over the body would work well?" She pinches her bottom lip between her thumbs and forefinger and stares at the wall, in thought.

"I would do bottoms of the feet. They're a lot more sensitive than people give them credit for. There's a bunch of nerve endings in them."

"Yes! I like the way you think," Chewy says, briefly glancing at me with dancing eyes.

"What the hell is happening?" I hear Nat ask Remy, Remy shrugging in reply.

"You ever thought about using CO2? It's the same chemical that builds up in the human body when you're suffocating. The victim will be wide awake and alert enough to panic over and over again until you end them," Chewy offers up after a moment of thought.

"Oh," I say, patting my boobs, looking for my notebook. "Oh that's good," I pull my notebook out from my bra, along with the little pen and start writing stuff down.

"Aw shit, please Nat, Remy, someone tell me these two aren't bonding?" one of the guys says.

"We're totally bonding," Chewy answers. "Hard."

"Noooo," another voice whines before moving away. I don't even look up to see which brother it is, I'm on a roll and have to note down this stuff before it flits straight out of my head.

"Morning ladies," a deep voice says from behind me.

"Morning, Tank. Here for the geek show?" Nat says, snickering a little.

"The geek show? What's going on?" he asks, coming to a stop at the seat next to mine.

"Chewy and Mira just realized they can exchange torture methods," Remy replies.

"Oh, shit." This time Marx's voice sounds out. "Please don't tell Chewy about that scene in 'Devil's Heat'."

My head snaps up to stare at him, eyes wide.

"I mean, I heard it's pretty rough. From what I've heard. Or read on the internet when I searched your name. Yeah." With that, he turns and stomps off to his office, the door slamming behind him.

"Well, that was weird," one brother says, the rest of the MC agreeing with him.

"Yeah, totally," I cough out.

Everyone finishes up breakfast and I try to take notes around being distracted by all the goings on. Blanche collects up the little kids, or Littles as they seem to collectively be called, then corrals them into the mom vehicle with the precision of an army drill sergeant. She's nice, but also very terrifying. The MC brothers seem to leave the clubhouse in packs heading out to work in the MC owned businesses, the only brother who isn't employed by the MC, Switch, eats his breakfast and then heads to bed after working the night shift at Rose Grove General Hospital.

Within half an hour the clubhouse is almost empty, save for Mama Debs in the kitchen and Marx in his office somewhere.

"You alright there Mira?" Mama Debs' voice calls through the hatch.

"Yup!" I call out, tidying up my mess, and popping my notebook back into my bra. I carry my dirty dishes through to the kitchen, cleaning them up and popping them into the industrial sized dishwasher. "I'm going to head home and check up on Mrs. McKenzie, she'll be all huffy with me for being out all night. But never fear, I will be back!" I turn to head out, but then spin on my heel and give Mama Debs a quick squeeze. Nothing too intimate, we only just met, sheesh! "Thank you for breakfast,"

"Anytime, dear. Anytime." She uses her strong mom arms to give me a big squeeze before releasing me out into the world, a huge smile on my face, and walking on air.

Chapter 4

Tank

"Another call out brother," Judge calls from the reception, giant mitt of a hand covering the bottom of the business phone.

"Another one? Holy shit, what is going on in this town?" I mutter to myself.

Walking past him to leave he holds a sticky note up with the location, name, vehicle and cell number of the caller. I snatch it out of his hand on the way past and give him a chin lift, taking a glance. "This is out old man Henderson's way. I'll pick up that case of 'shine for the old boys while I'm out there."

"Where's Tav? He usually does it."

"Yeah, but he and Blanche have that meeting with the school for Elio. Teachers don't take kindly to 5-year-olds making fireworks in the playground."

Judge snorts and shakes his head.

I pull myself into one of our two new tow trucks, blast Metallica and let my thoughts run away with me while I make the half hour drive. I've always been a thinker, much to

Gramps's chagrin. I think he would have liked me better if I was all brawn and no brains. Willing to do exactly what I was told, no questions asked. That doesn't get you home from deployment safely though. That gets you dead.

"Well, lookie what we got here. I didn't know they stacked shit so high," Old man Henderson teases in his rough 3 packs a day smoker's voice when I pull into his place. "Young Tombs slackin' today?"

"He has a meeting at his son's school." I let him know, shaking his rough, leathery hand and then following him to the porch where his premium quality moonshine sits, ready for distribution.

"Which one? The big one or the little one?"

"The little one, Elio."

He nods, roughly stroking his stubble. "Figures. First time that kid turned up here he asked if I could boil a human. Just like his aunt."

I let out a huff and carry his crates to the truck, the old boy following behind as if he's helping. "Yeah, it's nice that Elio has someone who understands him."

"Should probably keep him away from Sid though, unless Marx wants the boy as the next generation MC enforcer," He grins wide with a twinkle in his eye. "You wanna stay for a drink? We haven't played scrabble in a while."

"Sorry Bud, I'll have to take a raincheck. I'm on a callout and shit is busy over at Big Tow," I tell him, securing everything tightly. Can't lose a drop of this liquid gold.

"Shit, son, what the hell are you doing lollygagging here with me then? Get outta here and get to work, lazy bum." His eyes twinkle with mirth and I wave him off.

"I'll do next pick up and play a game with ya. Til then old

man," He flips the bird at me and heads back to his porch chuckling to himself.

Getting into the truck I fire her up and head out to the middle of nowhere. The GPS tells me I should be coming up to my location and yet there doesn't seem to be anyone out here. Checking both my left and right sides they're as empty as the road ahead. Punching in Judge's number I wait as the ring tone sounds out over the truck's speakers.

"Yo?"

"Yeah, you sure this was the location? There's no one here." I tell him, eyes searching. There don't seem to be any ditches or hills for them to roll down, but people are stupid so you never know what type of shit they get themselves into.

Judge reads out the GPS location the caller gave and I check my equipment, letting him know I'm in the exact spot I'm meant to be.

"Shit, I don't know what to tell you, brother," his gruff voice fills up the truck cab.

"Fuck it. They must have sorted themselves out. I'm coming in."

Judge hangs up abruptly, like he always does. I used to think it was just the way he spoke to his brothers, but I've seen him do it with customers too, so it's obviously just how he ends calls. I shake my head and I wonder whose fucking bright idea it was to have Judge and I work the tow company. I mean I'm not the chattiest guy in the world and Judge talks even less. Neither of us are fit for a front-facing role either, which is why every morning we play three rounds of rock, paper, scissors to decide who's working the counter. Not that it matters much these days seeing how often we're both out of the office most of the time.

Glancing into the rearview I notice a flashy, Fast and Furious matchbox car behind me. I have no fucking clue where they came from, but they're tailing me pretty fucking closely. I could do the decent thing and pull over, letting them overtake me, but I don't like the look of this greasy little shithead.

The car speeds up a little more, really tailgating me now, and it's pissing me off. I weigh up my options. I can speed up, slow down, or jam on the brakes and let him crash his piece of shit into me. Decisions, decisions.

"Call Judge," I growl at my phone.

"Yo."

"How much would it piss Marx off if I purposely got rear-ended?"

Judge's chuckle vibrates through the speaker. "A lot."

"Dammit."

I beat him to the punch and hang up on him this time, laughing to myself. I notice the junker behind me pull out to overtake, speeding up on my left. Our driver's side windows level out and I take note of the scrawny, greasy looking shithead driving and the bleach blonde in the passenger seat. Fuck, is that one of the old bunnies? Whitney? She gives me a little finger wave then leans into the lap of the douchebag driving, his tiny dick hanging out the front of his jeans. He stares me down, smirking as he presses her face to his junk and speeds past, veering in front of me, having barely cleared the front of the truck.

Fucker. I crank my music up so that I can feel the bass vibrate through me to calm myself and my thoughts. By the time I pull into the yard I feel better, but my mind is still busy playing the call out and crossing paths with Whitney over and over. Something feels a little off but I can't quite put my finger on it. Shrugging it off I crawl to a stop in the assigned garage and get busy unloading the crates of 'shine.

"Knock off time," Judge says as soon as I walk into the office.

"Thank fuck. That call out was a waste and to make matters worse, I had Whitney and her new little boyfriend riding my ass most of the way back to town."

Judge's brows pull in for a moment and he looks down at the papers in his hands, riffling through them. "That's the sixth bogus call since the complaint to Rose Grove's finest." He hands me the paperwork and I flick through it. He's right.

"You think someone is messing with me?" I ask, eyes still on the paperwork, waiting for something to jump out at me.

"Say so. Should give that shit to Wire and his team."

Nodding, I fold the papers in three and then put them inside my cut pocket. "Come on brother, I definitely need a ride now. And a drink."

And maybe an eyeful of a colorful, nutty blonde, working at the table in the center of the common room.

Mira

Holy moley! I can't believe it's almost been a whole week of DRMC and their clubhouse and all the stuff that goes with it. Which if I'm being honest seems to be a lot of gossiping, pranks and eating. I've yet to meet the rest of Chewy's family who are away helping the FBI and Blanche's brothers with something. I've been told this is highly unusual, as they have teams of people in their firm, but this needed "special skills" which I think is why Chewy's grandpa went too. I have no idea what any of these so called special skills could be, but whatever they are sounds intriguing. And maybe a little dangerous. Different brothers over the course of the week have told me to steer clear because the whole family is nuts, which doesn't seem likely. I mean Chewy's not nuts. A little different, but pretty sane. Although it did strike me as a little weird that the big, burly bikers seem to be wary of them. Maybe I need to get to know them better?

I mull over what their special skills could be for a little longer then remember I'm meant to be writing. I do that all the time, get sidetracked by thoughts and then have to somehow unthink them so I can get back to concentrating. So far, my heroine decided to not listen to any sage advice and go off on her own, even though the entire club is on lockdown and the hero is busy sorting out the cartel. I don't usually like to write heroines that wander off, but this one seemed hellbent on doing her own thing. That's the thing with book characters. People think the authors have all the control and power and it's simply not true. My characters write their own stories, I'm just here to type them into the laptop and do all the boring book admin.

I'm halfway through the scene when brothers start filing in from wherever it is they work. My eyes dart to the door, expecting Tank to walk through any moment now. I've gotten used to the movements around the clubhouse now, and I know that Tank and Judge get home from the tow yard between 6 and 6.30pm. Glancing at the clock, I note that it's 6.29. Huh. He's late.

Just then the door opens and in he walks, in all his big, blonde bikery glory. Looking all solid and manly and all "I can throw

you over my shoulder and spank your ass whenever I want."
I let out a little wheeze and try to contain the heat coursing through my cheeks. Jeez Louise, Mira Elizabeth Campbell, calm down. Nothing to see here. Move along. I give myself a mental talk down because I mean, otherwise I'll be all blushy and not playing it cool and that's what I'm meant to be doing, right? Playing it cool. Like a cucumber.

"Hey Writer Lady, how's the book coming along?" Tank's deep voice washes over me. As does his leathery, woodsy scent.

"I'm cool as a cucumber," I blurt and then cringe.

"I'm sure you are," he chuckles, eyes twinkling. He knocks twice on the table next to me with his huge ham-sized fist, "I better let you get back to it. I know how annoying it is to be interrupted." He smiles and then swaggers off.

What a tease. I bet he doesn't even know he's swaggering. Is swaggering the male equivalent of when a woman sashays? I quickly note that down. I should research that, it could come in handy with my writing.

"What do you keep in that notebook, girly? Secrets? You're writing about me, ain't ya?" Remy's dad Flack sits across from me, gently placing his beer on a coaster.

I grin at him. "Oh totally. I needed a wily, rough older character than can show these young guys a thing or two." He chuckles at that, his shoulders shuddering.

"If you're looking for an older, wily rough character, then you have the wrong man. You want Pops, Chewy's grandfather."

I point my bumble bee pencil at Flack, "Now you're like the 50th person who's told me that!"

His bushy white brow raises. "The brothers all been telling ya to write about Pops?"

"Well, no," I lower my pencil, "But everyone talks about Chewy's family like they're something special. Or nuts. A few brothers have said that."

"Well, the family are … unusual. Do you know how Chewy landed here?" Flack asks.

"Kinda. She broke into the compound, didn't she?"

"Well, me, Savage and Dex weren't on the scene then. We were friendly with DRMC, but we had our own shit going on, so I can only really tell you the story I heard. Chewy broke in because she was stalking the guy that murdered her parents."

I lean forward and whisper hiss at Flack, "And he was here?! DRMC?"

"Oh no, girly, keep your panties on. Nah, the guy she was stalking just so happened to be stalking Rhodie and the MC didn't know. Anyway, no one breaks into an MC, especially not a little woman like Chewy. But she had balls and just the right amount of crazy. With her came her family, August, Ana's husband, he's the one in control. A little highly strung, but a good guy to have around. You know Tav already. Jules is harder to peg. He's more of an asshole. Then there's Pops. Love the man, but hell he lives to piss people off. Word has it he survived a POW camp in 'Nam and came back with a 'particular' set of skills. Chewy is his apprentice."

I dart my eyes across the room to where Chewy is currently suspended in the air, arms around Rhodie's neck as he grips her butt and eats her face off.

"Would it be weird if I said that I can't wait to meet him?"

"Nah, he's a good stick. Apart from that time he made the brothers all wear sequined hot pants and shake their asses," He throws his head back and roars with laughter at the look on my face.

"Mira! There's a package here for you," Jimmy, the gate prospect who I met on my first day here, makes a beeline for me holding a plain, brown cardboard box.

"That's weird. How does anyone know you're here?" Chewy frowns, sidling over to me, looking at the package like it's a bomb.

"I have no idea. Or maybe I do. I dunno, sometimes I just talk out loud for no reason so maybe I told somebody? Although I don't remember. I woke up, came here and that's about it." I shrug, taking the package from prospect's outstretched arms.

Placing it on the table, I look for a return sender address, but find none. I start to pick off the tape so I can open it, but then there's a snick sound and Tank's big tattooed arm is reaching around me to slice the tape. How do I know it's Tank arm? Believe me, I know. I've committed all those tattoos to memory. For research. Obviously.

"There you go sweetheart," he says gently before leaning back again.

I open the flaps wide and start to lean in when a gruff voice belonging to a man I haven't met yet growls out, "Why the fuck does this place smell like liver?"

Chapter 5

Tank

Looks like having a keen sense of smell runs in the family. Chewy sniffs the air before leaning forward and peering into the box with her grandfather.

"Why do you have that?" Pops asks, his voice gruff.

"I have no clue. Someone keeps sending livers to me, which I agree is totally weird but also kinda handy because my cat loves eating them. But it's weird right? Unless I accidentally signed up to a delivery service and forgot. I did that once before. I kept having train trading cards delivered." Mira shrugs.

"There ain't no service that delivers human liver that I know of, girl."

"What!?" The whole room roars, all of us jostling for a closer look.

"Shit, he's right, they are human," Switch says in his booming voice, Mira blinking a couple of times at the sheer noise.

"Human liver has four lobes. One, two, three, four. Pig livers look the closest to ours, but they have five lobes." Chewy says calmly, as if it's common knowledge.

Mira is looking pale as fuck, her hand resting on her chest. If she had pearls she would be clutching them.

"Human? Like, from people?" she whispers.

"Mira, sweetheart, take a seat." I tell her gently, guiding her back into her seat. "This is Chewy's grandfather, Pops. He's Mama Debs' Ol Man." She gives him a tight smile and waves. "Pops, this is Mira. She's a writer."

He ignores the introduction. "Girl, who have you pissed off to have livers sent to you?"

"I, I have no idea. Oh, holy carp I've been feeding people to Mrs. McKenzie?" A look of pure horror washes over her pretty face.

"Who's Mrs. McKenzie?" Chewy asks, head tipped to the side.

"She's my cat. The one that's been looking fabulous thanks to a diet of delivered liver." She squeezes her eyes tightly. "Ew."

"Mira, how often do you get these packages?" Pops asks, eyes still on the box.

"Well, I've had maybe three or four since that day we went to the slammer," she says, looking up at me from her seat at the table.

"That was, what? Two months back?" I think out loud.

"If you've had four parcels, then that's every two weeks," Chewy adds. "How many do you get each time? And is it always delivered on the same day?"

Mira looks shocked at Chewy's quick fire questions, then nods, her curly blonde ponytail bobbing. "Well, the first time it happened was a Sunday. Then the next time I remember seeing Mrs. and Mr. Barklay in their nice church clothes when I was on the porch with the parcel, so another Sunday. But today is a Tuesday, so maybe it's just whenever they have livers?" Chewy looks at Pops and they do that weird no talking communication. "Oh, and I always get two in the box."

"Four bodies," Chewy mumbles.

"To Trap a Kiss," Marx's rough voice mutters.

We all spin to look at him, what the fuck is he talking about?

"Holy shirt balls, you're right!" Mira shouts. What in the fuck?

"Um, care to share?" Dex's voice pipes up. The whole MC is here, wanting to know why the hell the woman we've let into our clubhouse is having body parts sent to her. Not just her, but now us.

"In my book, 'To Trap a Kiss', the main character was investigating a killer who would remove the victims' livers."

"I thought you wrote sex books? Nothing about liver is sexy," Rider asks.

"Oh, well, the main character joins forces with a prickly single mom medical examiner that he had a fling with four years prior but doesn't recognize. He's super attracted to her and she hates him because he left without saying a word after they shared a wild weekend together. What he doesn't know is that the weekend they shared resulted in a daughter. So not only does he have to find a killer, but he also has to uncover the fact that the woman of his dreams hid a child from him, all while groveling enough to get her to give him another chance and heal his childhood trauma at the same time." Mira says, all in one breath.

"Oookkk. And how exactly did you know about this book -" Pops looks from Marx to Mira for the title.

"To Trap a Kiss-"

"– To Trap a Kiss? Well, Skid Marx?" Pops folds his arms over his chest, staring at Pres, his lips tipping up in the corners.

"I did my research, old man. Wire sent me Mira's background check and I dove a little deeper." Wire's eyes flick to Marx briefly before covering his surprise.

Pops narrows his eyes, staring Marx down and getting nowhere because Marx is one tough motherfucker.

"Whatever shit Marx does or doesn't know isn't important. What we need to know is how the hell the sender knew where Mira was to deliver it to her." Rhodie says, looking around at everyone, Chomper now nestled against his chest.

The room is silent, everyone taking in the new information. Remy comes to stand next to Wire, handing him his laptop. I was so busy watching Mira that I didn't even notice that she had left the room. We're all assembled, including the prospects and our wider family – the rest of the Tombs back from Louisiana, Lovely and Blanche and the big kids; the Littles, bored with the drama, have gone to join Debs in the kitchen.

"Jimmy, were you on the gate when this was delivered?" Marx gruffly asks.

"Yes, sir. An older man in a white Honda Civic. Works for a florist in town and was asked to deliver this rather than flowers."

"Did he say which florist?"

"Yeah, Flora's Buds," Jimmy answers with a snicker.

"We did their security install." Gus says. It's good to know Flora's Buds has a Tombs Security system. "We may be able to get a look at the person who ordered the delivery. Jules?"

"I'll talk to Flora," Jules says

"Whoa, who are they?" Mira whispers.

"Jules Tombs, pleasure to meet you," Jules says, winking,

fucking winking at Mira. And looking less bitchy than usual. "This is my older, less handsome brother, Gus."

"I said the inside part out loud didn't I?" Mira's wide eyes look around for confirmation, her shoulders slumping as we all nod at her. "Your good looks gave me a brain fart." Jule's brows fly to his hairline. "Have you ever thought about modeling for romance covers? You both totally have that alpha hole look going on."

Both brothers look bewildered, Ana cackles, and across from me Flack frowns and mouths 'alpha hole'. I have no idea what an alpha hole is, but judging by the women swooning, well, all the women except Chewy, an alpha hole must be a good thing.

"You'd be a cinnamon roll hero," Mira whispers to me, patting my stomach.

Sure, I may not have a lean, hard looking body like Jules or Gus, but I hold my own. Also, what the fuck is a 'cinnamon roll hero'?

"Thanks for your help Tombs'," Marx's gruff voice breaks into my train of thought, putting me and the rest of us back on track. "We need to know who the hell is sending this shit." Before Mira can speak, Marx holds up a hand, "Not just for you, but by delivering this shit to our home, he's involved us now. Chewy and Pops, can you two dispose of these remains before fucking Rose Grove PD gets a whiff? With fuck all movement on who tried to frame Tank, we gotta keep our noses clean. I want you all to go about your normal routines until Wire can pull some information we can use."

"Aye aye Captain!" Chewy salutes. "Elio! We have a lesson!" She calls out to her nephew, stopping to drop a kiss on Chomper's head, then Rhodie's lips before carrying on her forward momentum into the kitchen to find Elio.

Tav has his mouth hanging open, as does Blanche. Pops stops, placing a finger under both their chins and effectively closing them. "Don't stress yourselves, we'll tell him they're pigs livers."

Mira turns to look at me. "Dispose of them how?" she whispers.

"You don't wanna know."

Mira

After the big revelation that I've been feeding my poor cat people-liver, things move fast. Remy and her very handsome Ol Man hit the internet in search of people selling body parts. I think? I actually have no idea. I tried to keep up with their conversation but they seemed to talk in half sentences, the other person knowing inherently what they meant. From what I could gather there are dark places on the web that specialize in that type of thing. Which is gross and horrific. Did I note it down for future reference regardless? Yes. yes I did. While they headed off to their "Control Center" to look into that a little more, most everyone else left to go about their lives as if this kinda thing was totally normal. Maybe it is in biker land?

"You holding up OK?" Mama Debs' soft voice asks from my side, where she's standing with a steaming cup of something and a plate of cookies which I eagerly take from her.

I'm a curvy girl. I like the way I'm built, which means I never say no to a home baked cookie.

"I have no idea. Twenty minutes ago I was a fabulous bubbly blonde writer in a clubhouse working on my new romance novel. Now I'm a woman eating cookies wondering who the heck I fed to my cat," I sigh. I can feel the tension in my shoulders and the place in my head that normally works a mile a minute, thinking of scenarios and sentences and characters is shockingly quiet.

"Would it make you feel better if I told you that DRMC has your back? And that they won't stop until they find out what the hell is going on?" Debs asks, taking a seat next to mine and laying a warm hand on my arm. Would it be weird if I crawled over to sit in her lap? "I don't think it would be weird, but it would definitely be a tight squeeze."

"Drummit!"

She laughs, a great big belly laugh, her whole body shaking. She's wonderful and warm and it makes me miss my Nana even more than usual. She's the one that encouraged me when everyone else said that writing wasn't a real career and maybe I should look at hospitality or retail. I tried those options, believe me, I tried. But it's hard to make tips when you don't have much of an inner monologue and are inherently nosey. Did I want to excel at being a server? Not as much as I wanted to know how you got that missing tooth.

After being let go from pretty much every restaurant in Rose Grove, my nana sat me down and told me I needed to say "to heck with it" and find my own path. With her encouragement, and my love of people and stories, I found my career. Taking the figments of my imagination and giving them backstories, loves and losses, trials and tribulations. I give them excitement and romance and all the things that the many people I've come across in my lifetime have, making my characters' lives whole.

Human. With a healthy dose of mystery and thrill, of course.

Looking around the room, I realize that since I've been here I've been more interested in getting the ideas out of my head than getting closer to the people that give this place its family vibe.

"Mama Debs? How the heck did you get from New Zealand, which, I'm not even entirely too sure where that is exactly, to this clubhouse half a world away from your home?" I turn my body fully, my knees touching hers.

"Well, you know my Ana works and is best friends with the Bratva, yeah?"

I nod, dunking a cookie into my tea, and then popping it in my mouth, the warm sweetness hitting my tastebuds. Heaven.

"Well, there was a little *raruraru*, trouble, and her boss and bestie, Roman, had to head to Russia. This caused an issue with her visa, and she had 30 days to leave the country. So Chewy's brother, August, swept in and suggested a marriage of convenience. I came to offer my support and of course meet my new son-in-law. It took me all of five seconds to realize that they were both hopelessly in love with each other. But, well, they are both stubborn and I'm sure Gus has anxiety or some issue, but that aside, it all worked out and now they have that very scrumptious fat baby of theirs." She smiles huge at me and I love how joy seeps out of her pores.

"I love that. But wait, how did you end up at the MC?"

"Well, with Chewy part of the MC and Gus friends with Marx, we somehow all just landed here. Marx asked if I wanted a job feeding them, and if I'm honest, I would have done it for free. They're good boys." She shrugs.

"And you and Pops?"

Mama Debs smiles softly, eyes twinkling. "We both lost loves.

But the universe decided to give us another go round, and, well, now I'm Sid's Ol Lady and I have someone to share all the good and bad with. After years of doing it alone, it's nice to have someone have my back again." She tilts her head at me, much the way Chewy does. "What about you, dear? Who has your back?"

"No one. My nana died two years ago and it's just been me since then. I mean, I have friends, they're all writers too. We chat all the time online and some of them I video call. We all met up in Vegas over Christmas. But, I mean, they're not here with me. If I got sick they wouldn't call by with soup or cough syrup. But that's alright, I have Mrs. Mac and I'm pretty sure she wouldn't eat my face off if I died in my sleep. Although I guess she's had a taste of human now, so maybe I shouldn't discount her eating me. But other than that, I'm fine. It's not as sad as it sounds," I end with a laugh. It was meant to be light but to my own ears it sounds unhinged honk.

Mama Debs' lips twitch and she pats my hand. "Well, you have a dozen people who have your back now, *kotiro*," My brows pinch, not knowing what that word means. "It means 'girl'," Mama Debs smiles.

"Oohhh, that's cool. It's like 'Yuss Gurl'," I snap my fingers, "But more exotic."

Mama Debs throws her head back and laughs, "If you say so,"

"Hey, can I ask you something?"

"Anything, *kotiro*," she winks.

"Why is the Tombs family so good looking? Like, it's not right."

She bursts into laughter again, and I join her. We're still laughing when Blanche, Lovely and Ana come to join us.

"What's so funny?" Blanche asks. She's the most abrupt of the women, except Chewy, but I'm guessing with the number of kids she has she probably doesn't have time to mess around with words.

"Mira asked why the Tombs family are so good looking," Mama Debs answers, still chuckling.

"God, I know right!?" Ana exclaims. "When you get them all together it's like looking directly into the sun, that's how hot they are."

Blanche points at her and nods emphatically, Lovely joining in with the nodding.

"They obviously take after my man," Mama Debs says, grinning.

"I think you're right. But, that doesn't explain why everyone else around here is so good looking," Lovely says. She has such a sweet, gentle nature about her.

"That's a good point. There isn't a fugly in the whole bunch. Even your scary ass boss is hot," Blanche says, nodding toward Ana.

"Roman is a sweetheart. He just comes across as a hardass. You should see him at home, facemask on watching 90 Day Fiance," she laughs.

"Is that before or after he's offed some poor bastard?" Blanche teases.

"Definitely after," Ana says then presses her hands to her breasts. "Right, I gotta go. These girls are going to start leaking like a faucet soon, which means I gotta go feed."

She stands and heads down the hall. It's the first time I've noticed that she didn't have her baby with her. Neither does Lovely.

"Ah, where are the babies?"

"We left them in one of the spare rooms with matches and alcohol unsupervised to see how long they could survive," Lovely answers with a straight face.

A laugh booms out from behind me, causing me to jump and a little pee come out.

"Oh, she's got jokes now, huh?" Marx teases.

A slight blush comes over Lovely's cheeks and she beams at the gruff man. "Thanks. I've been working on my repertoire."

My eyes dart between the two. I wonder if anyone else can see what I'm seeing? Catching Mama Debs' lips twitching, I see I'm not the only one.

Marx clears his throat, turning to me, "We have a nursery down the hall, had to put one in because we have rug rats coming out of the woodwork." He gives a big sigh, as if it's a terrible hardship, but I can see by the look on his face that he enjoys being an uncle. "Mira, can I have a word?"

"Oohhhhhh what did you dooooo?" Blanche teases, her and Mama Debs making gasping noises while Lovely grins.

"I swear it wasn't me! Please don't send me to the chokey!" I exclaim. Instead of laughter all I hear is.... Crickets.

I turn to look at my new lady friends and they all look puzzled.

"You know, the chokey? The place where Trunchbull sends the naughty kids? Matilda? Both a book and a film? Oh come on people!" I throw my hands up in the air when I realize they have no clue what I'm talking about.

"Lady, we grew up in a cult and she's from New Zealand. Who even knows what they get there? Just know that pop references are beyond us." Blanche shrugs.

"That's it, I'm making a list. You lot and me have a date later, I'll teach you all you need to know. I got you, *kotiro*." I look to Mama Debs who grins and nods. Yes, I nailed it. "OK, Marx, march me toward the gallows."

He rolls his eyes and leads the way.

Marx

I can hear her quick footsteps behind me as I stomp my way into my office. I could slow down to let her catch up, but what can I say? I'm an asshole sometimes and I have a lot of shit on my mind.

I indicate she take a seat in the chair across from me, and I lower myself into my own ergonomic chair. It was a total pain in the ass to assemble, but it's worth every fucking penny.

I watch as she looks around as if she hasn't ever been in here before. Weird given that she was in that exact same spot last night.

"There's like, so much to look at in here. Like who are those guys? Why are the walls nicotine yellow? Do you smoke?" She stares at me, waiting for the answers.

"The guys who started the MC, the ex pres smoked, and no."

"Ha! Good to know. Anyway, you wanted to talk to me? About important, secret stuff I'm guessing seeing as I'm in here and not out there," Mira indicates with her head.

I let out a sigh. "I think you need to go through the plot of 'To Trap a Kiss' and see if you remember anything else. Has the sender of the livers reached out in any other ways? Phone calls and then hanging up like they did in the book?" She shakes her head. "Maybe think through anything weird that may have happened to you recently and see if any of that matches any of your books. Whoever is doing this must be a fan." I say, drumming my fingers on the top of my desk.

It was fucking close out there, blurting out To Trap a Kiss once I put together the similarities between Mira's book and the shit happening in her life. I'm not ashamed that I read and love Mira's books. I just don't need the headache of my men finding out and giving me shit about it. They're like kids. The lot of 'em.

"That's a solid plan, Mr. President. I never thought of that. AND if I put all the threads together then you can stop pretending that you don't read my stuff," she gives me an exaggerated wink and I roll my eyes.

"Exactly. I don't need fuckers on my case. I don't know if you've noticed this but they can be pains in the ass."

"Nope, they've all been nice to me," she replies with an empathic nod.

"Give it time," I mutter.

"OK. I'm going to head home and love on my poor cat who's been eating people." She stands and heads toward the door before turning around. "Oh, and I'll try to not have any more body parts sent to you." She grimaces at the last part. Having that shit sent to you, as a single woman, must be scary as hell.

"You're not on your own, Mira. We're all in this together. Got me?" Her shoulders slump and I can see where she was putting on a brave face. The woman may be loud and not shy at all, but that doesn't mean that this shit isn't messing with her head.

"Oh my gosh thank you so much. That makes me feel a little better."

"Don't mention it." I give her a nod and she turns toward

the door.

She grasps the handle and then spins around once again. "How long have you had a crush on Lovely?"

My quick intake of breath has me choking on thin air and I burst out into a coughing fit. Holy shit I'm going to die choking to death on air. A hand beats the hell out of my back and I swallow madly, hoping that saliva may be able to stop the choking. Deciding that's a shit idea I grab my bottle of whiskey, pour two fingers and shoot it back.

"Holy shit, what the fuck are you on about woman?" I manage to wheeze out.

"You and Lovely out there. How long has that been going on?" she asks, eyes wide, twinkling at the look on my face.

"We're friends. She's Blanche's sister, so that makes her family." She stares at me as if I'm talking out my ass. "Look, she's been through a lot, had men treat her like shit. She needs to find who she is as a person before she can even think about having a relationship. With anyone." I stare at Mira, hoping my words are enough to convince her there's nothing going on with me and Lovely.

Because it's the truth. From what Blanche has shared, Lovely's life would have been hell. Royal was an absolute mean fucker, and that sweet woman was married off to him in her teens. Now she's out here making a life for herself, and I want her to succeed at anything and everything she puts her mind to. She needs our support, not me or anyone else trying to get into her pants. Besides, even if there was something in the way we interact, interest or whatever you want to call it, we wouldn't be right together. Lovely is sweet and kind and she sees the absolute best in people. I'm a hard fucker, downright nasty at times, and the life of a Pres' Ol Lady isn't for Lovely. She deserves the picket fence, the dog and the fucking accountant or banker to come home to her and their children every night.

"That's very noble of you, Pres. Very noble indeed." Mira smiles and gives a bow. "Right, I gotta get going, I've got to check in on my cat and write an anal scene. Oh, and I'll write a list of weird stuff that's happened recently and cross reference my books. I'll see you tomorrow."

I have nothing to say to that. Asking would just engage the woman in a conversation about anal and I'm not ready for that at this time of the evening. Shaking my head, I try to clear it to get on to my actual job, paperwork for all our businesses. Not thinking about Lovely.

Chapter 6

Tank

Cruising into the compound I let out a sigh of relief. Today was fucking exhausting. If Judge and I thought we were busy last week, then today was a rude awakening. We were so busy in and out of Devil's Big Tow we had to call in reinforcements in the shape of Savage, Flack and Rider. Savage and Flack worked well together, getting the old tow truck out on the road while Judge and I worked the newer trucks as usual. Rider, well, his help in the office was appreciated. Even if it wasn't as efficient or professional as it could have been.

Parking Winnie in my spot, right next to Judge, I shut her down and sit for a moment, waiting for Judge to do the same.

"Shit, brother, I think we need a couple more employees."

Judge nods, sitting with his thoughts. "Yeah. Today ran well with Savage and Flack pitching in. But shit, having Rider work reception was a big fucking help."

I give him a chin lift and throw my leg over my bike to stand, gathering my shit out of my bags.

"I'll take it to church. Business has been steadily growing and you and I don't have time to run reception and go to call outs."

"You got my vote, brother," Judge replies, walking alongside before stopping abruptly. "Shit."

Parked in the parking lot is a police cruiser. Not any cruiser, Sergeant Davies' cruiser.

"Fuck."

A hand lands on my shoulder, giving me a little shake. "Breathe, brother."

We head toward the door, me wanting to get this shit over with; Judge having my back. Before we even get to the door it swings open, Nitro marching out, Davies by his side.

"What the fuck?" Judge mutters, staring at the men walking past.

"You're off the hook this time, brother," Nitro winks at me on his way past, not a care in the world.

Davies, again looks relaxed and as with me indicates Nitro take the front seat. Nitro doesn't look too pissed, but you can bet your ass Fox will be. Pushing through the door my brothers and the Ol Ladies are gathered in the common room. Wire on the phone most likely calling his momma, everyone else looking to Marx for instruction.

"What in the hell was that?" I ask the room, hoping someone will fill me in.

"Some fucker laid a complaint with Rose Grove PD. Same MO as you, brother," Fox seethes.

Swinging my head toward Marx, the Pres confirms with a nod. "Someone out there is fucking with us. Was bullshit when they hauled in Tank, even more bullshit with Nitro now. Davies knows it's a waste of fucking time, but the man has to follow all leads."

"Why the hell does this town have such an efficient police department? Most towns would shove that complaint into some shitty dark room somewhere," Flack grumbles. Coming from a one percent club in Roxburgh where half the force was in their pocket, I can see why this is blowing his mind.

"Don't know. But we've had two fucking complaints against us now. Wire, I need you to see if you can find anything." Wire nods, taking Remy by the hand and leading her to their control center. "We also have this whole Mira thing. Usually we wouldn't get mixed up in civilian issues, but that package coming here is a problem. With us on the RGPD radar, we don't need them turning up when we have a box of fucking human parts on the table."

Chewy puts her hand up, waiting patiently for Marx to give her the go ahead to talk. He nods in her direction and she shares a look with Pops.

"Speaking of livers, we did our research and we can say that the liver was fresh."

"How fresh?" Savage asks.

"Less than 24 hours outside of the owner's body." She answers confidently.

"Could the livers have been stolen from some place that does transplants or something? Something less messed up than we think?" Nat asks from her seat on the couch, where all the Ol Ladies except Remy and Chewy sit.

"There's no sign of them being on ice or kept in a cooler and the condition they were in was consistent with the type of degradation that the human body experiences after blood stops pumping." Pops answers.

"They're right," Switch says, agreeing with the Tombs.

"How the hell do they know all this stuff?" Dex mutters under his breath.

"Decomposition was a special interest of ours for a while," Chewy answers, shrugging a shoulder.

"Mira was going to do a deep dive into her books in case this fucker is a fan and is basing his moves on one of her characters," Marx says, looking around at us all.

The Tombs brothers step forward and I hadn't even noticed that August and Jules were here, although I guess it makes sense. Now they're back from whatever secret mission they were on, they've been here every day since. "Jules met with Flora from Flora's Buds," Gus says, tipping his head to his brother.

"Yeah, checked the footage. The perp was clever enough to stay out of full sight of the camera. Any glimpses we got were from behind. No way to do facial rec."

"I spoke to Flora's husband, he's their delivery driver. He said he had no contact with the person who placed the order, and he just does whatever his wife tells him to do," Gus adds.

"What about whoever took the order?" Rhodie asks, Chomper attached to his chest, his arm slung over Chewy's shoulders.

"Yeah, about that. Flora is, um, unusual?"

"That's my mom you're talking about!" We all spin to the doorway to see Sergeant Davies standing there, a dark look on his face. "But yeah, you're kinda right in your description." He lets out a sigh.

"Why the hell are you back? And how much did you hear?" Marx growls, stepping toward him. Fuck this cop has a lot of balls. Or no brains.

"We never got out of the lot because pretty boy here forgot his phone." He rolls his eyes as Nitro comes ambling in, grin on his face.

"Why the fuck would he need it?" Fox asks, bewildered.

"To call one of you to pick him up?"

"You let him come back to pick up his phone?" Chewy asks, brows pinched in confusion.

"Yeah," Davies answers.

"He's letting me sit in the front, too!" Nitro crows.

"You are the worst policeman ever," Chewy says with a frown.

"Look, we all know the charge is bullshit, but it's my job to take him in and ask questions and fill out the paperwork. It works in your favor, too. Being seen as cooperative goes a long way with the department. As for how much I heard, that doesn't matter because my mother called me, found out where I was and wanted me to pass on a message."

"This whole situation is fucked up," Flack whispers to Dex who nods back.

"Mama said that the person who placed the order had," he looks down at his phone, presses a couple of buttons and then reads from the screen, "an orc build, small piggy eyes, hair like the big man from Moana with the magic tattoos that sings and has the voice of a crab." He looks up from his phone, grins smugly at us, and gestures to Nitro to follow him. The door bangs after him and we hear the asshole's booming laughter on the other side of the closed door.

We stand in silence trying to figure out what the fuck that even means. Looking toward Jules I ask "Did Flora say that to you too?"

He shakes his head. "No, she told me he was as wide as three rich women's bouquets and the type of face that invites fists."

Marx scrubs a hand down his face. "Right. So a solid man that

Miss Flora obviously hated on sight. Got it. Fuck if Wire can find anything from those descriptions he'd be a fucking genius. Jesus." His shoulders slump before he continues. "Fuck, why can't we ever catch a break and weird shit bypass us for a change?"

As soon as the words leave his mouth, Mira comes swanning in with an arm full of books. "Whoa, what did I miss? Why does everyone look so serious?" Her gaze travels around the room. Once. Twice. "Hey, where's your boyfriend?"

"He's not my boyfriend!" Fox barks.

"Oh, soz. My bad. I just always see you together so I figured you were together, together. Nothing wrong with that." She dumps her books on the nearest table. "You guys are hot individually. Together you would be scorching hot. Fire and ice." She brings her fists together, fist bumping herself making explosion sounds, drawing her hands out making jazz hands.

The women all start talking animatedly about reverse harems, whatever the fuck they are, and then Marx's whistle rends the air.

"Listen up, we have church in 20 minutes. Chewy, help Wire and Remy, see what they can find on all the shit we got coming at us. The rest of you ladies, would you mind reading some of Mira's books? We need clues. Fuck, anything that can lead us to whoever is messing with Mira and now us."

The women all nod eagerly and descend upon the pile of books on the table.

"I want everyone in church, including prospects. Gus?" He tips his head towards his office and Gus drops a kiss on Ana's head, then his son's, and follows after Pres.

Since the arrival of Chewy, Pres and Gus have become close friends. It's a development I never saw coming, given how uptight Gus can be, however the man is a machine when it comes to security and safety. He may not be ex-military like the rest of us, but his training is on point. Thanks to him and his family, the MC has state of the art weapons and gadgets. I can only imagine their meeting currently will be for some new tech or shit. That's always Marx's number one. Keep his men and the rest of our ragtag family safe.

"Penny for your thoughts? Or maybe a quarter? What with inflation and all," Mira quips, her arm brushing mine as she gesticulates, her soft and yet spicy vanilla scent enveloping me.

"Just thinking about security systems."

She lets out a low whistle. "Wooooooow, that sounds very boring. Here, have a book."

She shoves a book into my hands, the shiny cover a moody purple and blue. 'Stabbed in the Feels' is written in swirly gold script and I can't help the chuckle that bursts out of me.

Looking up, Mira catches my eyes and gives me a wink, then carries on handing them out to everyone, not just the women.

"There's too many for just the *kotiro* to read, so we'll all have to pitch in. Do you guys have a whiteboard?" She asks, spinning this way and that, looking around the room. "Or, like a really big paper? Somewhere I can write all the weird and wonderful things that happened to me recently so we can cross reference and catch this sucker?"

"Gimme a minute," Takoda says, disappearing into the storeroom behind the bar. Within moments he returns, carrying a big ass whiteboard.

"Shit, who even knew we had that?" Rider says, pointing at it. "Why do we have that?"

No one seems to know the answer, not that it matters as we

all watch Mira draw bullet points on the whiteboard and then in large, pretty handwriting the weird shit that's happened to her.

"Rescued from a rogue dog by a fighter pilot?" Judge asks, brows in his non-existent hairline.

"Found a strange garden gnome in your petunias?" someone else says.

"She's an interesting one, your little writer," Jules' mono-tone voice says to my left.

"She isn't my anything." He raises his brow at me. "Fine. We're friends. I like her. She's … comfortable with herself" "

He stares at me a moment, assessing, his gaze uncomfortable. I've stared down worse men, but something about Jules Tombs makes it feel like he sees straight through you. Unlike his siblings, he isn't quirky like Chewy, or anal retentive but controlled like Gus. He's not even friendly and congenial like Tav. Jules Tombs is more intense, reserved, and because of that fact I know he would be one hell of a man to have at your back.

He looks toward Mira, then turns back to me. "Weird friendship. You say fuck all and she says too much."

I grunt at his comment. "Works for Fox and Nitro."

Something glints in his eye, and his lips twitch. "Yeah, guess it does, doesn't it?" With that, he saunters off, leaving me more confused than when he arrived.

Typical Tombs.

Mira

"Girl, what the hell type of life do you lead? This shit is nuts!" Nat exclaims, Savage chuckling as he stands behind the couch she's sitting on, rocking their little girl in his huge arms. He leans forward, gently passing Rosie to her and drops a kiss on the top of Nat's head. It's all very swoon worthy.

"Be good, baby," He murmurs before following the rest of the men into church. Apparently today is their usual church day, and given the livers and whatever happened with Nitro, they could be in there for a while.

"Accidentally ran into Old Man Matheson on my bike," Lovely reads out loud.

"He would have deserved it too. That Old Man Matheson is a total asshole," Blanche loudly adds, causing Lovely to gasp.

Both of them are sitting side by side on the small two seater couch, Nat, Ana and their babies are sitting on the other. Chewy is sitting on the floor cross legged with Chomper on her lap. Remy is perched on a bar stool between the two couches and Mama Debs is on Pops' knee in the recliner.

"Blanche is right. He is an asshole," Pops adds over a yawn.

"Can I ask you all a question?" I say, looking at eight pairs of eyes. Or sixteen eyeballs. Seventeen if we count that I can only see one of Rosie's, the other side of her face nestled into her mom. Who has a fantastic rack. I wonder if it was like that before Rosie?

"Nah, they were way smaller. Ana here has an amazing rack both pre and post Junior." Nat says, giving me a wink. Dag nabbit, why inner monologue, why!?

"Oh yeah, she does too! Here, look, poke her in the boob,"

Chewy says in what I'm guessing is her excited voice. "They feel amazing." Ana slaps her hand away and Chewy frowns at her.

"You wanted to ask us a question, *kotiro*?" Mama Debs asks gently, getting everyone back on track.

"Oh, yeah. Were you all friends before becoming Ol Ladies, or did you become Ol Ladies and then friends?"

"I didn't have any friends when I first got here. Then Rider and Wire became my besties and Rhodie became my lover," Chewy says, side eyeing Ana.

"Ugh! Stop referring to him like that. It grosses me out."

"Why? He is my lover." Chewy answers in her flat voice.

"ANYWAY, I met Chewy when she freed me from a trafficking ring," Nat says. Wait, what? "And Remy and I were friends because we came from the same MC." Remy nods in agreement, smiling at her friend.

"I met Chewy when the MC and Bratva were working to-gether," Ana adds.

"I met all these women pretty much at the same time. Including Lovely. I didn't even know she existed until she broke out of Eden's Keep." Hold up, aren't they sisters? Between that and Nat's revelation, we are definitely circling back to this conversation.

"And now we're all part of Chewy's girl gang," Lovely beams.

Chewy stabs her finger in her direction. "Yes! We need to induct Mira into the gang! Pops?"

"On it girl." Pops answers in his rough voice, like he's been gargling rocks all his life.

"Wait, what are you planning?" Remy asks, looking a little worried about the whole thing.

"A surprise. Trust us," Chewy says and I can see everyone

does not, in fact, trust them.

"Every time we let you and Pops organize girls' night we get into trouble," Remy replies.

"Oh it was one time I hired police strippers. You make out like I hire them every girls' night," Chewy huffs.

"I double dog dare you to. With the brothers being taken in all the time and Mira's body parts they'll be all on edge. Police strippers would be the perfect way to settle everyone down," Blanche says with a sly grin.

"You really think so?" Chewy asks, head tilted.

Blanche nods her head vigorously up and down while Ana and Remy try to hold her still. From where I sit I can see Pops' phone screen and it looks like he's researching male strippers in the area.

I'm very intrigued and kinda want to see how this turns out, but my brain is screaming that we should be working on the matter at hand. I don't really want any more body parts turning up. Especially not here, they've already got a mystery person trying to frame them for things. An evil doer trying to destroy what the men have built here. An unscrupulous person, a formidable foe that we'll all have to pool our resources and fight on all fronts to keep the MC safe. Oh that's good stuff, I quickly note that down.

Putting my pencil down I turn to look at the people still arguing about police strippers. After a long time alone, and a lifetime of very few real life friends, I'm really hoping I can keep these women. I peek around and note they haven't paused their bickering, meaning my thoughts must have stayed in my head that time. Yay for me! I don't want them to have to be my friend just because my brain can't use an inside voice. Anyway, I shake that off and turn back to the whiteboard, racking my brain for other weird happenings. I guess I could add the time I met Tank, so I do. Only the incident, not the actual meeting. The meeting is something I like to keep to myself. For a short moment in time that big, blonde sexy biker man was part of my life. I mean, he kinda still is, but I enjoyed having him all to myself. Men like him don't look twice at a woman like me, so to have him to talk to, and then help me home, well, that was the highlight of the year, maybe even decade. I may have even bashed out a novella with a sexy blonde convict and tall, curvy woman. Shoot, I better get back to the task at hand. It's bad enough these people have been lumped with my crazy fan. They don't need Brain Mira drooling over their quiet MC brother at the same time. I take a breath and think.

"Oh! I remembered another one!" I definitely say out loud and write 'Accidentally killed a chicken escaping from a bad date', the whiteboard pen making an annoying squeaking sound.

"No, like seriously, what is your life? How does all this weird stuff happen to you?" Nat asks.

"Did you take it hostage, threaten to kill it and when the bad guy called your bluff you were forced to kill the chicken?" Chewy asks, almost looking more excited than when she sees her gator.

"Oh nice one, girl," Pops says, giving his granddaughter an appreciative nod.

"We need the details. On all of these actually. Because there is no way these all happened to you. Like over how long a period?" Blanche asks, pointing at the 19 bullet points of weird things that is my life.

"Um, since just before the first delivery, so maybe, 4 months?"

There's a squawk and exclamations of "spill!".

With the spotlight on me I try to explain to the best of my abilities. Which is harder than you think for an author. Where in my books I can tell the story in a linear fashion, lay out the characters, their motivations and deep dives into hot sexy times, in real life with real people, my story telling is not linear at all. These poor people, my prospective real life friends, sit in confused silence as I let them into the inner world of Mira. The good stuff like Mrs Crispin's delicious pies that she makes me because I'm a "good girl", right through to two weeks ago when I returned a lost kitten to a hoarder and accidentally bumped a stack of newspapers from 30 years ago and it caused a domino effect, knocking over four more piles. By the time I finish telling them I accidentally killed a chicken by jumping over it to escape the farm maze my boring date took me on, they all sit silently in shock.

"So, let me get this straight. This shit happens to you all the time?" Pops rasps.

"Um, yeah. But I'm pretty sure this stuff happens to everyone every so often."

They all look at each other, as if to wonder what the heck is wrong with me.

"Whatever you say dear," Mama Debs soothes.

"OK. So we have to track down some of these people. That's easy work. The hard part is figuring out who these people are, if any of them has it out for you, if they would hate you enough to threaten you in any way and if any of them are fans of your work. Only fans would know about the liver stuff. We also need to cross reference some of these other weird things –" Chewy points to things I've found inside my house or garden that I know weren't there before. "with your books and figure out if any of them could be coincidental."

"Oh when you put it like that it'll be easy," I quip, rolling my eyes. "We may as well solve whoever's trying to frame the MC while we're at it."

"Trust us, Writer Lady, we'll figure this out."

Chapter 7

Tank

I file into church behind my brothers, catching one last glimpse of Mira working at the whiteboard. I didn't lie to Jules, I think we are friends. I mean, I'm not going to deny that she's a beautiful woman. Tall, curves for days and a beautiful face, she's exactly the type of woman I go for. But it's more than that. She's clever and funny and genuinely interested in people. Pretty much the opposite of my reserved, quiet self. Where most women would ditch me in favor of some of my more outgoing brothers, Mira looks at me as if I'm interesting. Or something. Shit I dont know anything other than my dick's been hard every time she's in the vicinity.

I'm snapped out of my confusing thoughts by the banging of Marx's gavel. I shouldn't be thinking about what type of relationship Mira and I have. I should be focusing on who the hell is messing with us.

"Wire, got anything for us?" Marx grunts.

"Between Chewy, Remy and myself we managed to 'find a way'-," He does comma fingers, "- to get into the RGPD

"

files. Tank's complainant was one Miss Kelly Maree Birkhead. Nitro's complainant is Miss Clarisse Louise Welch."

"Who the fuck are they?" Rider voices what everyone is thinking.

"You'd know them as our old bunnies, Whitney and Kelly."

"Wait, Whitney's real name is Clarisse?" Fox asks incredulously.

"Yup. Looks like our old bunnies are fucking with us." Wire sits back, letting the information settle.

Marx looks less than pleased. In fact, he looks pissed. "So you're telling me that Whitney and her little sidekick were so pissed at being kicked out of the club that they're now wasting police time by making false claims against us?"

Wire nods. "All four of the ex-club girls live together in an apartment on Hillcrest Ave. They all four work at 'Spinners', the strip club in Roxburgh."

"They're commuting that far for work?" Flack asks, clearly shocked. Roxburgh is an hour and a half away from Rose Grove. A long ass commute after a long night.

"Seems that way."

Dex and Savage share a look, one that doesn't go unmissed by Marx.

"What do you know?"

"Spinners is owned by a nasty little fucker, David something or other. Big D. Was a pimp on the streets, built up a crew and pretty much bullied all the other lower street criminals until he was top dog. Rumor has it that if you want anything, drugs, girls, information, then Spinners is the place to go." Savage says with a dark look on his face. "If these women don't bat an eyelid accusing men of assaulting them, then they won't bat an eyelid to sell information to anyone who wants it either."

Marx runs a hand down his face and curses. "We need to neutralize the threat. They all signed confidentiality agreements when they signed up. That includes keeping their mouths shut after a contract has been terminated. Rhodie and Rider pay them a visit, reminding them of their obligations. Prospects, I want you on shifts to watch them, just so they know we have eyes everywhere."

"If that doesn't work?" Rhodie asks his brother.

"We send in the women." Marx's eyes track around the room looking for any disagreement. He finds none. "Good. That's settled. Prospects? Draw up a roster, I want two on them at all times, up to you how you all work it."

"Got it Pres," they murmur, from their places along the back wall.

"Good. What do we have on Mira?"

"Not a lot. As we heard out there Flora's Buds was a bust on getting anything out of the security cameras or Officer Davies' mom." A few brothers snort and Wire keeps giving his report. "Chewy set up a program, it's going through all of Mira's social media messages as we speak. It's set up to flag any fans that may have questionable behavior."

"Dude, she writes romance books with really hot sex and people being murdered. I'd be surprised if any of her fans don't have questionable behavior," Tav says.

"How do you know that her books have really hot sex in them?" Rhodie asks, turning to look at Tav.

"I flicked through one of her books while I was waiting for church. There's some good stuff in there. I'm going to try it on Blanche when the kids are in bed." He waggles his brows and we all groan in unison.

Marx sits drumming his fingers on the dark, scarred wood

of our church table. It feels like we're fighting on all sides, and yet it's nothing like what we've been up against in the past. It feels like two annoyances, although I know as well as any brother around this table that small annoyances can turn into big fucking problems. My mind drifts back to being stationed in Afghanistan. I lost brothers who went on short low danger missions to never come back after running into landmines, or ambushes.

"If we can't work out who's behind this, maybe we can find out where the body parts are coming from? Are they being bought on the dark net or is it something else?" This is the first time Sniper has spoken this meeting, and he has a fucking valid point.

"Remy and I had a quick look, but most of the organs for purchase are all for donation, so they would have to be kept on ice. Chewy said that there's no sign of that," Wire frowns. I know my brother struggles with not being able to find the answers for things.

"Well, maybe it's not as bad as we think." We all stare at Rider. "OK, so four people have died, but we haven't had a visit from Roman in a long time. When that asshole turns up you know it's going to be bad." What Rider's saying does make sense. Maybe it isn't as bad as we think.

Banging has all our heads snapping to the doors of church, hands on weapons. Fuck! The Ol Ladies are all out there and all of us, including prospects, are in here.

"Oh Maaaaaarx!" Chewy's voice sing songs, the tension in the room dropping by a mile.

Marx runs a hand down his face, then waves at Rhodie to see what his Ol Lady wants. Rhodie makes his way to the door just as it swings open with such force that I'm certain that little lady must have kicked it.

"Babe! What's wrong?" Rhodie asks, dodging the swinging door.

"Roman's here. Has some important information."

We all groan, Dex shooting daggers at Rider. "You just had to, didn't you? Speak his name and the Devil appears."

"I thought that was more Pops, but OK, I agree with you. But, like, really, what were the chances that Russian dick would turn up out of the blue like that?"

"It's Roman," Marx says in a tired voice.

"Yeah, alright. My bad." Marx stares at Rider before waving Rhodie to let Roman in.

The tall, dark Russian strides in like he owns the place and my mind goes to Mira and if she's OK. Although, I'm sure if anything happened the women would have taken care of it. And Roman isn't dangerous per se. He's more the bringer of shitty news and problems.

"Well, isn't this a treat? You've never allowed me into the inner sanctum. I must say however, that I do have the name of a great decorator should you ever wish to use their services."

"You know, I was just thinking the other day how peaceful Christmas was with you all the fucking way over in Russia, keeping your business to yourself." Marx says drily.

Roman smirks at Pres, "Aw, Marx, did you miss me?" Roman comes to a stop next to Rider.

Rider arches his neck until he's staring directly at Roman. "Can I help you?"

Roman continues to stare and even though I know Rider can be just as violent and tough as the rest of us, I know that prolonged eye contact with another male will get him squirming any minute now.

"Fine!" Rider jumps up and moves to lean against the wall, muttering "Fucker," and flipping him the bird.

Roman takes no notice, unbuttoning his suit jacket and using his hands to toss both sides out before taking Rider's seat, crossing one leg over the other.

"Roman, I can't be bothered with your bullshit today. Say what you need to say and then you can go back to wherever the hell you've been hiding lately."

His lips twitch and then he schools his features, glancing around. "Ana asked me to keep my ear to the ground regarding body parts. As you well know I'm not in the business of transporting anything human, however I have heard of a family-owned funeral home who have been, shall we say, losing things."

"What kind of things?" Fox asks.

"The kind of things that get sent to beautiful authors."

Great. So Mira somehow has crossed paths with some madman who has been stealing parts from the dearly beloved. On the upside, it makes the sender a little less dangerous if the organ owners are already dead.

"We're gonna need the name and location of this home, Roman," Marx says in a bored tone.

Roman admires his nails a moment, picking at them, not even looking up at Marx. "I'm not sure I can do that." He holds his hand up as Marx starts growling. "You see, this particular funeral home is under my protection."

"Why?" Savage demands.

"They're family friends. They've worked hard to make it in the great United States. The founder knew my babushka. Take your pick."

We all sit and stare at Roman while he continues fucking

around, pretending that we aren't staring directly at him. Any other man would have shit himself by now, but not the man who seems to live to piss us off.

"They take care of your disposals don't they?" Sniper says in his quiet, measured voice.

At this, Roman looks up, assessing Sniper for a beat. "Well, you can't expect me to get rid of all those bodies myself do you? Disposal of any type of mammal is very tedious."

"Is that how you disposed of Diego Cordoza and his men?"

Diego Cordoza was moving women and Roman's stolen drugs for Eden's Keep. Roman took care of the problem, but it still doesn't sit well with my brother. I know there is history there, but that's Sniper's story to tell. If he ever wants to.

"Diego Cordoza and his men did not deserve such pleas- antries. Their heads were sent to their families, minus the tongues to encourage them to keep their mouths shut." Ro- man's cold gaze meets Sniper's, sharing a look with him before my brother tips his chin and relaxes back in his seat.

"The name and location of the home, Roman. All we need is to get eyes on it, run surveillance. We don't need to talk to anyone," Marx rumbles.

Roman lets out a sigh. "Fine. I think that can be arranged. However, I may need something in return."

I try to hold in my groan, Rider and Rhodie are unsuccessful. Marx doesn't answer, just glares at the other man.

"There's a strip club in Roxburgh. Spinners. What do you know about it?" Roman says, ignoring everyone around him.

"It's run by a dodgy little shit head that loves to deal in drugs, women and information."

"Exactly. I've heard that there's a few loose lipped women in there. I would like my "relationship" with the DRMC kept quiet. These *shlyukhi,* whores may jeopardize that."

"Consider it taken care of. Now, the name of the funeral home."

Mira

Well, turns out the planning/investigation meeting with the girls didn't go quite to plan. Instead of nutting out who could be doing this and why or how, we ended up having cocktails to get the thinking juices flowing. I'm not sure how good any of our suggestions are, given that I can't even read my own handwriting on the whiteboard and my eyes are fuzzy.

"Ana, tell me again how you met that hunk of spunk Roman. He's so pretty," I feel my head roll back on my shoulders, so I use my hands to put it back where it belongs.

I blink, and then close one eye to help my focus. Nope, I was seeing things right the first time. Lovely is sitting on a chair, and Chewy is trying to drape Chomper over her shoulders, like a fur stole. Once he's in place, his funny little under bite snout hanging dangerously close to Lovely's boobs, she stands and sashays across the room to cheers and claps.

"These people are seriously nuts, but not you hot viking guy. Wait!" I lean closer to a gorgeous blonde man that I have never met who is sitting next to me, feet up on the coffee table next to mine, Nat painting our toes for us. "Where the heckerly doo dah did you come from?"

Viking man chuckles, the sounds vibrating through me, his

giant, hard bicep touching my soft, jelly bicep.

"I came with my husband, he's managed to make it into their little meeting. He'll be crowing about this for the next two weeks."

"Ohhhh Saaasha! We met before when you came in with the hot vampire looking guy!" I pat his head because I don't know why and then I have another sip of the delicious cocktail. I hold it up in the air, the light hitting the bright pink liquid in my glass. "Compliments to the chef!"

Everyone else calls out their compliments to Mama Debs and Pops who are our alchemists tonight. They're good at it too, possibly a little too good, but I feel great and not stressed about deadlines or livers or not having real people friends and no boyfriend and oh my God I'm going to die alone aren't I?!

I try to fight down the tears but the only place the emotion can go is directly out of my eyeballs. And not in a cute way. In a very ugly, very snotty waily way.

"Oh no, we've broken her," someone whispers. I think it was a lady voice.

"It was a matter of time. Besides, she needed a factory reset. Have you seen the weird shit that happens to her?"

"Chewy, that is not her fault."

"Whose fault is it, then?"

The silence suggests that they don't know which has me spiraling again. This time with loud sobbing.

"Hey, it's OK, drunky, let's get you into your room, yeah? You can sleep off whatever the hell happened here," a deep, gentle voice soothes.

"Hey! I know that voice. That's Tank's voice. It's so warm and it vibrates me. Like my whole body goes all vibratey. Even my special parts. The ones that Nana said I have to save for good. Am I floating? It feels like I'm floating. Like a massive, chubby angel floating to gift presents to children and take their teeth to make furniture for my teeny house." My inside thoughts are so funny sometimes.

Whatever is helping me fly makes a funny rumbling sound and my head bounces around making me feel a bit sick. OK, maybe a lot sick.

"I don't feel well Mr. Rumbly Voice," I say weakly before lurching.

"Shit! Hold on!"

There's some banging, actually lots of banging and then I'm on something cool, a white cold thing touching my face. Oh that feels nice. There's a warm pressure on my back, moving from the top of my neck all the way to almost my bottom, and then back again. Petting me like I'm that big luck dragon from The Neverending Story.

"He died you know," I sniffle, moving my face to get more cold white onto it.

"Who died, sweetheart?"

"Falcor. He was the very best luck dragon. He was trying to find Ellora Dannon's mom."

"Ugh, I think she's from Willow, not The Neverending Story," the magic Tank voice says.

"Oh, do you know it?" I raise my head a little, I don't feel so sick now that I'm not flying anymore.

"Yeah, I remember watching it when I was a kid. My neighbor loved it." His voice sounds smiley. Usually his voice is measured and rumbly, not light and smiley. I like it.

"Oh, can you please sing me the song? My nana used to sing it to me when I didn't feel good. Like now. If she was still alive she would be sitting right here with me, singing the theme song, making me feel warm and soft inside." I sigh, closing my eyes and picturing my nana. Her gentle face and funny crooked fingers. There's moisture on my cheeks but I keep my eyes clamped shut, so I can keep seeing nana in my mind.

"Shit, you're killing me, sweetheart."

"I know," I whisper, a funny echo whispers back, and then buzzing in my mind.

No, not a buzzing, a hum. Why does the humming sound like the theme from The Neverending Story?

* * *

I roll over and a loud groan escapes. What in the jeewillikers happened to me? I crack one eye open and try to roll the dry eyeball around, taking stock of the room around me. It's not the same one as the one I was in last night. Or was it the night before? What day is it? Who am I? My hands drift up to my face and I pat it, hoping that everything will feel familiar. Check. Everything feels like it should do. To be sure though I do a quick squeeze of the girls.

"What are you doing?" Holy Moses and that sea he parted, the rumble and grumble of Tank's sleep-roughened voice punches me straight in the vagina. In a good way. A good vagina punch.

"Um, checking to make sure I'm me," I squeak out.

Opening both eyes I turn my head toward the furnace that's on my left side, coming face to face with Tank. Big, blonde, Howdy Doody gorgeous Tank. His blue eyes twinkle as he looks at me and his lips pull up, causing the crinkles around his eyes to deepen.

"Like a big, wise, jolly old walrus."

"What?" he chuckles, the movement shaking the bed gently.

"Nothing. Just normal things. Normal people thoughts. Anyway, how did this all happen?" I wave my hand around in a big circle, encompassing me, Tank and the room in general.

"Seems last night turned into a girls' night induction party for you. I was carrying you to your room but when you started looking like you were gonna be sick I brought you to my room. Bigger attached bathroom that I knew would be clean." His eyes dart between mine, as if looking for signs of me being uncomfortable being brought to his room, but there are none. In fact, he can bring me in here anytime.

His woodsy man scent is everywhere in the room, enveloping me in what feels like safety and hope. Oh, that's a good line. I'll remember that for later.

"You with me?" Tank's voice breaks through my thoughts, and his eyes dance as he tries not to laugh.

"Oh yeah. Totally. Was just, um–"

"An idea for your book, right?"

I beam at him. "Right. Exactly that. How did you know what I was thinking?"

"Let's just say I used to love English class as a kid."

"Well, aren't you Mr. Full of Surprises! I would have guessed bunking out of school. Kissing behind the bike stands. Smoking in the bathrooms. Real bad boy stuff." He rolls his eyes at what I picture young Tank to be like.

He rolls onto his back, his hands coming up behind his head and stares up at the ceiling. Well, I think that's where he's looking. I wouldn't know. I'm too busy staring at the bulge of his biceps in this position. Moving my eyes to his profile I take note of his straight nose, pouty lips and long curly eyelashes that I spend a buttload of money trying to get. How unfair.

"I was a pretty geeky little kid. My parents were both in the army. I think I came along by accident. They were both career focused and I was dropped off to my grandfather's pretty soon after I was born. He raised me."

"Wait, did you ever see your parents?"

"Whenever they were stateside they'd stop by for dinner and things. Sometimes my dad would come watch a ball game or whatever. For the most part though, it was just me and gramps."

I roll further onto my side, tuck my hands under my cheek and curl my legs in, giving Tank my full undivided attention. Something about this man tells me that he doesn't often demand the limelight. The fact that he's here, telling me about his childhood is something precious and I won't take it for granted.

"Gramps made sure I did well in school. I was good at most subjects, but English was my favorite."

"What did you like about it?"

"Stories. I liked the stories and how they can transport you to anywhere or anytime. I liked hearing about the characters and their journeys. What they're going to do and if they'll survive." He shrugs a massive shoulder. A boulder of a shoulder. My fingers tingle, itching to touch the tanned skin, pulled tight over the boulder shoulder and marked with dark, swirling tattoos.

"I've not told anyone this, well, other than my gramps, but I like to write." He coughs, clearing his throat. "Um, I like writing stories. It was relaxing when I was stationed overseas." His cheeks pinken a little and he stares at the ceiling, almost trying to avoid my gaze.

"I love that! I would love to read some of your work."

"Hell no! No way. They're pretty shitty. I just like doing it to get out thoughts and things. Nothing like your novels."

He lies stiff as a board, as if embarrassment or shyness has taken over his body. This huge man, probably dangerous to those who threaten him or his family, is shy of me. Mira Campbell, kooky writer lady who wears too much color and is too noisy and has no inner monologue. My hand finds itself landing gently on Tank's cheek, turning his head to look at me.

"Writing my novels is me getting my thoughts out. Same as you." The intensity of his gaze almost takes my breath away. Swallowing, I give him a wobbly smile, so as to not show him how affected I am by the feel of him beneath my palm, his eyes boring into my soul. "I would love to read your thoughts someday, Tank."

"Tyson," he rasps, leaning into my hand a little.

"Tyson."

Chapter 8

Tank

"I need your help."

Savage, Rhodie, Wire and Tav all look up from Mira's books, where they've been studying them.

"Of course brother, need an extra driver at DBT? I've got the day off from bunny watch and I've already dropped the kids off at school so I'm free until school pickup," Tav says, moving to stand.

"No, it's ah, not work related." I rub the back of my neck. What the fuck was I thinking?

"So, what is it related to?" Savage asks, eyeing me up, Mira's book still open in his hand.

I lean my head back and blow out a breath, sorting my thoughts. My brothers wait, knowing I like to get my mind in order before saying anything. Apart from when I blurted out that I needed help just now. Mira has me twisted up in knots and not quite myself. Her little problem that is now our problem has us planning and waiting for the right time to move forward. The tech team has been working hard to hack into the funeral home's security and bank accounts and we've planned to send a team in for intel tomorrow. The rest of us are reading through Mira's back catalogue to find anything that may be of use and I should be helping but instead I've been busy fantasizing about the bubbly blonde that brought this all to our door.

"I want to take Mira on a date," I blurt out. The four assholes in front of me all put down their forgotten books, sitting forward.

"Mira? The writer lady?" Wire asks, brow furrowed. "The one with no inner monologue?"

"Yes, yup, the same one." I nod and then stand tall, straightening my spine and squaring my shoulders so I can take whatever shit they'll dish out. Instead, I'm met with confusion.

"Why are you asking us?"

"Because you are the only brothers with Ol Ladies. You must know what you're doing." They all look at each other before looking back at me.

"OK, let's help a brother out," Tav shrugs, clapping his hands. "Do you know where you want to take her?"

"No."

"What about what you want to do?" Rhodie asks, brow raised.

"Also, no. I haven't dated since high school and that was just a movie," Fuck, I'm in deeper than I thought.

"Well, she's being sent weird shit, but there's no real threat so you can pretty much go anywhere," Wire points out.

Four pairs of eyes stare at me as I stare back. She's different from any woman I've ever met before, which means I can't just take her to a bar and feed her wings and beer. It needs to be better than what I usually do.

"Have you thought that maybe the guys in these books -" Tav waves Mira's book in the air, "- are what she's looking for? Maybe do whatever they do."

"Well, the guy in this book liked to turn his cap backwards and lean over the woman in doorways and shit," Savage says, looking distastefully at the ripped guy in the cover.

"Yeah, mine seemed to just growl and grunt a lot. And murder a lot of people with his bare hands."

I let out a breath and pinch the bridge of my nose. "I'm not going to do any of those things. Any other bright fucking ideas?"

"What about a meal at the diner? I took Chewy there for our first date and look at us, still going strong." Rhodie grins wide and looks a little starry eyed at the mention of his Ol Lady.

"Yeah, but you also shut down the bathrooms with unconscious bodies and I think Tank wants to avoid violence when he takes Mira out," Tav points out.

"Wait, what the hell happened on that date?" Savage asks Rhodie with a confused look.

"It's a long story, but it all worked out in the end," Rhodie replies. He spots his Ol Lady walking through the front doors and gives her a grin, then blows her a kiss. This is met with a frown from Chewy who weaves her way toward us.

"What was that for?" she asks Rhodie, dropping a kiss on his lips before taking a seat on his knee.

"I was just telling the guys about our first date and then your beautiful ass walked in and I thought I'd show you my love by blowing a kiss."

Chewy's frown deepens, "That makes no sense. You can't blow a kiss. The act of the kiss itself is for lips to make physical contact. If you blow a kiss at me all you're really doing is blowing warm air my way."

Rhodie's body jiggles Chewy on his lap as he laughs silently. "Yes, you're right babe, total waste of time. Anyway, we're trying to help Tank come up with a first date idea."

She nods once and then turns toward me, her eyes on my shoulder. "Who are you dating?"

"I want to ask Mira out."

Chewy's lips tip up so I guess that's a good sign. "OK. I will be able to help because I like Mira and I'm a girl." I give her a smile and she leans forward, almost conspiratorially, "She loves books. And picnics. She told me." She leans back a little, then moves forward again, "OK, she actually told Lovely when Lovely asked if the guys in the books are what she's looking for in a man. She said no. She said she wants a nice thoughtful man that would take her to bookstores and on picnics and crap." I nod, this is all good shit. "She also said she would prefer a thick cock to one that's thin." She stands and moves to leave while my brothers and I all cough and splutter at that bomb drop.

Chewy walks toward the hall before spinning, "You're welcome."

We all watch her go and I'm not sure what to think. I mean, I have a pretty decent cock, definitely got good girth, if I do say so myself, so hopefully it's satisfactory. But shit, I never thought women thought about cocks like that. What else do they think about?

"Yo, man, you OK?" Savage asks, snapping his fingers in my direction. "I wouldn't worry about the state of your junk. First you gotta impress her enough to even want to see your junk," he grins.

"Is that what you did with Nat? Get her interested enough to want to see your junk?" I raise my brow.

"Nope. I didn't even know his name. We met at his sister's wedding. It was meant to be one and done in the reception venue bathrooms but once I met his junk I couldn't get enough of it," Nat beams, plopping their chubby little girl in her daddy's lap.

"I still had to work hard to get you to stay around though, babe," Savage says, staring up at his Ol Lady.

"That you did, baby." Nat drops a kiss on his lips and sashays off into the kitchen.

Watching first Rhodie and now Savage I decide that's what I want, and the only way I'm going to get it is if I stop fucking about and start dating.

"OK, I'm going to ask Mira out."

"Wait, I thought we already knew that?" Tav says, looking around at the others.

"You did. I've had a thought and I'm gonna run with it. Thanks brothers," I hold out my fist and bump knuckles with them all, heading out the door.

"Tank?" Mama Debs calls out. I take a detour to the kitchen, knocking twice on the doorjamb.

"Yeah, Mama?"

"Don't forget your lunch! I know you and Judge work through your breaks and I need you to stay strong and healthy,"

My lips twitch as I take the two big lunch boxes by their handles, dropping a kiss on Mama Deb's cheek. "Thanks, Mama."

I turn and head out the door, but not before Mama Debs calls out "Let me know if you need me to organize a picnic for the lovely Mira and yourself, I'll get it all sorted." I give her a grin and a wave and leave out the back door, beelining for my bike.

Securing the lunchboxes in my saddlebags, I throw my leg over my girl and start her, letting her vibrate my nerves away as I pull up my phone and type out a message.

Tank: Hey Mira, it's Tyson. Would you like to go out with me?

Mira: Yes! I'd love that! When? Today? This evening? Will there be food? Will I need to wear pants?

Her enthusiasm and wild texting has a smile on my face as I shake my head. I thought we would schedule for later this week, but shit, if she's keen for tonight then so be it.

Tank: Tonight if you're not too busy? I can pick you up, wear pants, and something warm. There will be food.

Mira: Then I'm in like Flynn! You know where I live! ;)

Smiling to myself I put my phone away, rev my engine and pull out, heading toward the gates. Looks like I'll be needing Mama Deb's services sooner rather than later.

Mira

Oh my god oh my god oh my god! Tank, I mean Tyson, asked me out! Me! Weird old Mira. Big, tall, weird old Mira. Big, tall, too loud, weird old - OK, that's enough freaking out. I have things I need to do. Like finish this one section I'm working on and then very calmly get myself ready for my date. With Tyson!

The squeal and little happy clap jog I do startles Mrs. McKenzie from where she likes to sit her fluffy ginger behind on my desk.

"Oops, sorry Mrs. Mac. It's just I have a date, old girl. So I need to concentrate on my work and then think about what I'm going to wear." I stroke her bright ginger fur, running my fingers through the silky strands, and think about running my fingers through Tyson's chest hair. I've seen the dark blonde strands that stick up out of his shirt and I would love to know exactly where all that hair goes. Hopefully, it's all over his chest and not just in a funny little patch at the top of his throat and then nowhere else, because that would be odd. Note to self: Perhaps write my villain with odd chest hair. I type that note in my list of notes that perpetually sits open in a tab on my laptop and flick back to the scene I'm working on. It's a classic part of romance, the third act breakup. This one is made slightly trickier by the fact that not only does the heroine have an evil identical twin, but so does the hero. Shaking my head to myself I marvel at some of the weird stuff I come up with. Maybe I should move to the small town romance genre. I'm less likely to be sent body parts by small town romance fans. I think.

I let my mind get into the scene I'm writing and everything flows through my fingers, without me even noticing. That's the thing about writing. I may be in charge of typing and doing all the admin stuff, but the characters themselves are who dictates the scene. If they want to torture their identical twin for information then so be it.

I type away like this, letting the people from inside my head tell me their stories, and it's only when my alarm to stretch goes off I notice the time. Holy sands of time, Batman! I have an hour and a half to get ready and it's not enough time! Jumping up in a panic I startle Mrs. Mac from my desk, her giving me the stink eye as she walks away.

"Argh, sorry! I just need to get ready for a date, Mrs. Mac

and I don't know where to start! Should I wash my hair? I will shave but how far up do I go? To the knee? Or higher? All the way up? HELP ME!" I screech at my cat, who looks at me calmly and slowly blinks before jumping up onto the couch, plopping her fat cat body down and going to sleep.

"I don't know why I even bother talking to you," I mumble at her as I speed walk to the bathroom, turning the shower on to heat as I throw my clothes off.

For some god unknown reason Nana has a full-length mirror in her bathroom. It was probably some weird old timey weight loss thing. You're so disgusted by what you see it spurs you into eating less. Not me though. I just ignore it. Well, usually I do. Today though I stare at myself and try to imagine what Tyson sees. I have good legs, I'll give myself that. They're toned and shapely, probably from carrying these gigantic boobs around. They droop, because big boobs always do, but I don't mind that. I'd look weird as heck if they were up under my chin all the time. Running my hand down my soft belly I grip the little overhang when I get to it. I would prefer a nice toned tummy but alas, I work a sit down job. Although I did see this treadmill thing where I could walk while working. Grabbing my phone from where I left it on the countertop I search up 'treadmill' and am inundated with images of treadmills and standing desks. And would you look at that! Amazon has a special on treadmills AND even has a standing desk to go with it. AND the price is phenomenal! I press buy now, work through my details (lets face it, Amazon knows me on a personal level) and hit buy now.

Feeling buoyed by my new purchase I step into the shower tub and get to work lathering everything up. And when I say everything I mean EVERYTHING. I start at the bottom. I have one hairy toe so I defuzz that little guy first. I make my way up my legs, front and backs. I feel like this date calls for that. I have been set up a couple of times and on those dates I only defuzz the front. Don't want to put too much effort into a dud. Tyson however, he is definitely no dud. Which is why when I get to my knee I decided to go a little higher. So high in fact that I'm now sporting a new hairdo down below as well. Nothing too crazy, just a jaunty little triangle pointing to the main event. You know, just in case. I mean, I haven't really had anyone enter the Batcave before, but there's always hope that the right man will venture in there. For a bit of spelunking. I snort to myself because that's a funny word and keep on with my grooming.

Before long I'm sitting on my bed in a towel staring at my wardrobe wishing I was a normal woman. With a normal wardrobe. The very cool heroine in my book would right now be slipping into some jeans that make her butt look all round and amazing, and she'd own black motorcycle boots and a leather jacket. I on the other hand own a pair of jeans with sunflowers embroidered on the butt, I only own colorful sneakers or colorful heels, and all my coats are embellished with either fur or sequins. Letting out a sigh I pull on my jeans, a red sweater because everyone knows red is romantic, and top it off with my navy blue cape, complete with pompoms. I know I should probably wear sensible shoes, but I'm not going to. It's a date after all! I go for my bright yellow heels and nod at myself in the mirror. It may not be biker lady chic, but it is Mira chic and I'm good with that. I blow dry and smooth my hair, giving it a little curl so it bounces around my shoulders and I finish off with a quick spritz of hairspray and a slick of red lipstick just as the doorbell rings.

I fling open the door, startling Tyson on the other side. Tyson who looks finger licking good in his dark jeans, forest green button up and his cut. Why this man is still on the market is a mystery to me. Unless he's hiding psychopathic tendencies. I try to get a good look at him from under my lashes, all covert like.

"Are you OK?" Tyson's gruff voice asks me, leaving me to believe that I was not pulling off 'covert spy woman'.

"Oh, peachy," I grin up at him.

He smiles back at me, a little shy, before his eyes travel down my body and back up again, eating me up with his gaze.

"Mira, shit, you look stunning," he breathes.

A little shiver works its way through me and the man in front of me looks at me with a mixture of awe and heat. My down belows clench at the heat I see there and I have to remind myself that I, Mira Elizabeth Campbell am a virgin and that means that I cannot, should not mount this man on my front porch. Yet. My traitorous eyes dart toward Tyson's crotch and I try to use my non-existent xray vision to see what he's packing. I know that as someone yet to lose her V card, that I should be hoping for something small. Tiny even. But Nana always told me to look for a man with a thick appendage. According to her, "Long and thin goes too far in, they do not please the ladies. But short and thick does the trick and manufactures babies."

A guffaw has my eyes snapping up, to where Tyson is leaning against the doorjamb. But not in a sexy book boyfriend type of way. No, he's leaning against the jamb to hold him up because his belly laughter has weakened his knees.

I let out a sigh, not even questioning if I said that out loud, and make my way to Tyson's bike. He pulls himself together and jogs down the steps behind me, moving to my side, his hand resting on my lower back.

He presses a kiss to my temple. "You, Doll, are a fucking breath of fresh air." He chuckles one more time, shaking his head and repeating what I said under his breath.

I gaze up at him. It's so nice to see him this way. From what I've seen of Tyson around the clubhouse he seems to be reserved, happy to watch from the background, just quietly going about his business being a good brother, a good worker and a good man. Watching him cut loose a little, especially with me, feels really good. I want to know everything. His thoughts, his ideas, his dreams. I want to read his writing and workshop ideas for my books with him. Most of all, I like making him laugh. I gaze up at him as he gently lowers a shiny motorcycle helmet onto my head, letting him get it placed just so, gently brushing any trapped hair out of my face.

"There," he murmurs at me. I knock the side a couple of times, reveling in his smile, perfect white teeth on display as he shakes his head at me.

"Your chariot awaits milady,"

He mounts his lovely matt black and chrome steed. Holding his hand out he takes my hand, showing me where I should put my feet, talking me through how to get on. The butterflies build in my tummy and it could be because I'm not the most graceful woman, but it could also be the fact that very soon, my hooha will be pressed up against the back of Tyson, being hit by vibrations from below.

Breathe Mira, you can do this. I repeat over and over in my mind. I repeat it when he starts the bike, I repeat it again when he stands the bike further upright. I repeat it when he wraps those large hands around my denim clad thighs and pulls me tight into him and again when he gently, slowly leads us out of my drive.

"Breathe Mira, you can do this. You're doing great. Look at you go!" inner Mira says. I give myself a mental pat on the back, smug in the thought that I am a total biker babe.

"I'm going to go a little faster now, OK Doll?" Tyson's voice washes over me.

"Go as fast as you want dude. I got this," I tell him, patting his thick slab-like muscles in his abdomen.

He gives me a smirk over his shoulder and opens her up.

Inner Mira starts screaming. We most certainly have not got this! We are not doing great! Do not look at us go, WE'RE GOING TO DIEEEEEE!

Chapter 9

Tank

I try to hold in my laughter. This woman is nuts in the very best way. From her hilarious little rhyme about dicks, to her pep talk that has now turned into what sounds like a eulogy, it all has me wanting to get more of her and that doesn't scare me quite as much as it once would.

"Doll? You can get off now." I squeeze her denim clad calf in the jeans that made her ass look absolutely phenomenal. Those little sunflowers on the back pocket drawing my eye directly to her curvy heart shaped ass.

"Wait, when did we park up?" She opens her eyes and looks around her.

"We've been parked for a couple of minutes. I was waiting for your freakout to subside."

She makes a cute little huffing noise, "I wouldn't have freaked out if you weren't going so fast." She throws her leg over the bike, and me. Jesus, how flexible is this woman?

Shaking those thoughts out of my head I kick down the kickstand and dismount as well. "Doll, we were going 10 miles the whole way here."

She gapes at me. "What?! No way, why did it feel like 1000 miles an hour? Aw man, I'm a terrible biker passenger," she pouts, a little crease appearing between her brows.

I rest my hands on her shoulders, the round bally pom pom things on her coat ticking my palms. "You were a perfect passenger. I'd take you on the back of my bike anytime." She beams up at me and I feel about 10 fucking feet tall. "Come on, let's go."

I take her hand and lead her to the first part of our date. She tugs me to a stop. "Tyson, why are we going to the bookstore?"

"Because this is our first stop. You choose three books, I choose three books and we swap and read each other's choices."

Her eyes light up and she jiggles, clapping her hands. "And then we tell the other one all about it? Like a two person book club! Eeeeeee!" She screeches, stomping her yellow heels and taking off into the store. Two seconds later she comes screeching back, "This is the best date EVER!" She grabs my hand and drags me in her wake. "Come on! We have books to buy!"

After an hour and a half we finally have our purchases. Surprisingly, Mira didn't choose all romance. She chose a thriller, a poetry book and a small town romance, but unlike her writing, this one doesn't have a murder to solve. I tried to get a selection of genres too. I figured that Mira probably doesn't want to read a book on motorcycles, so I choose a murder mystery written by one of my favorite authors, a chick lit that seems quite popular and like Mira, a poetry book.

"Up on the counter, Doll. I got this."

"No way! I'm an empowered, independent woman, I can buy

my own books." She tries to elbow me out of the way. Even though she's tall and curvy, she's shit outta luck trying to move my bulk.

Turning, I look at her square on, resting my hands on hers holding her books. "Doll. Mira. I asked you on this date, so this is my treat. Let me do this for you, yeah?"

Her cute yellow shoe taps out a beat on the wooden floor then she rolls her eyes at me. "Fine, caveman. But I get the next bunch!" she crows, relinquishing her book pile.

She hums a happy tune while I deal with the teenager behind the counter, and I watch her out of the corner of my eye. She's strong willed, but also doesn't hold a grudge. I feel like that will come in handy in the future.

"OK, so now we go home and read?" She looks up at me hopefully.

"Not quite, Doll, Come with me."

The bookstore looks out onto the town square, right where Tav is setting up a cozy little picnic for me and my date.

As soon as Mira sees it she beams up at me, "A picnic!" She grabs my face in her soft palms, squeezing tight, pressing her lush soft lips to my fishy lips. She gives me one last squeeze and then trots as fast as her heels can take her over the grass to where Tav has finished laying out the food.

"There's tiny quiches, Tyson! Tiny quiches!" She throws her head back and laughs and I watch the pure joy emanating from her. I don't deserve a creature quite this glorious but fuck if I'm not gonna try to keep her.

Mira

OK, so I'm not going to lie, I haven't been on many dates. Ever. I don't know if it's just because I'm big and loud and that scares men sometimes, but the few dates I have been on have all been terrible. Usually they're shorter than me and have that little man syndrome thing going on. Which is fine, I don't mind a short king, but usually those short kings want to talk about themselves and order me the salad. Tank, Tyson, he took me to buy books and arranged a picnic. This is wet dream stuff right here.

I sit myself down and scooch a little to the left, trying to get comfortable. I'm not sure what's happening in my jeans, but they're feeling a little odd this evening. I'm not sure if it's because I've been on the bike earlier or what, so I wriggle a little more to get comfortable and try to ignore it.

"Holy shit, Prospect did good," Tyson mumbles under his breath, looking at all the miniature goodies spread out in front of us. He picks up a tiny quiche in his giant paw and nibbles on it delicately, sending me into a fit of giggles.

He frowns good naturedly at me and then continues nibbling his way through his treat.

"This is so much fun. Thank you, Tyson. This has been the best date ever!" I tell him enthusiastically as I decide to dive into the sweet stuff, taking a bite from a fruit kolache.

He smiles gently at me, and if the light wasn't so dim, or the streetlights were brighter, I'm sure I'd be able to better see the color on his high cheekbones.

"Are you blushing?" I tease him. I try to wriggle a little in my seat, my leg is feeling a bit pins and needle-y. I give it a little shake to get blood flowing through it.

"Maybe a little," He mutters. "I've never been on an actual date. Or organized one. But I did get some advice from my brothers with Ol Ladies." The corner of his mouth tips up slightly.

I think through his words and my tummy starts flapping wildly like there's a chicken doing the bird dance in there. This big, gruff, quiet man, my polar opposite, went so far as to ask his brothers for help organizing this date. I lean over to press a kiss to his cheek and, thanks to my leg that has now gone dead, I tip wildly sideways. With a gasp I inhale some pastry from my kolache which sends me into a wild coughing fit. Still listing sideways I throw my hand out to catch myself, unfortunately getting a whole handful of cream pie which slips sideways, sending me crashing flat onto the picnic rug.

There is silence, not even the crickets want to wade into this one, and then there's a guffaw. Then a choking noise, and wheezing. Gentle hands scoop me up and place me upright, but there are no comforting words as Tyson tries to hold in his laughter. His body is vibrating and his cheeks are puffed out. He looks awful and it shocks a bark of laughter out of me, the kolache pastry I was choking on shooting out of my mouth in his direction. I stare at him in horror and the floodgates burst, Tank leaning forward, gripping his stomach, losing it. I join him in hysterical laughter, the two of us, heads tipped back laughing like mad people in the middle of the town square.

Mrs. Crankshaw, who is one of the grumpier members of the Rose Grove community, stops on the sidewalk and narrows her eyes at us, shaking her head slowly from side to side. I try to contain my laughter, but that all goes to heck in a handbasket when Tyson flips the bird at her back as she shuffles away.

"Tyson!" I screech-laugh, holding my stomach, cream all over my hand and now my cape.

"What? She's a judgey old cow. She once told Jovie off for laughing too loudly at the Rose Grove Christmas parade."

"Oh, in that case," I answer, flipping her off behind her back as well.

Our giggles settle and Tyson looks at me, his eyes still wet from laughter. "Are you alright, Doll?"

"Yeah, my leg went to sleep. I don't know what's wrong with it."

Tyson stands, brushes himself off and offers me his hand. "Kick off those heels and let's get some blood flowing back into those long legs of yours, huh?"

I look at my cream covered hand, and then at Tyson's.

"Hold up. Tav is an over planner." He mumbles, bending and looking through the picnic basket.

Hopefully, he doesn't find what he's looking for anytime soon, because in this position I have an eyeful of his firm butt right in my face. I bet it looks amazing naked. Although from this angle, naked, I'd also be able to see his balls, and as far as I'm concerned testicles aren't that sexy. Kinda like a lumpy purse. Covered in plucked chicken skin. Now I feel a little grossed out, and that coupled with my sticky hand and my dead leg that is somehow numb and really painful at the same time is making my face collapse. I know it has when Tyson turns around triumphantly, holding a packet of baby wipes only to frown and drop down next to me.

"Mira, are you alright, Doll?"

"Oh yeah, I was just thinking that I can't feel my leg but at the same time I can feel it really hurts. And that ball sacks are very unappetizing."

He stares at me for maybe a beat too long before blinking and shaking it off. "OK then. Well, here you go."

He opens the wipes then tears a few out and hands them to me, patiently waiting for me to clean myself up, then stands, offering me his hand again. I take it and pull myself to standing. Or at least I try, before my right leg gives out from underneath me.

Tyson catches me with a grunt and pulls me to stand, leaning against his front. "Mira, I need you to shake that leg out. Wiggle it around and get it moving. It must have really gone right to sleep, huh?"

I nod and do as he asks, but instead of blood flow lessening the pins and needles, I get a shooting pain, one that takes my breath away. Tears prickle my eyes and I can't believe I'm going to have to cut this perfect date short because my body is having a body breakdown. This is what happens when you sit down all day and scoff at all those women out walking in the streets in their activewear.

"You good Doll?"

I shake my head, a tear breaking free. "I'm sorry Tyson," I can feel my lip wobble and I try to act brave. "I think I need to go home."

"Are you sure? I can take you back to the clubhouse and get Switch to take a look at you?"

I hide my face and shake my head again. Would I like to spend more time with Tyson? Heck yeah! But I want to do it when my leg, and now my crotch, isn't on fire.

"No, I think maybe I need a hot bath and some pain meds. I'm sure I'll be fine. It's probably from sitting too much or something. I'm so sorry, this has been the most wonderful, fabulous perfect date I've ever been on and my stupid fire crotch is ruining it." I want to stomp my foot in protest but even putting weight on it feels excruciating.

"Wait, what's wrong with your crotch?" Tyson leans back to look into my face, his large hands wrapped around my biceps,holding me steady, the heat of him warming me.

"Oh, nothing. I think I pulled something."

He stares at me for a moment, then wraps an arm around me, holding my weight as his other hand fishes his phone out of his pocket. He texts someone and then places his phone back, his free hand coming to wrap about me, rubbing my back gently. I sigh into him, soaking up his steady warmth and the scent I now equate to him and him alone. Leather. Wood. Tyson. We stay like this for a minute or maybe more, just leaning on each other in Rose Grove Square, the sound of people moving around us, but we stand solid. Peaceful. The type of peace my mind never has, and yet Tyson magically quietens everything inside me. Like a man-sized weighted blanket.

"Hey there, daters. I've been called to chauffeur you two crazy kids." Tav's cheery voice sounds out, breaking me out of my thoughts.

"Thanks Brother. Let's get Mira in the car. I'll drop her home if you want to pack this up, then I'll come back for you and my bike." Tyson says to Tav, who nods and follows his instructions.

I start taking unsteady steps toward the SUV, the pain in my groin getting worse by the second. Tyson takes pity on me and swings me up into his arms, carrying my heft to the car like I weigh nothing. I'm shocked and delighted all in one. He would *definitely* be able to lift me up and bang me against a wall.

He places me gently in the passenger side, secures my seat belt and then walks around the front of the vehicle, stopping to take something from Tav before joining me.

"Are you sure you don't want Switch to take a look?" Tyson asks, his gaze imploring.

"No, I just need to go home. Thank you anyway," I rest my hand on his.

He turns his hand over, and our fingers twine, gently holding on to each other as he navigates the quiet streets until he pulls up to my little cottage, the lights on from when I left.

"Tyson, I had a wonderful time and I'm so sorry I had to cut it short." I pout a little, letting him know that going home with a crotch on fire, and not in a good way, is the last thing I want.

He smiles gently at me. "Me too, sweetheart. But look at it this way, it just means we'll have to do this again to finish what we started." He winks at me and then gets out of the car, tapping a beat on the hood as he makes his way to my side.

Ever the gentleman he opens my car door, gently lifting me out and carrying me up the front steps of my little house, holding me just so as I unlock my door. He waits for me to push the door open then carries me in, depositing me on the couch.

"Do you need anything? Tylenol? A doctor? Anything?" HIs brows furrow and I know leaving me here like this is killing him.

I would love to sit here and argue with him over my health and wellbeing all night, but at this point I need to get rid of him so I get out of these infernal jeans. They didn't feel that tight when I put them on. Maybe a little riding up in the front and back but nowhere near enough to it feel like it's cutting off circulation in my legs.

"Tyson, I'll be fine. You go and do biker man things and I will rest up and hopefully see you soon?"

"That's a guarantee. I mean, the clubhouse is your office

now," He grins and winks at me, then bends and presses a gentle kiss to my forehead. "Get some rest and I'll see you soon, Doll."

He takes one last look at me and then heads out, shutting the door gently behind him. I wait until I hear his car door slam, then the SUV starts up, and then the sounds of it driving away, getting fainter and fainter.

"Oh, thank god!" I breathe out, pull myself up to stand, undo my button, yank the zipper down and tear my jeans off, throwing them across the room for good measure.

Looking down at my right leg, the one that is both on fire and numb, I notice it's a weird mottled color. I let out a squeak and then slowly it dawns on me that my jeans are across the room but my leg is still on fire. What else dawns on me is how gosh darn uncomfortable my underwear is. I decided to wear this fancy, lacy thong that I found in my drawer and haven't worn in around ten years. Looking down at myself I frown when I catch half of my muff hanging out the side of the tiny front triangle part.

"What the heck?"

Sucking my tummy in for a better look I notice not only is the muff part askew, but also that one side, the left side that arches over my hip is a lot thicker than the other side. Hooking my thumbs into the tiny thong I draw it down my legs, realizing that I put it on wrong. Somehow it got turned around and my legs are sticking through one leg part and the butt string part. The butt string so thin and tight that it cut off my circulation to my right leg. I know this to be true because now that they're around my ankles I can feel blood rushing back to my groin like a tidal wave.

My date was foiled by my inability to put my underwear

on properly. The realization has me collapsing on the couch, naked booty to cushion, a long groan escaping me.

Tyson 0. Thong 1.

Chapter 10

Tav

"You sure you've got this?" Tank checks in with me for the third time.

"Brother, we do this shit all the time. Wire and Chewy have already hacked into the funeral home's security cameras, we just need to investigate the mortuary part. I got this. I was chosen for this specifically because I can handle it. I mean, it's nice that you're worried about me, but we'll be fine." I slap him on the back and turn, but not before I hear Nitro mumble "You were chosen because of your old ass grandfather." I choose to ignore that hurtful comment.

"Ready?" Gus asks, glancing between me, Jules and Pops. We all nod, ready to get this show on the road.

We climb into the Tombs Security SUV ready to pull out, Tank and Nitro following behind in a DRMC SUV. For stealth. As much as these guys love riding their bikes, bikes aren't that covert and that's what Pres wants. Tank and Nitro need to blend in as they're our assigned backup. Not that we need it, but I think he just wanted them safe and away from any police poking around. So he's sent them on perhaps the easiest job my brothers and I have ever been on. Maybe.

It's around a 30 minute drive to Ironwood, home of the family-owned funeral home Roman likes to use. And also the place where body parts seem to mysteriously go missing. The drive passes with little drama, other than having to listen to Pops regale us with gross stories about how much he loves Debs and trying to give us all pointers on "How to make love right".

"AND we're here!" Gus yells over the top of Pops' story as he parks in the lot. He turns to eyeball me and Pops in the back. "Remember, we are a loving family wanting a tour and information on the best way to say goodbye to a loved one. No need for full theatrics, got it?"

I give Pops the side eye, but he's already out the door walking to the back of the SUV. "Keep him contained." Gus gives me the stink eye and I don't know why. I'm the normal one in this whole damn family.

"Hurry up shitheads, I got a funeral to plan," Pops yells from his now seated position in the wheelchair he procured from somewhere or other. "We're burning daylight and I ain't got many days left!"

He cackles as he wheels himself toward the door, flicking his head at Jules to open it for him. He pushes forward, the rest of us following behind, stepping into a foyer full of marble. Like a ridiculous amount. Marbled floors, walls and table tops, with giant vases full of wedding looking flowers surround us.

"Holy hell! Death must pay well because this garish shit would have cost a bomb," Pops says. Loudly.

The woman greeter inhales quickly at his comment, looking completely put out. Stepping forward I try to smooth the waters. "Oh, please forgive my grandfather. He's lost his mind." Pops makes a choking sound behind me, "He's not got long to go. His faculties and body are starting to break down at a rapid pace. I'm so sorry," I give her the big puppy dog eyes and she waves a hand at me with a soft smile.

"Of course, Mr. Tombs, is it?" Her name tag reads "Svetlana" and so does her severe blonde slicked back bob. If I could draw what a "Svetlana" looks like, it'd be this woman.

"Yes. Actually, we all four are Mr. Tombs, so why not call me Tav?"

"Of course. Now, you wanted the full tour and a few options for when your grandfather -" Her eyes flick to Pops who is grinning at her with his finger in his nose, "-leaves this mortal coil?"

"That's correct. This is Gus," Gus steps forward, "and our other brother, Jules." She nods at them both. "Please, if you wouldn't mind leading the way?"

She takes off at a quick pace, her high heels tap, tap, tapping away on the veined marble. I trail behind Pops, who is wheeling himself surprisingly well.

"Psst, you and I, let's veer off. I want to see the mortuary," Pops says with the excitement of a kid at Disneyland.

I want to argue with him, I really do, but I kinda wanna see it too, and we have surveillance we want to get set up. If we get caught I'll just blame the kook in the wheelchair. We come to the door with 'Mortuary' written on it. Gus catches my eye and gives me an imperceptible nod while angling the woman away from us as she explains the virtues of cremation over burial. Focusing on our task I turn the door handle and open the door a crack, listening for an employee on the other side. When I'm satisfied that the coast is clear, I widen the door and shove Pops through.

Pops lets out a low, impressed whistle, "Now THIS is what I'm talking about!" He takes his phone out of his pants pocket and starts taking photos of the layout and setup.

Looking around there are four people laying out on stainless steel tables waiting for whatever farewell their family has decided on. Moving toward the body closest to me, I take a peek under the sheet, noticing immediately the silvery line down one side of his abdomen.

"Pops," I whisper, breaking him out of his research or whatever the fuck he wants those pictures for, "Check this out,"

He comes to stand beside me, checking out the dead guy's stomach. He runs his finger along the silvery line, then places his hands on either side, palms flat, and then moves them slowly in opposite directions, observing the skin the whole time. Once he's satisfied he holds the sheet up higher, taking stock of everything on the body.

"Huh."

"Huh what?"

"Not sure yet," he answers, moving to hold the dearly deceased's eyelid open and peering into the eyes of a dead man. "You get that shit set up and I'll poke around."

I nod in reply and head toward the shelves along the back wall. There are two rows of supplies on the shelf, so I set up our tiny spy camera on a tallish bottle at the back that looks like it isn't used often. Our camera and mic will be able to sit there unnoticed for a good while.

Turning to Pops I see him still poking around the bodies, humming and hawing but not really saying anything. By the time he stands by the last body he looks like he has an inkling as to what's going on, but before he can confirm the door handle jiggles. Pops dives back into his wheelchair and ends up spinning it, hitting a metal bookshelf and leaving him facing into a corner.

"Who the hell are you and what are you doing in here?" a male voice with a slight Russian accent demands.

"I'm so sorry! My family is on a tour with Svetlana and we lost my grandpa. I found him in here so I was just collecting him and heading back out."

I grab the handles of the chair and spin Pops around. Pops, who has a suspicious wet patch and his junk out of the open zipper of his chinos. The mortician guys eyes grow huge as Pops yells about Vietnam and communism.

"I'm sorry, so sorry!" I apologize, through clenched teeth to hold my laughter in. "Come on grandpa, it's probably time to get you home for supper."

The Russian guy nods and waves us out, but not before slipping on something wet on the floor. I don't want to know what that could possibly be so I power walk Pops out of there, running into our group in the hall. Pops still has his dick hanging out, pulling a yelp out of Svetlana.

"Get me outta here! These people are crazy! Blonde scary lady, help me!" Pops pleads with her as she shakes her head in horror, taking two steps back to escape the crazy old man. "I don't want them to cremate me and grow a tree out of my ass!" He hollers, drawing the attention of a family group and three dodgy looking fucks in cheap suits.

Jules' lip is starting to tremble and I know we've got about 30 seconds before my stoic brother loses it. I start grabbing pamphlets from a wall of information, shoving them onto Pops' lap while my brothers apologize. I leave them in my dust because I cannot keep this shit in. I run out to the car, pushing Pops in front of me and explode into giggles at the back of the SUV.

"Aaaaaand end scene."

Tank

"No offense brother, but this feels kinda weird."

Nitro's voice snaps me out of my thoughts. Thoughts of Mira and our date last night up until I had to drop her home writhing in pain. I turn and take in Nitro's profile before letting out a sigh. He's not wrong. Being on a stakeout with him does feel weird. For as long as I've been in DRMC, I've always partnered with Judge for shit. Work, runs, stakeouts. He's the same, Fox always has his six. To be sharing an SUV with each other does feel a little off.

"Yeah. I get it." Pres has us placed as backup to the Tombs' at Roman's preferred place of disposal. I can see why Roman chose it. It's out of the way and looks classy as hell.

"What do you think of Sergeant Davies?" Nitro asks after a beat.

He's not the usual type of power hungry cop you get out there. The ones that hate MCs and all we stand for even though we keep our noses clean and help the Rose Grove community as much as we can.

"For a cop, he seems like a good guy. I didn't have any issue with him,"

Nitro grunts in return. "Me neither. Pretty much told me straight up that it was a bullshit charge. Not even a charge, more a complaint that they have to follow through. Fucker even let me sit in the car when he pulled over some kids joy riding. What the fuck kind of cop does that?"

We both share a look. A snort escapes me and I shake my head. I can't tell if Davies is fucking with us, or Rose Grove's useless as horseshit sheriff. The sheriff who only cares about rubbing shoulders with the country club assholes.

"Heads up," Nitro nudges me and points toward the funeral home Tav has just come running out of. "Wait, is Pops in a fucking wheelchair?"

We watch and Pops yells and shakes his fists, Tav shoving him around the back of the SUV and bending over.

"What the fuck?" I'm about to get out of the SUV when Gus and Jules come wandering out, pace slow and steady until they get further from the funeral home entrance when they bolt behind the SUV and join Tav in the same position.

"Are they fucking laughing?" Nitro asks, his voice high pitched, face scrunched in confusion.

Their shoulders shake, and Tav almost falls to his ass. Pops stands calmly, zips up his high as hell chinos and opens the trunk to throw the wheelchair in. Is that a wet patch on the front of his pants?

Gus, Jules and Tav finally get into their fucking SUV and pull out. We follow behind, winding our way back to Rose Grove, pulling over once we get to the diner. We follow the brothers in, taking a seat when the teenage waitress tilts her head to a large table in the back, letting us know she'll be with us in a minute.

"What the fuck are all those?" Nitro gestures as he sits

heavily in the booth next to me.

"These are all the different types of services that families can opt for when they lose a loved one," Tav answers, flicking through them as if they're the most interesting things in the world. "Like did you know that place offers to not only cremate your loved one but also send some of the ashes to this lab that can create diamonds out of you." Gus rolls his eyes as Jules sits deathly still.

We all quieten down as 'Taylor' fills our cups with steaming hot coffee. We place orders for a light meal, which apparently means everyone gets the all day breakfast special and we wait for Taylor to wander back to her post.

"Gus, did you find out anything? And why the fuck is the front of Pops' pants wet?" I turn and ask him. Tav is busy planning to turn Pops into a pimp ring and you get fuck all out of Jules on a good day.

"Yeah. Got the full tour. Security is almost nonexistent apart from the cameras that the team already hacked into. No guards, nothing. Be real fucking easy to acquire things, so to speak." Gus answers before taking a sip of his black coffee.

"Pops and I found the mortuary and some of the shit there looks less than above board. Pops wet himself to get us out of there." Tav adds.

"No I fucking didn't! When I went flying into that shelf and a bottle of embalming fluid fell off and spilled. I was trying to throw him off our scent. Make him think I was an old, crazy, infirm geriatric."

"So you pulled your dick out of your pants and hollered random shit?" Gus asks.

"Worked, didn't it, asshole?" Pops fires back.

We all settle down, leaning back to be served our breakfasts,

Pops throwing his grandsons stink eyes. We eat in silence, mainly because I don't want to risk setting off the fucking Tombs' again. Wishful thinking as with no provocation whatsoever Pops starts bickering with Tav over not wanting to have his ass turned into a diamond.

"Enough!" I throw down some cash and a generous tip. "Let's get back to the clubhouse and update Pres."

Hopefully Debs can wrangle Pops, a sane Tombs' can update the crew and we can start getting some answers. And once all that is taken care of Mira and I can finish what we started last night.

Mira

Ugh. Writer's block. Writer's blocky block block and there's nothing I can do about it. I've tried all the tricks. Having a glass of water. Going for a walk. I've fed Mrs. McKenzie (NOT livers) and we've played with the laser pointer thingy she likes. I tried writing an alien romance as a palate cleanser and still nothing. Just the incessant flicking of the curser on the bright white page taunting me. On the up side the blood flow to my groin is back in full force and I now have two working legs and the ever present mortification that I had to cut my date short because of a wardrobe malfunction. I bang my head on my desk twice and try to get the ideas flowing.

I thought infiltrating the MC would make this way easier but somehow it's made it harder. And all because of one man.

Tyson. Tank. Wrongly accused hot biker man. I thought he was hot and delicious before I got to know him, but after waking up next to him and how sweet and shy he was when he revealed he likes to write. Then he takes me to the bookstore on our date, pays for the books AND arranges a picnic. Now my panties are constantly on fire for the man. In a good way. Not a diseased way. Ew. Although in order for me to catch a disease I'd have to have had intercourse at some stage in my life and alas, I have not. I'm a fraud. The most fraudulent of frauds, writing spicy romance without ever having reached my peak with another real life human before. But the readers don't know that, so I'll keep that little secret between me and Big Ricky.

Not that any readers will notice my lack of love life seeing as there are no words on the page. I let out a long groan and flop forward, my head hitting the table gently, over and over again as I bang it hoping to rattle some ideas around. A rattling sound on the porch draws my attention and I frown. It's midday and I never get visitors outside of my neighbors but they're very polite and will always text first. Actually it's less because they're polite, and more because they've caught me doing some weird stuff for book research so it's best for all of us if they text first.

Mrs. McKenzie jumps down from her perch and wanders toward the door, stopping halfway to look back at me, as if telling me to get my big behind up and check to see what that noise was. If I'm being honest I'm a little leery about doing what my cat wants me to do, and let's face it, she only wants me to do that because she's probably wanting another yummy human liver. I try not to gag as I make my way to the door and peek out the little spy hole thing that Nana insisted on.

Nothing looks amiss. The gnomes are exactly where I left

them, even that weird interloper gnome that just appeared one day. The chubby bent ladies are also in place. Humph. It was probably the dreamcatcher brushing up against something. I turn to head back to my little office but something stops me. What if there's something on my welcome mat? A note, a parcel, a little surprise. Most likely one that I don't want, but still, if I was writing a scene this is exactly what would happen. I mean, my scene would also probably lead to a kidnapping and definitely don't want that to be happy. Well, not unless the kidnapper is actually a criminal with a heart of gold who is only kidnapping me for my own safety. He'll keep me in his beautiful mansion and be harsh and brutal to everyone except me. He'll also have a scar on his face, maybe even two. His laugh will be rusty from lack of use and oh my god Mira just open the darn door!

Taking a fortifying breath, I unlock the door and slowly inch it open. OK, there isn't anyone hiding out on my porch, so that's a good sign. Everything seems ordinary. A breeze brushes over my skin, then something flutters out of the corner of my eye. Tucked into the screen door is a "Sorry we missed you" note. Plucking it out and turning it over to read the back I'm met with friendly, flowery handwriting.

"Your package has been redirected to Devil's Rose MC."

Huh? I twist and turn a few times and then drop the card and start flapping. OK, breathe, Mira, breathe. Maybe it's just a normal package? This is a smallish town, and people gossip, so perhaps the delivery man knows I'm writing at DRMC? *Or perhaps the weirdo is messing with you again.* Ah cheese and rice. I have to get to the clubhouse.

Rushing around pulling on shoes and throwing my laptop, notebooks, fidget toys and pens into my backpack I stride toward the kitchen door, heading toward my garage where my glorious bike lives. My hand is on the handle when a low, long meow sounds out.

"Aw, Mrs. McKenzie, I know I've been away a lot the past few days, I'll make it up to you, I promise." I give her smooches and turn to head out once more when she moves to stand in front of the door I'm trying to exit and lets out another pitiful cry. I stare at her for a moment before letting out a long sigh.

Dropping my bag on the counter I move efficiently, scooping some food into a little baggy and popping it into my backpack.

"OK, lady, let's get out of here."

I heft Mrs. McKenzie's bulk up into holding her to me with one arm while I use my other hand to open the door and flick the lock before slamming it shut behind me. I hot foot it into my garage, hitting the door opener, the garage door screeching a little before rolling up. Now for the hard part.

"Mrs. McKenzie, I need you to behave alright? We need to get to the clubhouse and remember, you didn't want to be left at home so you'll be calm and enjoy the ride."

I'm certain she rolls her eyes at me and lets out a sigh and I plop her into the very roomy front basket of my bike.

"Good girl," I coo at her, throw my leg over, sit on the softest bike seat to ever have been invented and set off.

DRMC, here I come.

Chapter 11

Tank

"What in the...?" Nitro mumbles under his breath and I follow his line of sight.

There, on a powder blue push bike with a sequin rainbow backpack is the woman who seems to always be in my thoughts.

"What the fuck is she doing?" I growl.

She's weaving all over the main road out to the clubhouse. At one point she wobbles dangerously before righting herself.

"Why the hell is she dressed like a fucking rainbow threw up?" Nitro asks, slowing down as we pull up beside her.

"Writer Lady, what in the fuck are you doing?" I growl at her through the open window.

"Oh, hi Tyson! I've got to get to the clubhouse, I had a missed package delivery. They said it was redirected - whoa! Calm down Mrs. McKenzie! - argh, anyway, I'm on my way to the clubhouse," She beams up at me while she has one hand on the fattest ginger cat I've ever seen, the other hand white knuckling the handlebar. "Mrs. McKenzie you settle down right this instant! You wanted this!" she screeches.

"Fuck this." I mutter under my breath. "Mira, pull over, you too Nitro." Nitro drives ahead of Mira, pulling over to the side of the road.

As soon as the car comes to a halt I get out, walk to the crazy woman, scoop the fat ginger cat up in one arm and carry him to the SUV. The Tombs' stop their SUV further ahead, checking in on us so I wave my arm in a circle in the air then point straight ahead. Gus gives me a thumbs up out of his driver's window and pulls back onto the road, heading to the clubhouse.

"Hey! What are you doing?"

"Mira, get in the car. You'll hurt yourself biking with this fatty," I yell back to her, placing the so called Mrs. McKenzie gently in the back seat.

Turning to look back at Mira, she has her arms crossed over her chest, pushing up those plump tits of hers, but her lips are twitching as she watches me. I gesture to the car and she rolls her eyes, dismounting her bike and pushing it toward me.

"I can bike the rest of the way if you want to take Mrs. McKenzie?"

"Nope. Get your pretty little ass in the car with that monster cat of yours and I'll load your bike in the back."

She grins at me and then sashays off. "He said I had a little ass," she squeals to herself.

"Pretty little ass." I correct her, shaking my head as I push her bright yellow bike with goddamn spoke decals to the trunk, opening the back and placing her bike in the back of the SUV.

Shutting her up nice and tight I climb back inside, slamming my car door behind me, staring straight ahead, waiting for Nitro to pull out. I can see his asshole grin from the corner of my eye but I ignore him and the beautiful menace in the backseat.

"Thanks for the ride guys. I didn't think Mrs. Mac would be such a pain on the bike but alas, cycling is not in the cards for her." Mira laments, giving her cat pets on its fat belly while it snores in the backseat.

"Why the hell were you biking with a cat anyway?" Nitro asks.

"Oh, I heard a noise on my front porch and when I went to look I saw a card saying I had a package delivery, but it was redirected to the clubhouse. It seemed hinky so I was making my way to DRMC to intercept it." She shrugs one shoulder, the motion causing her tits to jiggle in the brightly colored blouse she's wearing.

"Shit. Do you think it was the guy?" Nitro asks her.

"The guy?"

"You know, the guy that's doing this," Nitro answers.

I flick my eyes to the rearview so I can gauge her reaction. Her brows are furrowed and she's chewing on her plump lower lip. Why the hell does she have to be so sexy? She frowns for a moment then shakes her head, her blonde hair flying in all directions.

"How do you know it's a man? It could be anyone. Most of my fans are women."

I spin to look at her. "Do you think it's a woman doing this?"

She looks out the window as we pull into the DRMC and park the SUV behind our garages. "I'm not really too sure what to think, Tyson. I'm a good person. I pay my taxes and give to charity and I talk to all the old people in the supermarket and ask how their grandchildren are. I mean, there was that one time that I laughed when a teenager slipped in a mud puddle, but I feel like anyone would have laughed at that. And he had good bones and stuff so I knew he was fine."

Nitro turns to look at me and blinks once, then twice. "Good luck with that one, *Tyson*," the asshole then snickers and gets out of the SUV, slamming the door extra hard.

"Come on, let's see what this package is."

She nods, slides her backpack on one shoulder and then scoops her cat up, cradling it in her arms the same way Chewy does with Chomper and the ladies do with their babies.

"Oh, it's after work time! Everyone will be in. I love it when everyone is in. There's so many people to talk to and watch. Everyone is having fun." She turns to me as we walk side by side to the main doors, "That's what I like most. You must love it. It'd be like living with your family every single day." She beams up at me and I think through her words.

I know that deep down the DRMC is family, but it's only really just started feeling like since Chewy crashed into our lives. Before then we would call ourselves a family, but it was more like a frat house. A place for us to crash when we arrived stateside. Safe, people that understood what it's like to readjust, and businesses we could all work. Since the addition of Chewy, the Tombs', the Death Riders, all the Ol Ladies and now the kids, now it feels more like a family.

Clearing my throat, I think of the best way to put my thoughts into words. "I never really had much of a family, just me and my gramps. Now I have nieces and nephews and brothers and uncles. Shit, even a bunch of little sisters that run riot in there. "It's," I swallow, "It's the best thing that ever happened to me."

Her eyes twinkle at my sharing my thoughts, and I love when she smiles softly, not needing me to elaborate or explain. She just gets me. I hold her gaze for a moment, then the door bangs open.

"Hey Tank, hey Mira. Whoa, that's a fat cat!" Sage calls in her sweet voice. Niko follows behind her looking a hell of a lot bigger than the day he turned up with his three siblings in tow.

"Hey Bigs, where are you going?" I ask, moving my bulk aside so they can get past.

"Sage has cheer squad and I have football practice. Before you ask, Takoda is off spying duty and is on drop off and pick up." He grins at me on his way past.

I'm not even going to bother asking how he knows what the prospects are up to. Kid has grown up with an investigator mother, and now a security expert father. He knows how to ferret for information. Shit, even his younger siblings are experts at it. He slaps me on the shoulder and I just smile and shake my head at him. Sage is a lot sweeter as she rests her hand on my forearm and moves past. She doesn't pay me too much attention, probably because her eyes are on Takoda this whole time.

"OOhhhh, I see what's happening there," Mira whispers as she watches the trio head for the SUV.

I catch her eye. It's so nice to not tower too much over a woman. I can look at Mira without getting a crick in my neck. "What do you think is happening there?"

"Well, that girl has one hell of a crush on that barman biker. Maybe one day she'll go to college and then when she comes back all grown up she'll meet him again. He'll be all burly and weathered and have had some type of biker trauma. Ooooh maybe he lost a leg in a shootout! And now he's got bad self esteem or something because he used to be a ladies' man and now all the shallow women are all like 'ew! A one legged biker!' and it will be all up to Sage to show him his worth through her love." Her fat cat yawns and jumps out of her arms, making its way into the clubhouse as she lets out a sigh and stares up at me with dreamy eyes.

I stare back at her, not sure whether to kiss her or run. On one hand her brain and her imagination have me in awe. She's talented, clever and colorful. On the other hand I will never be able to live up to the men in her imagination and that scares the hell out of me. I like her, like really like her. I can see us spending time together talking about books and her methods, and just maybe I could get back into my writing. Nothing as serious as hers, of course, but as a hobby it's a great outlet for my thoughts and worries and stresses.

"Sorry Biker Man, did I freak you out?"

I stare at her a beat longer and think, "Fuck those imaginary men," before slamming my lips onto hers.

Mira

Holy shitballs! Yes, that's right I am cursing! But it's in my head so it doesn't matter and Nana won't even know what's happening. Just like she won't know that right at this very moment the very hot, very sweet Tank has his firm lips on mine. After the initial shock that his mouth was touching my mouth I felt myself lean into his strong, hard body. His large hands move to cup my cheeks and he softens the kiss, gently nibbling at my lips drawing a moan from me. Taking that as a sign his tongue runs along my bottom lip, seeking entrance. Even trying to get his tongue into my mouth he's a total gentleman. I sigh, my tongue meeting his as I melt into him.

He angles my head and deepens the kiss. I feel it all the way to my toes, butterflies going wild in my stomach. He pulls back slightly, sipping from my lips. I expect him to step back, maybe apologize or tell me he made a mistake, but instead he pulls me into him and wraps his arms around me.

"Thank you, Doll."

I have no idea what he's thanking me for, or really what in the hell just happened then, but I like it. A lot. I like him a lot. I like hearing about his inner thoughts. I know that he probably doesn't share them much and I'm not sure why. He has things to say, and things to contribute. Instead, he sits watching, listening. He thinks through what he wants to say, or if he even has anything to say. He's the exact opposite of me. I'm not sure if it's because he discredits his own thoughts and opinions, but when he's with me I want to hear them all. I will always have time to listen.

"You ready to go in?" He asks me and I snap back into the reason I'm here in the first place.

"Oh yeah. Um yup, yes. Yes I am ready. Are you ready?" He grins down at me and shakes his head and chuckles.

"Definitely."

I take a deep breath and lead the way into the clubhouse, Tank holding the door open for me. Everyone seems to be hanging out in the common room. All the Tombs' are here, which makes sense because I've noticed they congregate wherever Mama Debs is, with her ever present apron and the delicious food smells emanating from the kitchen. The little kids are all on the couch taking turns petting Mrs. Mac, the Ol Ladies are at the table in the corner that seems to be where they always sit and the brothers are spread out between the couches and the bar.

"There she is!" Chewy stands, pointing directly at me causing the room to go silent. Crickets.

My pulse starts to rise and I want to hide somewhere. Anywhere. I hate being the center of attention. It reminds me of all the times I played the lobster during the Nativity play and all the adults laughed. The memory of how awful that was twists up my bowels and I need to disappear. Figuring standing behind Tyson would be a great hidey hole, I slide slowly behind his bulk, hoping that no one noticed me.

"Ah, Doll? They can all see you," Tyson's choked voice says. I just know he's trying to hold his laughter in.

"Shhh! On the count of three I need you to slowly shuffle backward toward the door," I whisper yell at him. "THREE!"

"Um, where is she going?" Chewy's voice asks someone. Someone who just laughs in reply rather than answers. "Mira! Writer Lady! Where are you going? There's a package here for you and I'm dying to see what it is!"

Shoot! I forgot all about that dumb package. The whole reason I was here in the first place. My brain must have gotten addled, what with the bike ride from hell and Tyson kissing the living daylights out of me and then cuddling me. God that was so nice. Being all up in his warm, hard chest. A thick arm wraps around me, Tyson's hand gently gripping my forearm, tugging me to move from behind his wide back, and moving me to stand beside him. He doesn't let go of my arm however, no, he slides his hand down my forearm, meeting my hand, his fingers twining with mine. He gives my hand a little squeeze, giving me the strength I need to stop bricking it.

"OK. Yes, I'm here for the big package unveiling!" I decide

to cover my discomfort with bravado and drama. I wave my free hand in a jazz hands type of way and let Tyson's chuckle soothe me.

Chewy gets up and power walks directly into a table, bouncing off, Chomper's legs in the front pack jolting slightly. "Hate when that happens" she mutters, righting her course and beelining her way toward the table in front of me, coming to a stop next to a boring brown box.

"Huh. That's a lot bigger than the last one," I mumble under my breath.

I slowly tiptoe my way closer. I don't think there's a bomb in there, but still, I'm a big girl. I don't want to accidentally jostle it with my giant Fee Fi Fo Fum footsteps. Looking up I notice everyone's rapt attention. Running my fingers over the top of the box I start to pick at the tape at the end, jumping when Tyson rests a hand on my hip and flicks out his pen knife.

"Sorry, Doll," he murmurs in my ear, the thumb of the hand on my hip stroking back and forth hypnotically, causing a good fire in my groin. Not like the one on our date.

He easily slices through the tape along the top of the box, and then the sides, waiting for me to open the flaps. Looking around the room, at the audience waiting for the unveiling, I take a deep breath, let it out and then gingerly open the flaps, first one, then the other.

Nothing jumps out at me, so that's a good sign. Peering inside I see pink tissue paper. Huh. Not really wanting to touch it too much I use a pincer grip to take up the edge and slowly move it out of the box, dropping it to the table once it comes away clean.

"Ugh this is taking too long! Want me to do it?" Chewy asks, almost vibrating with excitement and wonder.

I wave at her to step forward. I'm not a scaredy cat, but I'm also not one to steal the moment off someone who really would appreciate it. She claps her hands, then high fives Rhodie before taking excited little tippy toe steps to the box. She dives straight in, like a kid in a lucky dip barrel, hands first, peering over the top of the box.

"Ahhh, something is afoot!" She announces, mirth on her face as she steps back with a foot in her hand.

There are yelps and shouts and it all sounds very, very far away. Like I'm in a tunnel. Or like there's an ocean in my ears. But not in a good way like when you go to the beach with your nana and listen to shells. No, this is like the type of ocean you hear when you're drowning.

"Chewy! Put the fucking foot down!" Marx barks, just as Chewy mimes kicking Rhodie's behind with it. She places it back in the box, but not before turning it this way and that, having a good ole looksee.

"Switch, mind taking a look at it? Tell us what you can,"

Chewy goes to open her mouth to report back, but Marx silences her with a hand up.

Switch, the loud ginger doctor man I've chatted to once or twice, pulls a pair of glasses out of his pocket, rests them on his face, and takes a look at the appendage in the box. While he's doing this, Rhodie looks at the box from all angles, mumbling something to Rider.

While the MC look further into the goddamned (sorry Nana) foot I've been sent, Tyson guides me toward the worn leather couch, takes a seat and then pulls me onto his lap. HIs arms wrap around me, holding me tight. I never knew how touch starved I've been lately, since nana died, but this right here brings it home. It feels so good to be given a hug when I'm not feeling on top of things. Usually I get deep into my head and think up the worst possible scenarios. But here, in this moment I feel calm, in control, and warm.

"You holding up OK there, Doll?" Tyson's voice vibrates through me. I melt further into him, letting him take my weight because I know he can handle it.

"Well, I've never received a foot before. I've also never seen one not attached to a body either, so I guess it's a day of firsts for me," I tell him honestly, not knowing whether to laugh or cry. He squeezes me tighter and I watch Switch continue on with his foot-topsy.

"Well, it's the lower extremity of someone who is advanced in age." Switch booms. He has the loudest voice of anyone I've ever met. I like it.

"That tracks to what we found at the funeral home," Tav says, stepping forward, Pops right behind him.

"Yeah, by the looks of it they've been having a go at the freshies. The four we looked at all had scars on their abdomens, not autopsy incisions either," Pops says, effectively shutting down Savage before he could even ask. "These ones were small incisions, then glued back together. If you weren't looking closely you'd never even notice they'd been tampered with."

"Yeah but taking a foot from the ankle down? Surely a family member will miss that?" I'm not sure who said that, as there's so many brothers asking questions and I don't know them well enough to tell them by voice just yet.

"Yeah, dunno, that does seem extra fucked up," Pops shrugs.

"Not to mention the bodies we saw had their feet," Tav adds.

Marx lets out a long breath, "Gus, what else can you tell us about the funeral home?"

"Definitely on the take. Place is covered in marble and there are way more staff than a place that size should need," Gus, the hot one married to Ana says.

"Any long haired orc motherfuckers?"

"None that we saw. Unless they keep the ugly people out the back, all we saw was creepily good looking Russians," he replies.

Marx has his hands on his hips, head down. "Does anyone have any ideas why Mira was sent a foot? Anything in any of the books?" he asks, raising his head to look around the room.

"Oh," Lovely says, sitting up in her seat abruptly, "Hang on, I think I might have something." She rummages around in her gigantic baby bag, then pulls out one of my books. She flicks through it quickly, frown on her face, tongue sticking out the side of her mouth, her brows pinched. "Here!" She says triumphantly, "In 'Night Peril', the bad guy sends the heroine the foot of her lover after he accidentally stepped on her toes at the debutante ball," she beams.

"How the hell is that meant to be romantic?" Rider asks.

"Well, he's not really the bad guy. It turns out the one foot man is the baddy. The murdery guy is romantic, he'd do anything for the woman he loves. Even chop off feet." Lovely answers with a sweet smile on her face. The girl gets it. I didn't think she would, what with being the loveliest woman on earth and all.

Rider gives her an odd look then leans back in his seat, a confused look on his face.

"Right. So whoever is doing this is most definitely a fan of your books, Mira. Computer team, how far did you get with scanning Mira's social media?"

"Not that far. Turns out that Mira's fans are enthusiastic, and a little crazy. We've had to tighten our parameters and run it again," Wire grumbles.

"Fuck. So we're no closer to knowing anything other than the funeral home is on the take and Mira's fan somehow has access to elderly body parts. Maybe at the home, maybe not. Fucking great." Marx scrubs his face in frustration. "Prospects, tell me you have something a little more promising?"

Tav, Jimmy the gate prospect, and the one with the panty melting voice, Takoda I think his name is, they all look to one another before Tav decides to do the talking. "They got our warning. Three of them agreed to keep quiet, but Whitney laughed and slammed the door in our faces. After that they've laid pretty low, going to work in the evenings, and then coming home at the end of the shift. Their boss has a car pick them up and drop them off each time."

"Their apartment is high end as well, in that gated area of Rose Grove. Whatever he's paying them is big." Melty voice Takoda adds.

Marx curses under his breath and I feel Tyson tense beneath me. I had almost forgotten he was there, too busy watching the exchange in front of me. I would normally be taking notes, but this seems personal, the private inner workings of the DRMC and I won't sully it by taking notes like they are a side show or something.

Turning in Tyson's arms I hit him with a stare, "Are you OK? Don't the bunnies have something to do with you and Nitro being taken into the slammer?"

He huffs a laugh, the tightness in his body melting away slowly, "I'm good. How'd you know about the ex-bunnies anyway?"

"Do you know how much this MC gossips? I've been here for what, four, five days writing at that table over there, I hear pretty much everything,"

He raises his brow at me but before he can say anything I rest my fingers gently over his lips, "It's OK. I'm a vault," I beam at him as a slow smile spreads across his face.

"Good girl."

Aaaand there goes my underwear.

Chapter 12

Tank

Great, so we are back at square one again. There has been no movement on anything. No headway. Well, everything apart from the bubbly blonde in my lap. That seems to be progressing very nicely. A little too nicely. I'm hard as rock, my cock on an uncomfortable angle as I didn't want it digging into the crack of her plump ass. She may write romance, or what did Remy call it, spice? Whatever it is, she may write about sexy things, but she's still a woman I want for myself which means showing restraint and respect and not just digging my erection into her at every turn. There will be plenty of time for that once we're on the same page. Or at the very least once some sick fuck stops sending her body parts. I can't imagine any of this is arousing, probably quite the opposite.

"I have an idea," Chewy says, chewing her lip, looking everywhere but at Marx.

Marx raises a brow in her direction, Rhodie giving her a pat on her ass, murmuring something in her ear.

"I say we act completely normal. Usual movements, take

Tank and Nitro out of lock down or whatever laying low thing they're doing. We act totally unbothered." She flits her gaze around the room. "Mira, you act normal too. Do whatever random stuff you get up to, make it seem like you never got the package at all. Whoever is doing this is watching you, shit, maybe all of us. We act normal they'll think we didn't get the foot and get desperate."

Pres stares at his sister-in-law then nods his agreement. "Desperate people make mistakes."

"Yup. Then BAM! We lay a trap, catch them and torture information outta them. It'll be beautiful."

"Wait, don't you mean get them help?" Mira looks at me with her big green eyes, then everyone else. "Like, this person is seriously unwell. They probably need psychiatric help or something." She's met with silence. "Don't they?"

We all stare at her a moment before Nat clears her throat, "Yeah, totally." She eyeballs all the OI Ladies who then start nodding enthusiastically in agreement with her. Blanche even going so far as to start a diatribe on the state of mental health care in this country. Tav slaps a hand over her mouth just as her lips start to twitch and her voice breaks with a giggle.

"Exactly! Definitely in need of mental health care. That poor person." Mira then frowns to herself. "Although, Mr President, I do think we should probably kick their butt a little, I mean, they shouldn't be desecrating people's loved ones. That's just wrong."

"Noted." Marx nods once. "Prospects, I want you to stay on the bunnies, but maybe take turns rather than pairing up. Chewy is right, we need to show it's business as usual. Tank and Nitro, you're back to business as usual as well. If you want to go to a bar and pickup then do so," He nods my way and I feel Mira tense up.

"Settle down, Doll. He's saying that for Nitro's benefit. I'm not the type to pick up strange women in bars."

"Just strange women you meet in holding cells?" She's facing away from me, but I can see by the rise of her cheeks that she's smiling.

"Didn't you know? Criminals are hot," I whisper in her ear, causing a shudder to go through her.

Her breathing is a little quicker, I can feel her chest rising and falling under my tight hold. "Tyson?" she breathily sighs.

"Yeah, Doll?"

"Can we go back to your room and hang out?" She twists in my arms to look at me, the tops of her cheeks a little pink. "Oh, if this whole impromptu meeting thing is over. Shoot! Should I do something about the foot? I mean it *was* sent to me and all," She twists this way and that, jiggling around and I have to hold in my groan. She's wiggled my hard cock right into the cleft between her cheeks.

I know when she feels it because her body goes ramrod straight, not moving a muscle. Shit, I'm sure I even hear her gulp. She's silent for so long I start to get worried, gripping her by the hips to move her gently off my lap and away from my harassing cock.

The movement must have snapped her out of whatever haze she was in because she jumps up, "I have things to write about!" she loudly announces to the room. "Important things. And, and I need Tyson, Tank, to help me with it. He has experience with, um, language that will help the scene I'm writing." She starts walking toward the mouth of the hall then spins abruptly, "It's not an anal scene!" she yells in a shrill voice.

Everyone stares at her. Well, my brothers and the Tombs

men stare at her, once one of the women cackles it starts a chain reaction of giggles. She stares at me wide-eyed, and I can't do anything but follow her. Anywhere. Everywhere. Wherever she wants me to go, I'll be there.

I rise up out of the couch, discreetly tuck my cock so I'm not walking past my family with a tent pitched and start to follow. First off, I let the brain in my head do the thinking, rather than the little one in my pants. "Chewy, you'll be dispo-"

"Yup, I'll take care of disposal. I have an idea," She waggles her eyebrows in my direction, her line of sight on the foot. "I wonder if Elio wants to see an old foot?"

"NO!" Elio's parents yell in unison and I take this as my cue to get out of there before I have to hear any Tombs arguments. Trust me, Tombs arguments take on a life and logic of their own.

By the time I make my way out of the common room Mira is down the far end of the hall waiting by my room door. She's twisting her hands with a concerned look on her face until her head snaps up at the sound of my heavy footsteps. She beams at me, and before she can stop it her eyes dart to my junk, before snapping to my face, wide as hell.

"I wasn't perving! It, it just kinda happened because out there he was all like -" She puffs her cheeks out, lips pinched as she makes a big circle with her hands, then moves them up and down like she's jacking a huge dick. "Huge. It felt huge. Which is kinda weird because it was nestled by my butt and my butt is *not* small. In theory it should have seemed waaaay smaller. Miniscule even. Like when you sit on the remote but you can't feel it there, even when someone accuses you of sitting on it and you swear black and blue that you're not and that you'd feel it and then the accuser makes you stand so they can check and it's right there. On the seat where you said it wasn't." She tips her head back to look at me and I can't help myself. I lean forward and take her plump lips.

I nibble at them gently then leave a peck, pulling back just a moment, "I love the way all your words and thoughts spill out of these lips." I press my lips to her again, hers curling up beneath mine in a sweet smile, a happy sigh leaving her.

We stay like this a beat longer, before Mira pulls back. "Let me in there, Tyson. I got ideas."

"As you wish, sweetheart."

Mira

Mira, play it cool. Whatever you do, do not blurt out that you're a virgin. A 27-year-old virgin. You'll look like a total weirdo.

"I'm a virgin," I blurt out, even before Tyson has shut the door behind us.

He freezes for a split second, then presses the door shut with a soft snick, turning to face me. He doesn't say a word, just stands there, looking at me with an unreadable look on his face.

"I don't have it because I took a celibacy pact or anything like that, I just, um, never got round to getting rid of it?" I have no idea how or why that sentence turned into a question but it did. "It's not like I haven't tried to lose it. I've tried loads of times. And I guess if we're talking about the actual, physical virginity then that's gone, thanks to big Ricky. So in that sense I'm not a virgin, but-" I'm cut off when Tysons big finger comes to rest on my lips. In not an attractive way either, I mean, I was mid sentence, so my top lip is a little askew and I'm sure my bottom teeth are showing.

"Doll, it's OK. I'm not coming in here to maul you." He smiles softly at me, removing his finger, using the same hand to gently run the backs of his fingers down my cheek. "I like you. A lot. We can take this as fast or as slow or not at all. It's your call, Mira. Got it?"

I nod, then swallow, trying to straighten out the thoughts that are zipping around in my brain. There's too many, and yet none at all. My body is on fire. Not in a burning up way, but in an achy way.

"I want you, Tyson. So much it almost hurts. My skin feels too tight, too hot. I'm going to say something incredibly not sexy, but it feels like my crotch is on fire for you, in a good way. Not like the other night," I let out a shudder, because what the heck even was that?

"Well, I'm glad it's not on fire in a bad way," Tyson's lips twitch and I know I'm being weird, but jeez, I can't help it. When I get nervous, things get weird.

"Good. That's good. Great even. So, um, even though I've never done it with a real man, I feel like my down belows should be fine. Like no tearing or anything. They're probably in tip-top shape really. Well, at least I hope so," I frown down at my down belows.

Tyson's chuckle reaches my ears, breaking through the fog. "Mira, let's just relax. Kick our shoes off, and sit on the bed for a while. You can tell me what this great idea of yours was. And who the hell big Ricky is."

I watch as he toes off his boots and a snort bursts out of me when I see his colorful socks. I don't know why but I guess I was expecting those thick wool worker man socks, not bright yellow socks with little dogs all over them. He scrunches and wiggles his toes, a goofy smile on his face as he looks down.

"What? I like colorful socks," He shrugs and then kicks his boots into position near the bathroom door, the toes just touching the wall.

I look down at my bright pink and blue sneakers then toe them off, picking them up and depositing them next to Tyson's huge motorcycle boots. By the time I stand and turn he's sitting on his bed, back against the headboard. He gently pats the spot next to him and I jump up, landing on my knees beside him, then getting cozy against the headboard, mirroring his position.

"Comfy?" he asks, eyes twinkling as he looks down at me.

"Very," I nod, letting out a sigh.

"So, tell me about big Ricky."

By the time I've touched on big Ricky and then regaled Tyson with stories of my childhood and all the weird and wonderful things that have happened to me throughout my life, both Tyson and I are half reclined, slumped down, my whole right side pressed up against his left.

"Wait, I still don't understand how you managed to get a dead leg from putting your underwear on wrong,"

"Neither do I, dude."

"You are the weirdest, most wonderful person I've ever crossed paths with, Doll. I'm glad they banged me up in the cell next to yours." Tyson's eyes shine with mirth and I take the compliment modestly.

"Yeah, I am pretty awesome," I reply cheekily.

He chuckles and then presses a kiss to the top of my head, drawing a sigh out of me.

"I know you can't really go into club business with me, but what's going to happen with the old club bunnies or whatever you call them?"

Tyson lays still for a moment, working through his thoughts. I listen to his steady breathing and wait, knowing that he likes to think things through before he says them.

"I'm not sure. They all signed confidentiality agreements when they came here. Marx likes to keep things all official and above board. Their jobs were to cook and clean and they could have fun with the brothers if they wanted. They always had a choice. Anyway, they got a little jealous when the Ol Ladies started claiming brothers, and they had to be let go. Now we need to keep an eye on them to make sure they honor the contracts they signed."

My brows pinch as I think through his words. "Are they honorable ladies? Will they keep their word?"

"I thought they were. A little possessive and all, but I thought they were good people. Now I'm not so sure."

"The, um, the things they know, will it be big enough to sink DRMC?"

He runs his hand down his blonde stubble, "It may be enough to sink us and the Bratva." He holds my gaze and I know that he's asking me to keep what he's told me to myself. Not that I have anyone to tell, but I nod sincerely at him.

"Vault." I pretend to zip my lips, lock it and throw away the key.

He cups my face in his large rough palm, running his thumb over my lips, then tugs me closer to him until we're a breath away from each other. We hover there and I just know he's asking me to close the final distance, giving me the power to decide what happens next. I know what I want to happen so I press my lips to his, my body angled over his as he lays back, letting me take the lead. Well, a little of the lead. His tongue gently licks at me, drawing a moan out of me and entrance to my mouth. He tastes, licks, sucks at my tongue, the dueling becoming more and more heated.

One moment I'm hovering over him, the next I somehow find myself fully on top of his hard, thick body. My thighs are spread wide on either side of his, bearing down on that delicious erection I felt earlier. My core clenches at the thought of having him inside me. Tyson's hands grip my hips and he works me up and down his denim clad length, letting me rub against him like a cat in heat. I'm almost there, I can feel the pressure building within me but just out of reach. I tear my lips away from Tyson's on a whine and that's when he rears up, tugging my top down, revealing my tight nipples, puckered in the cool air just begging for relief. Tyson sucks my left nipple into his hot, wet mouth, batting the bud with his tongue, his rough hand pinching the other.

My body feels like it's touched a live wire, everything is zingy and jolty. My hips have a mind of their own and I desperately need something... more. The desperation must be written all over my face when I glance down at Tyson, because he stops for a moment, pressing a soft kiss to my breast.

"I've got you, Doll."

He leans back on his haunches, then runs his hands over my thick belly, moving my top up as he goes until it's all the way over my head. I lean up slightly to divest myself of my bra, his gaze drinking in each sliver of skin that gets exposed.

"You're fucking beautiful Mira," he runs his hand reverently down my side, stopping when he gets to the waistband of my stretchy pants, flicking his eyes to me for permission.

I nod, letting out a whine and he takes no time in stripping me of them, along with my industrial strength panties. I start to wonder if they've rolled themselves up in my pants only to have that thought shocked out of me when Tyson licks me from ass to clit. "Sorry Nana!" I screech in my head just before all rational thought flies out of my head and I orgasm all over Tyson's handsome face at an embarrassingly quick pace and fall into a dreamless sleep.

Chapter 13

Tank

I wake up to see Mira still asleep, blonde curls spread over my pillow and a soft smile playing on her lips. I lick mine, in the hopes that some of her sweet essence may still be lingering, although fat chance seeing as I brushed my teeth last night after tucking her under the covers. I snuggle closer, pulling her lush body into mine marveling that she's here with me.

"Why are you so hot?" she mumbles, letting out a little sigh as I run my fingertips down her arm, gently down her pointer finger and then back up again.

"I'm a big guy."

She cracks a bemused eye at me. "That's it? You're a big guy so you have to be boiling hot? That doesn't make any sense!" She giggles, her morning voice hoarse. Or that could be from the orgasm I gave her last night when I ate out her sweet pussy.

That thought must have played over my face because Mira gets all shy and hides her face in her hands. "I can't believe I O-ed all over your face and then fell asleep! How's your peen?

Is he OK? I ignored him! Lemme at him, I'll make him feel good, I've watched videos!"

She scrambles up, her gorgeous big tits bouncing around, her large areolas home to tight plum colored nipples just begging to be sucked. Rearing up I go to cup one but she slaps my hand away, rummaging in the covers to get to my stiff cock.

"Mira, babe, you don't have to do anything for me. I saw that little pink pussy of yours and needed to taste your cream. It's not an exchange. He can wait for next time to come out and play,"

I try to tuck my covers over my legs, and my dick that is probably giving me the evils right now. I know he'd love to be balls deep inside her, but after finding out last night that she's a virgin, I want to make our first time special.

"But you didn't get to come last night!" she pouts.

I tilt my head at her, "What makes you think that?"

"Wait, what? When did you come? I'd remember that!"

I try to hide my grin. "I'm not sure you would sweetheart. I blew my load into my boxers when I sucked your hard little clit into my mouth and you exploded on my chin."

She gasps, slapping her hands on her cheeks like that kid from the Home Alone movie. She sits like that a moment before her eyes go wide and she leans in, "Did I scream your name so loud everyone heard it?" Her eyes are huge and she looks mortified.

"Well, not quite," I answer, rubbing the back of my neck.

"Wait, what did I do? It was something weird wasn't it? Nooooo!" Before I can answer she throws herself face first onto the bed. "Don't tell me," her muffled voice says. She then sits up abruptly. "Actually, no, tell me. I need to know."

She braces herself and I try to school my features. "You, ah, you screamed 'Sorry Nana!'"

She goes stock still. Not even a muscle twitch to let me know how she feels. Well, up until she throws herself back down onto the bed and covers her face with the pillow. I can hear muffled screams and as much as I'd really love to comfort her, my mind has blanked out because her tits are on display, just begging for my touch.

The door bursts open, my reflexes are just quick enough to throw the covers over the two plump wonders of the world.

"Why is she trying to suffocate herself?" Chewy asks, standing with her hands on her hips, not in the slightest bit worried that she never knocked and pretty much kicked my door in.

"I'm suffocating myself because I'm an embarrassment to all women. Maybe even humanity!" Mira's muffled voice calls out.

"Right. Well, can you maybe do it after we go on the Ol Ladies shopping trip? All the men are on babysitting duty while we find Lovely's style." Chewy says the last part in air quotes and I can't tell if she's happy to be included in the trip or not.

Mira flings the pillow against me and sits up, clutching the covers to her chest.

"Aw shiitake mushrooms! What time is it?"

"We're aiming to leave at 9am on the dot, and it's 8.47 so you have 13 minutes to put a bra on and meet us out front." Chewy informs her in her very efficient manner.

"It doesn't take me 13 minutes to put on a bra." Mira argues with her, glancing down at her boobs.

"That man-" Chewy points at me, "Looked like he was saying goodbye to his deceased grandmother with how sad he looked when you covered up those amazing boobs. I'd say he wants to give them a very heartfelt goodbye when you strap them into their holders." She smirks in my direction. "Anyway, you have 12 minutes now, so chop chop." With that, she spins on her heel and slams the door.

"She's a funny woman," Mira says, staring at the doorway.

"You have no idea," I mutter. "Now, let me say goodbye to my very dear friends." Mira squeals with laughter as I pull her into me.

I watch her plump ass walk out the door exactly 12 minutes later and lie back in bed for a moment, gathering my thoughts. DRMC life has been changing for the better since Rhodie fell for Chewy. Then Gus wifed up Ana, Wire fell for Remy, Savage joined with his Ol Lady and then my prospect somehow managed to convince Blanche to take a chance on him. While all my brothers were falling, I had front row seats to how they all fundamentally changed, and I'd be lying if I said that I didn't want some of that for myself. Was I expecting to find someone in jail? Not really, but I guess you never know when life will kick you in the ass and give you a gift at the same time. That's what Mira is. A total gift. Crazy, sure, but crazy good fun at the same time.

Now all I have to do is not fuck up whatever this is that we're building.

"Yo, you gonna get up so we can get to work sometime today?" Judge asks, poking his head around the door.

"Yeah, gimme ten and I'll be there."

"Good. I got Rider coming in to work reception again."

I narrow my eyes at him. "Are you banking on him bitching to Pres about how busy we are over there?"

"Fuck yes. We'll have someone on reception in no time and won't even need to take it to Church," Judge grins.

"I like the way you think, brother."

Mira

I follow the Ol Ladies around the mall as they all oohh and ahh over the styles on offer. I can tell by watching their interactions that they've been a unit for a while. Chewy is the longest standing DRMC Ol Lady. The others sort of all landed at the DRMC in quick succession after that.

"Do you know what you're looking for?" Blanche asks Lovely as she holds up a flannel shirt. Blanche's style tends more toward tough mom mixed with covert spy clothing.

Chewy seems more alternative with her darker colors and her ever present Doc Martens boots. Remy and Nat seem to veer toward more biker chick which makes sense as they've been in the lifestyle longer. Ana is classy and high end and then there's me. Not that I'm an Ol Lady or anything, but I'm joining the outing and definitely not blending in with my floral wide leg pants, purple blouse, big pink plastic hoop earrings and green sneakers.

"Well, would it be weird to say that I want something that expresses my personality and not the cult we were in?" Lovely says in her soft voice.

"Fuck no! That cult had the ugliest clothes I'd ever seen in my life!" We all spin at the sound of Pops' voice to find him behind us, holding a glazed donut in his hand. "What? I stopped at Dunkin'," he shrugs.

Ana stares at him unblinking for an awfully long time, Pops mirroring her position.

"Who do you think is gonna win?" Nat whispers.

"My money is on Pops," I whisper back, Nat nods sagely.

"I'm picking Ana," Remy says, tipping her head in their direction.

"She would have learned that move from Mama Debs and I bet that look works on Pops all the time."

"Ugh fine! I'm here for security. AND you know I always come on the girls' trips and girls' nights! You've been leaving me out lately and I don't appreciate it," Pops huffs, donut forgotten as he waves it around to get his point across.

"We always invite you! It's not our fault you got an Ol Lady and now you'd rather make moony eyes at her than hang out with us," Ana argues.

"Can you blame me? She's fucking perfect!" Pops argues back.

Lovely rests a hand on Pops' shoulder, giving it a squeeze. "I'm happy you could join us. I need help to try to figure out my new style. Do you have any ideas?" She tilts her head sideways and smiles up at him. The man is putty in her hands. I hope I'm still around when the inevitable happens and Marx and Lovely act on their feelings. I have a hunch that the Pres will fold like a house of cards.

"Well, I think you need to find something that actually fits you properly. Since you escaped that shit hole you've been in hand me downs from your brothers," Pops replies, rubbing the stubble on his cheek.

"Then that's what we'll do. Mira, would you mind helping me choose some colors that might look good on me?" Lovely asks, eyes wide as if she's afraid I would ever tell her no.

"Heck yeah!" I say, fist pumping the air. "Let's do this!"
***

I'm exhausted and we're only halfway there. We've discovered that underneath all the layers of baggy denim, cotton and flannel, Lovely has a totally banging body.

"I cannot believe you've been hiding this the entire time!" Remy says, admiring Lovely's shape in a pair of purple leggings topped with a black off the shoulder top, similar to the ones I like to wear.

"I know! I'm so jealous!" Blanche laments, although I have a feeling that under her oversized sweatshirt she is probably hiding the same thing. Just on a shorter body.

"Well, in Eden's Keep women had to be modest at all times, so even I didn't know I could look like this in clothes that fit properly," Lovely giggles. "OK, I'm bushed, so I say we buy all the keep outfits -" she waves to the colorful pile next to me, filled with all manner of things: leggings, sweats, dresses, fitted jeans, blouses, the gamut. Lovely wanted to shop for comfy mom things but also things that would make her feel cool and hip. "-and then let's get food and drink. I'm starving!"

"I agree! Let's blow this joint, ladies," Pops says, eating another glazed donut. I have no idea where he's getting them from, as I'm pretty sure he's been with us the whole time, but who knows.

I help Lovely carry her things to the counter and notice that the Tombs seem to be holding back. Throughout the shopping trip Pops and Chewy have been murmuring to each other, eyes watching something outside the store. Blanche joined them in conversation a few times and I notice her eyes darting to a different spot outside. I think maybe something is going on, but I can't tell if it's a scary something or an exciting something. Or maybe both! Maybe they've spotted a threat and they need to find a way to distract us so they can neutralize it? Although I have no idea what type of neutralizing an old man and two little ladies, one of which is pregnant, can do, but I'm down with it. Oh, what if it turns out that they're actually really dangerous? Like trained in jiu jitsu or something? Didn't Pops say he was in 'Nam? I bet he knows a thing or two.

"Ready, Mira? You kinda checked out a little there," Remy asks, her dark brows furrowed.

"Oh yeah, sorry, I do it all the time. Have a thought and my imagination runs away on me." I wave it off.

"Speaking of, how is the book coming along?" Remy says, falling into step beside me as we follow Nat and Ana power walking through the mall, beelining for the food court.

I let out a sigh, "Not as good as I was hoping. There have been ... distractions?"

Remy chuckles, then links her arm with mine and it feels so nice and so accepting like for once in my life I'm part of the cool kids club and not one of two big girls who spend their time in the school library reading romance and daydreaming about their happily ever afters.

"Oh, distractions. Is that what we're calling that big, blonde hunk of biker huh?"

I can feel myself blush and dip my head to hide it. "Well, yeah. I mean, I'm not sure what we're doing or how serious this all is. I might be the distraction."

We come to a stop at the table and I keep my gaze on the ugly formica.

"Mira, look at me," Remy implores, "You are not a distraction. I've known Tank for a while now and not once have I ever seen him smile or laugh or open up the way he does around you."

My head snaps up, "Really?" Remy nods and when I drag my gaze around the table everyone nods in agreement.

"If we're being honest, I thought he might be a little special. You know, like a mute or a simpleton or something. He just never really did much other than loom," Pops says, taking a bite out of yet another donut, this time accompanied by a cup of coffee.

"You did not!" Ana says, jabbing a finger Pops way.

"Well OK, maybe not that bad, but I did think there was something wrong with him. No man should be that quiet."

"He talks more than Judge," Lovely points out.

"He's weird too," Pops harrumphs and then winks at me when the rest of the group start protesting.

I suppress a smile. I'm onto him now.

"*Anyway* Mira, you better get used to us because I have a feeling you'll be joining us permanently," Nat grins, plopping down into a seat and stealing a bite out of Pops' unattended donut.

The women tease and gossip and chat but all I can think about is that maybe, just maybe Tyson won't get sick of me and he'll choose to keep me. I've never been chosen first for anything. Not as a kid, not as an adult. I did come close to being chosen second one time, when the girl picking the volleyball team saw my height and thought I was athletic, but that was soon snuffed out when one of the mean girls pointed out that I fell over for no reason on the way to the locker room. I would wish her ill but I don't need to because she grew up to marry her boyfriend right out of high school who had a promising college football career until he dislocated his knee on an ice skating date with her. He was never the same after that. Had to become a carpet salesman and fat and bald. Actually, I think the fat and bald were probably something he wasn't aiming for. Either way, she's bumping uglies with him and I rubbed my vagina on Tyson's face last night. Eeeeeek!

Pops sprays his coffee across the table, coughing and spluttering as the women all cackle. Aw dogs nuts I really need to sort out this inner monologue.

"Yeah girl, you really do," Pops coughs.

I bury my face in my donut and try to ignore the chatter around me. Well, the chatter from most of the gang, but not Chewy, Blanche and Pops.

"Is that Whitney?" Ana says all of a sudden, pointing to someone on the other side of the food court.

"Oh my god, yes! That bitch! She's the reason Tank and Nitro got taken in," Remy says with such vehemence that it shocks me. She's usually such a proper lady.

Chewy and Blanche share a look and then start to stand.

"Where are you two going?" Lovely asks, looking up from her muffin.

"We're going to talk to her," Chewy says at the same time Blanche answers "To beat her ass."

"Maybe that too," Chewy shrugs.

"Wait, do you want backup?" The Ol Ladies start putting down whatever was in their hands, apart from Nat who picks up the knife that came with her food.

"No. If this goes South we don't want you hauled in away from your babies. You lot stay here. Any trouble happens call Marx, Blanche says. She's so impressive. Like I know she isn't that much older than me, but whoa, that whole Mom power thing gives her such a commanding edge. Like a lady Marx. Oh oh, maybe I can have a spin off of my MC series and it can have a lady Pres. I reach into my bra to take out my notebook and realize I never slipped it in there in my hurry to get dressed this morning.

A napkin comes sliding my way across the table, and I follow the hand pushing it toward me finding Lovely's smiling face. She reaches into her bag and hands me a pen, then turns back to watch the Chewy and Blanche show.

"That doesn't make sense! You're pregnant, Blanche," Ana points out.

"Yeah, but I have an ol man that isn't going to go all caveman on me. He knows I've got this."

"And I have an ol man that gets extra horny when I get into trouble," Chewy adds, waggling her brows at us.

"Imma kill that fucker," Pops mumbles under his breath. He also doesn't weigh in to the whole who's going who's staying debate so I'm guessing if he's fine with his pregnant granddaughter-in-law going to beat up an ex-bunny, then we all should be.

"OK, well if you need help just let us know."

"Aye aye captain!" Chewy salutes Remy and she and Blanche wander off.

"Um, should we be worried? What if this Whiney woman is dangerous? Like some type of crazy woman scorned who has this whole elaborate setup plan thing going on?" My concern is met with blank gazes which then turn into grins.

"Trust us, she's not the dangerous one."

Chapter 14

Chewy

"How do you want to play this?" Blanche asks, matching me stride for stride as I try my best to navigate tables and chairs.

This place is too loud and it stinks of too many things and I'm finding it hard to come up with a good plan. Not because I don't have a brain full of good plans, but because there are too many moving parts and variables in the mall. Hard to focus. I need to get her somewhere quiet.

"Get her into the bathrooms. I do my best work when there's a drain handy." Blanche nods, not asking for any more information. I like that. I turn my gaze back to Whitney, my face screwing up "What's wrong with Whitney's face?"

"Nothing. She's just looking smug. Did she always look like that? And is it bad to say that I don't like her even though I've never met her?"

"No. She sucks. Both figuratively and literally."

I walk through a haze of hotdog and body odor and I have an urge to cover my ears but I need to play it cool. Whitney has teased me before about being different so I won't give her the satisfaction. Rhodie says I'm perfect, and that's all that matters. Flicking my eyes back to Whitney I think Blanche is right, she does look smug. Maybe even a little too pleased. This may not be as easy as I think it will be. Glancing around the reason behind her false smile appears behind her.

"Chewy, that man behind Whitney, do you think he looks like a piggy-eyed orc with Maui hair? Like Flora described?" Blanche asks, clocking Whitney's backup at the same time.

I have no idea what Maui hair looks like, but he does look like a piggy eyed orc. Weird. The bunny messing with my MC and the piggy eyed orc messing with Mira in the same place at the same time is no coincidence. I hadn't calculated that the Tank thing would be mixed in with the Mira thing. Curious.

"The plan still the same?" Blanche asks, dodging a mom and her kid.

I pause for a moment, focussing on a dropped penny on the ground. The feet walking around it become a blur and all the noise and smells that were bothering me become background fluff, allowing me to formulate a plan better. "How do you feel about being kidnapped?"

Tank

"Fuck! Pack it up guys, the girls have been taken!" Rider yells from the front reception as he turns off the computer and flings papers around.

"What the fuck? Which girls?" I demand, Judge running in behind me.

"Dunno. Let's go."

We race out the door barely setting the alarm. If anyone needs a tow they'll have to fucking wait, our family is missing. We straddle our bikes and roar out of Devil's Big Tow, making the ten minute ride in 5 minutes flat. Jimmy rushes the gate open waving us in then shutting it up tight behind us.

Within moments we're all three stomping through the front doors to Pops, Lovely and the Ol Ladies, except Chewy and Blanche, all sitting on the couches being grilled by Marx while Wire, Savage and Gus stand at the backs of their Ol Ladies. With Chewy and Blanche missing, Tav looks like he's going to murder someone and Rhodie is cuddling Chomper for comfort. My eyes land on Mira and without even thinking I stride over to her, taking her lips.

"Glad you're OK," she blushes up at me and I move to stand behind her, like the other Ol Men. I'll think about why I like that so much later on, once we have our girls back.

"I don't know what you're so worried about," Pops waves his hand. "Those two are the best of the Ol Ladies to be kidnapped. They're probably worse than the guy who took 'em," he shrugs.

"I mean, when he puts it like that," Rider comments, earning a growl from Rhodie.

"We got any leads on who took them?" Dex asks, always level headed.

"Well, they were going to 'chat' to Whitney," Remy says, using air quotes.

"Whitney? What the fuck?"

"Is she shaped like a bobblehead? All tiny down the bottom and then massive boobies and a big head with really big blonde hair?" Mira cuts in, leaning back to look at me, which sends a weird thrill through my body, that she would look at me rather than my Pres or brothers.

"Yeah, that sounds like her. But with really bad makeup. Like no thought to contouring or blending," Nitro says, all of us turning to stare.

"Um, yeah she was there the whole time we were shopping. I like people watching and she was there lurking. And smirking," Mira says, drawing our attention away from Nitro and his apparent makeup knowledge.

"If Whitney took them they're probably on the way to Roxburgh and that club she works at with the dodgy boss. The bunnies aren't clever enough to pull this shit off on their own," Wire states then turns his attention to the Ol Ladies. "Exactly how long ago were they taken? I'll be able to approximate where they could be based on how long of a head start they've had."

The Ol Ladies debate if it was half hour ago they were taken or slightly longer. Wire pulls up a map and we all stare at it, pointing out where on the road they could be.

"Why don't you just check Chewy's tracker?" Pops asks in a bored tone.

"Fuck! You're right." Tav yells, pulling up his phone, "I gave Blanche a tracker necklace for Christmas for reasons just like this. I can't believe I forgot," he mumbles.

"Why didn't you give her an implant you cheapskate?" Pops frowns.

"She's pregnant, so we wanted to wait til baby comes. And she wants to know whether it'll give her cancer or something in the long run," Tav murmurs, tapping away on his phone.

"She'll be fine. I've had one for years and I'm healthy as an ox!"

"A little too healthy," Rhodie mumbles, earning a glare from Pops.

Tav taps a few more things on his phone and frowns. "You said they were going to chat to Whitney, yeah?"

"Yup. They were headed straight for her in the mall food court," Ana answers.

Marx holds his finger up and takes out his phone. He puts it on speaker, holding it so we can all hear Takoda answer.

"Prospect, how many bunnies are inside their apartment?"

"All four."

How can all four be there if Whitney has Chewy and Blanche? Mira must think the same thing because she frowns up at me.

"How long have all four been home?" Marx questions.

"Three of them were in when I took my post. Whitney was dropped off around 7 minutes ago carrying bags from the mall."

Marx's eyes narrow. "Know who dropped her off?"

"A greasy, scrawny looking guy, figured it's her new man."

"Same guy I've seen her with," I add.

"Thanks Takoda," Marx hangs up.

"This scrawny new man of hers look something like this?" Wire turns his laptop around, a mugshot of Whitney's new man filling up the screen.

"Yeah, that's the one. Drives like he thinks he's in Fast and Furious."

"Who the fuck is he, Wire?" Rhodie asks, gently rocking Chomper.

"This, brothers and Ol Ladies, is the owner of Spinners and a whole lot of other seedy shit. David Brian Tiffany. Or Big D on the streets."

"David Brian Tiffany? No wonder he grew up to be an asshole." Flack says.

"Right, we got Whitney fucking Big D and we know she's not one to keep her mouth shut if there's something in it for her. We've also got Whitney lurking at the mall and we've got two missing Ol Ladies. Got a hit on their location yet, Tav?"

"Well, if you're thinking that Whitney was a distraction and her new boss boyfriend has taken my Ol Lady and my sister, then you better think again. They're not headed toward Roxburgh." Tav says, eyes on the little screen of his phone.

"So where they fuck are they heading?" Rhodie barks. Chomper jumps in his arms and Rhodie murmurs and apologizes to the special guy.

"By the looks of the tracker, they're almost in Ironwood."

This has my ears pricked up ready to listen. Ironwood is where Roman's body disposal is located. My MC brothers recognize the location as they all stiffen at the mention.

"Now, what's a bunny that strips in Roxburgh got to do with a dodgy funeral home in Ironwood?" Pops asks, stroking his beard.

We all sit or stand around in silence, Mira's eyes are huge and I can see the thoughts ticking over in her mind. Up until now it's been quiet around the clubhouse, the only action she's seen was when Nitro was escorted to the police department. Now she's seeing what we really do.

"There's no paper trail from the funeral home to Spinners or vice versa," Remy says, her fingers flying over her phone screen.

"Nothing I can see either Pres," Wire backs her up, doing the same thing on his laptop behind her.

"Well, I don't care if there's a trail or not, I'm going to get my Ol lady, and then I'm going to spank her ass for getting herself kidna-"

The door flings open and for a split second I wonder why the fuck we have Jimmy on the gates if people are always barging through the door anyway.

"Honey, I'm hoooooome!"

Blanche

"Tav is going to lose his shit and then gentle parent me into never getting kidnapped again," I groan as I try to wriggle into a more comfortable position. Which is kinda hard as I'm lying on the hard floor of a big, blue van. I mean, could the kidnapper be any more obvious?

"I wonder how he turned out like that?" Chewy ponders from her position a few feet from me. Seriously, this van is huge. "You know, this van is very roomy. It's also not as gross as I would have expected."

I take in the back of the van and I have to agree with her. There's three single seats down one side of the vehicle, and a big lift type set up thing behind me. There is a wheelchair sticker on the back window so I'm guessing this guy has stolen this car from a needy person. What an absolute asshole. I tell him that fact, and he can hear every word as there isn't a wall or anything between us. Just the two front seats, a center console and empty floor space with me and Chewy rolling around.

"You bitches keep your mouths shut! I don't want to hear

your whiny bullshit." He glares at me in the rearview and I poke my tongue out seeing as I can't flip him my middle finger.

"Hey! Mr.! Is that a wheelchair lift back there?" Chewy calls out then looks at me. "This van would be great for moving furniture. Oh! Or like a piano, just roll that sucker on." She rolls over so she's facing the Maui Orc. "Hey, did you steal this van or is it yours? Are both your legs real or are you wearing prosthetics? I didn't notice anything unusual in your gait but I wasn't paying that much attention." His eyes flick to the mirror and I know by the resigned look on his face that he knows Chewy won't leave these questions unanswered.

"It's my van, happy? Now shut the fuck up." He speeds up, obviously trying to get rid of us sooner, rather than later.

Chewy flops around a little until she rolls to face me, then does some type of Raygun wriggle to move herself closer to me. "I'm gonna take his van," she whispers, waggling her brows, "The boys can give her a paint job and all that stuff. It's a good investment."

I stare at her. "Chewy, can you even drive?"

"Of course I can! I just choose not to." Her eyes dart away and I file it away to ask Tav. Ugh, he will be losing his shit right now. His overprotectiveness is bad at the best of times, but with me cooking our little nugget I can't imagine how he's dealing with it.

"He'll be fine, you know," Chewy says, looking me in the eye, earnestly, for a quick moment before looking elsewhere. "He's professional. He'll be able to set aside what he's feeling to do his job. I've seen him do it numerous times."

"You think so?"

"I know so." She nods, and it makes the sinking feeling in my stomach ease a little.

"Although, because he is so good at his job, we only have around a half hour, forty minutes tops to turn the table on the piggy man."

"Maui Orc."

"I don't know what that means."

"It's OK. You don't need to."

"I also don't like the way it feels in my mouth. And it's too long. I'm going to call him Morc."

"Fine."

She nods. "Good."

"So, what's the plan, oh great one?"

"We overpower him, take the van, and uno reverse the kidnap." She grins like this is the perfect plan.

"We're tied up, rolling around on the floor of a van." I whisper shout at her. "You're what? Five feet tall? I'm not much bigger and I'm pregnant. How the hell do we overpower Morc?"

She makes eye contact, eyes sparkling, "We overpower him with our minds." She grins and rolls back to face our kidnapper. "Ew, is that a Batman bobblehead on your dash?"

She wriggles closer to him, grunting with the effort, "You know Batman is the total bad guy right? Like he expects people to be sad for him because he lost his parents, waaaaaah, what a total crybaby. I'm an orphan too and you don't see me going around beating up innocent people."

Morc's head snaps around to glare at Chewy before his eyes flick back to the road, "Whatever lady. Clearly you don't know anything about Batman, so shut your fat mouth."

"Oh, yeah, you're probably right. I don't know that Batman was created by Bob Kane and Bill Finger and debuted in 1939. No way. I don't know anything about Batman," she sing songs.

Morc's jaw tenses and from the angle I'm lying on I can see his stubby fingers tighten on the steering wheel. "I'm sure you know way more than me. Like how in the 1940's Batman tried to prohibit killing because before then he was a total asshole? Beating up poor, defenseless men, just trying to make ends meet to feed their families."

"What the fuck are you on? Batman is the good guy!" he roars, swerving a little, sending me sliding into the side of the van.

"He's a gajillionaire and he goes around beating up poor people. The guys that are always loading vans in alleys. Batman maims them and then what? They have to live the rest of their lives on disability, costing the Gotham government more than what Bruce Wayne contributes. What's the bet he gets a buttload of tax breaks from his political buddies. The Joker, he's the real hero." Morc lets out a strangled cry but Chewy continues, "At least he's out here trying to give these guys jobs."

"That's it." The van swerves violently to the side, skidding to a stop. "I can't take this shit anymore. If you're not going to shut up, I'm going to make you." He unbuckles his seat belt and rummages around in the console, "I can't believe this shit. She's not paying me fucking enough to put up with this," he mutters under his breath.

"Whitney is a total douche, why the hell are you working for her?" I call out, my curiosity winning out over the fear of what the fuck this guy is gonna do to Chewy. We're at a total disadvantage, we have no hands free and I have no idea how Chewy is going to fight a seriously built guy with only her short legs.

His head snaps up. "Who the fuck is Whitney? And why the

fuck are you talking? I thought you were the quiet one."

"Whitney is the blonde bobblehead that met up with you, dickhead," I spit at him.

He squints for a moment, then maneuvers himself over the console into the back with us, "I don't work for no hookers. And I don't put up with shit from two mouthy biker whores either."

"Aw, good thing we aren't biker whores then isn't it?" Chewy says, from her position on the floor looking up at him with a smile. "Surprise!" She pulls her untied hands from behind her back, waving jazz hands at Morc before launching up and jabbing something into his groin.

He falls to his knees as Chewy stands, looking down at him. "Say goodnight, Bruce Lame."

And with that she swings a brutal right hook at him knocking him out cold. We both stare at his body for a beat.

"When were you gonna tell me you had a knife this whole time?"

"Couldn't give away my secrets," she mutters, climbing into the front and tearing the Batman bobblehead from the dash.

"So you were just gonna let the woman carrying your niece or nephew roll around tied up in the back?"

She turns to look at me. "You're fine. And I have loads of nieces and nephews. Besides, if it makes you feel better, I can let you do the honors?"

She waves the bobblehead around and then looks toward the bottom half of Morc and I follow her gaze. No. No way.

"What is it with you and butts?" I really need to know, it's not normal. I mean, sure, a little ass play is a good time, but Chewy is another level. She uses asses for good and evil.

"I like how it makes them squirm," she shrugs. "So, do you

want in on this or not?"

"I'll look through his shit, you do, whatever," I wave in her general direction and start pawing through Morc's crap. There's old fast food wrappers, papers strewn on the passenger seat and an employee swipe card for some funeral home.

"There! All done. Now move outta the way preggo, I wanna see how my new ride handles."

Chapter 15

Tank

"How in the fuck did you get here? And what's on your jeans?" Rhodie asks as he hands Chomper off to Dex who juggles the poor little guy before getting a good handle on him.

Rhodie strides to his Ol Lady and doesn't even wait for her to answer his questions, just cups her cheeks and starts devouring her face. Tav is doing much the same, on a gentler level, his hand cupping Blanche's small bump.

He pulls back then repeats Rhodie's question. "How the fuck did you get here?"

"In Chewy's new ride," Blanche replies, rolling her eyes.

"What!?" Rhodie, Gus and Jules all yell.

"Yeah! Come see it. I also have a little surprise in there for you all," She waves us all to follow her and we trickle out.

Mira's hand bumps against mine and I take it in my larger, rougher one. Real smooth like. She beams up at me and I hold her gaze, drowning in her emerald depths, until we're interrupted by a mechanical whirring sound.

"Is that a lift?" Mira's confused face watches as Chewy slowly descends to the ground on what looks to be a wheelchair hoist.

"Behold! My new ride. Isn't she magnificent? And look! We can move bikes, pianos," She gives the crowd a wink, "bodies,"

As soon as the words leave her mouth we all see the man slumped to the ground behind her on an awkward angle.

"Chewy, who the fuck is that?" Gus asks, a pained look on his face.

"This is Morc. Or the Maui Orc guy that had that stuff sent to Mira." She gives him a swift kick when he starts to whine.

I flick my gaze to Mira, trying to do a check in to make sure she's OK with what's going on. I mean, most normal people wouldn't be. They'd get one whiff of this and bail out. I'm half expecting that to be the case but when I glance at her I see...excitement. Her eyes are wide and there's a smile playing on her lips.

"You kidnapped the kidnapper!" She claps a little.

"Uno reverse motherfucker!" Pops crows, high fiving the girl gang.

Marx holds his hand out to Gus who hands him an antacid. He throws it back and takes a deep breath. "Men, you know what to do. Chewy and Blanche, debrief stat."

They nod, snuggle into their men and wander into the clubhouse, Takoda and Rider escorting Morc.

"This is so cool. Like can you believe those little ladies uno reversed their kidnapper? Like how the heck is that even possible? One of them is pregnant! That's total girl power right there, pow, pow!" Mira starts punching the air and giggling and I can't take my eyes off her.

How in the fuck my stoic ass has gotten this far with her is beyond me. I'm boring. Too quiet, too focussed, too inflexible, too messed up for someone this vibrant. I mean, if my parents couldn't even be bothered with me, why would this colorful creature?

"You're thinking," she glides her pointer finger over the pinched skin between my brows.

"I'm always thinking."

"Maybe just feel." She smiles softly then presses a feather light kiss to my lips, pulling back too soon. "Come on, I wanna hear the girl power story. Then I'm gonna emulate it and hopefully not get arrested. That's always a possibility you know." She tugs on my hand and I follow her into the common room.

It's silent. Gus is pinching the bridge of his nose and Marx has his head down, no doubt psyching himself up for some fucked up story. "What happened?"

Blanche and Chewy look at each other, from their positions on their Ol Men's laps.

"We wanted to have a word with Whitney," Blanche hedges.

"And then?" Marx presses.

Blanche tries to share a look with Chewy, but Chewy is looking elsewhere, tapping her fingers. This usually means she's put together something in her mind, or she's coming up with a not so honest story.

"And then we saw the guy she was with. The one that's now in the Rev Room," Chewy casually throws a thumb over her shoulder, accidentally jabbing Rhodie with it.

"And how did you go from having a word with Whitney and then being kidnapped? Hmm?"

"Oh for shit's sake," Blanche throws her hands up, "Whitney was there with Morc and some other gross, damp looking guy.

We got ourselves kidnapped, Whitney went off with the grossy and then we got unkidnapped. We-" Blanche points between her and Chewy, "are badass bitches who can handle ourselves. We caught a bad guy and we found out some stuff." Blanche crosses her arms over her chest and harrumphs, Tav burying his nose in her hair, his shoulders vibrating until Blanche spins in his arms and gives him a look that could shrivel a man's balls.

Marx lets out a long sigh, "I'm not saying you two can't look after yourselves. But you need to remember that you both are family, and when shit like this goes down it worries us all. Same as if one of the brothers was out there somewhere without us knowing. Just, try not to do it again, OK?"

Blanche's face softens and she nods at the same time Chewy mumbles, "I can't promise anything."

Mira snorts, her hand pumping mine a couple of times. I pump hers back and also try to hide my smirk. I glance at Mira at the same time she side eyes me and I have to look away before I get the giggles. What the hell have I become? Happy? Giggly? Smiley? I shake my head to clear it and tune back into what the girls have found out.

"There's nothing much in the van. Just some fast food wrappers and his employee badge to some funeral home in Ironwood." Blanche says.

"Wait, what's the name of the funeral home?" Nitro asks.

"Willow and Iron Funeral Home."

"He's our man. I'm sure if we show Flora a picture of him she'll recognize him as the Orc guy," Gus comments.

"He also has the opportunity to acquire the parts he's sending to Mira." Savage adds.

"I don't think it's him," Chewy states, matter of factly, her fingers tapping quicker.

"What the hell do you mean it isn't him?" Rhodie looks at the top of her head, puzzled look on his face.

"I don't think it's him either," Mira pipes up. She looks around the room before turning to look at me. I love when she addresses me and me alone, no one else. I'm sure a whore for her attention and I don't give a shit. "I have very few male readers," her eyes dart to the Pres before landing on me again, "It doesn't make sense that it would be him."

"Unless he's obsessed with you," Dex offers, causing a growl to escape me.

Mira grins up at me and pats my chest, snorting, "Nope, that's not a thing."

Marx looks thoughtful for a moment, before turning back to Chewy. "Why do you think he's not the guy?"

"Same reason as Mira. And he said 'she isn't paying me enough for this shit'. When we asked why he was working for Whitney in the first place, he said he wasn't. Someone else is pulling the strings, and it's a woman."

"You know, there is one very fun, very fast way to find out," Pops says in a bored voice.

"Rev Room?" Chewy asks, her face filled with hope.

"What's the Rev Room?" Mira whispers, leaning into me. Her warm breath teases my Adam's Apple and I have to fight to stay focused.

"Um, it's where Chewy likes to interrogate people. The Ol Ladies all chill out in here so you'll be in good company," I smile gently down at her and hope like hell she accepts that her place is here, in the nice warm common room that won't be filled with a grown man's screams for mercy.

"Oh I like the sound of that! I think I really need to see this place for research." She nods seriously.

"Doll, that's a no can do. It's not because you're a woman or anything like that, but it's for plausible deniability. We need to keep it strictly on a need to know basis."

"Will the Tombs' be in there?"

"Well, yeah, but they've been doing this shit for a long time. They may be a little different, but they've worked with the best of them, CIA, FBI, they know how to lock things down."

"And you don't think I can?" She turns to look at me front on, and I can see the confusion, and maybe even hurt in her beautiful green eyes.

"That's not it, Doll." I take a deep breath, letting it out slowly, gathering my thoughts. Mira waits patiently, as always. "I know you write torture and murder and all manner of horrific things, but writing it and seeing it happen to a real life person, hearing their cries and screams, is not something that you can ever forget. It'll take a piece of you and I can't have that. I love you exactly as you are, kind, funny, a little ridiculous and a lot clever." My big ham-sized fists, as she calls them, reach to cup her face, my thumbs grazing over the plump apples of her cheeks. "You're light Mira, in a world full of shade. Am I an asshole for wanting to keep you that way?"

Her eyes dart between mine, looking for the lie and finding none. A small smile plays on her lips, then grows in size, "Did you just say that you love me, Tyson Jingleheimer Schmidt?"

Laughter bubbles up in my chest and I set it free, tipping my head back, causing my brothers to throw me a few shocked looks. "That is most definitely not my name, Doll,"

She shrugs one shoulder, "Sounded good to me,"

Her eyes twinkle and I gently press a kiss to her plump pink lips, lingering for a moment. "I meant every word I said."

She lets out a gentle sigh, then turns to the room, jolting when she sees that everyone has been watching the whole exchange. "Um, hi," She sing songs and waves awkwardly. "Cover me," she hisses at me. "On the count of three we'll slowly edge to the doorway, escape all the eyes on us," she frantically whispers.

"You know we can hear you, right?" Rider asks, a cocky grin on his face.

"No! You didn't hear anything!" Mira yells, pointing in his direction then letting her finger glide around the room at the shit eating grins on everyone's faces.

"Another brother bites the dust," Fox laments, shaking his head.

Mira lets out a huff and speeds up her shuffling, her grip on my cut dragging me backwards in tiny increments because I'm a big, heavy fucker.

"Rev Room brother?" Marx asks, lips twitching.

"I think I'll sit this one out Pres."

"Fair enough. Have a good night." He nods once. "You have a good night too, Mira," he calls loudly.

Mira lets out a meep and scurries down the hall, leaving me to chuckle at her plump ass running away from me.

Mira

I race down the hall, burst into Tyson's room and throw myself on the bed. The thought of suffocation rolls through my mind but then I remember that I want to live a long, healthy life with the man who said he loves me so my self preservation kicks in and I make a little breathing hole. Although I do lament the fact that I don't have a blowhole. That would make this wallowing a little easier.

A warm hand lands on my back and Tyson does that thing where he pets me like I'm a massive cat. "You alright babe? You know there's nothing to be embarrassed of, right? Rhodie and Chewy are always eating each other's faces. So are the other couples. It's no big deal."

I roll my face sideways on the covers so one eye can peer up at his stupid handsome face. "I just didn't realize we were hard launching anything. Or that we even were anything. I'm me, and you're you, all perfect and hard and strong and silent and that jawline, I swear to god that jawline could cut cheese. Argh!"

Tyson gathers his thoughts a moment, then I feel his large hands under my armpits and in one swift move he scoops me up and plops me sitting up on the bed. "Alright, there's a couple of things in that sentence that we need to address. First off, this is most definitely something. Or at least I hope it is. Do, um, do you want it to be something?"

"God yes! So much that it makes my heart feel like it's beating out of my chest every time I see you. Which is all the time because my eyes find you as soon as you walk in. It's like I can't help but seek you out." I blow out a breath and peek at him.

He's beaming at me with his stupidly hot smile. "Well, that's good seeing as I hard launched us, as you called it." he runs a finger down my cheek. "Good, that's sorted. Which brings me to my next point. The way you think about me is the same way

I think about you. You're perfect and loud and fun and curvy and so fucking beautiful it takes my breath away. The way you seek me out is the same way I seek you out. I know when you're in a room because my heart settles, as if it knows my other half is near."

I blink the moisture from my eyes, trying not to sob with happiness, fear still gripping me. "What if you get sick of me? Get sick of my voice and my chaos? What if I'm not enough for you? We're polar opposites!"

"Yeah, we are. But I also know, in here," He taps his giant fist to his chest, "That you, my beautiful hurricane, are my perfect counterpoint. The other half to my soul. The part of me that is outgoing and funny and light and bright, that part of me is in you."

He smiles gently as I cup his face, pressing a kiss to my palm before leaning into it. I listen to him, as I always have, and let my fears fall away. "You, Tyson, are the other half of me. The calm, quiet, steady half of me." I lick my dry lips, swallowing and making sure I have his full attention. "I love you."

His lips crash into mine, nipping and sipping, licking and tasting, devouring me and my words. His hands gently push through my curls, cupping the back of my head, tilting me at just the perfect angle for him, for us. I grind up against him, the hips circling with need. I'm not even sure how we ended up with me on my back, Tyson between my splayed legs but I'm not complaining. I need this man, like I need air.

My hands explore his thick body, the heat of his skin almost scorching as I run my hands up under his clothing trying to get his shirt off. Without taking his lips off me he leans back, first divesting himself of his cut, then breaking our contact long enough to grip his shirt behind his neck and tug it off. Fuck that's hot! That's right Nana, I had to say it. No other words would suffice.

Taking his lead I quickly and unsexily strip off my shirt and bra, then grab him and pull him on top of me, wanting to feel him, skin to skin.

"Fuck baby, you're so soft, so sweet, so fucking perfect," he mumbles as he kisses down the column of my neck. I angle my head to give him more access, nipping at the skin of his shoulder when he hits a particularly sensitive spot.

My hussy hips are grinding against his denim clad length and I whimper with need.

"I've got you, I've always got you," Tyson pops the button on my jeans, pulls the zipper down excruciatingly slowly and then grips the waistband of my jeans, ready to tug them down.

"Tank!" A hard bang on the door jolts me out of my sex haze. "Need you brother!"

"No no no no!" I sob, "I was this close to having a real life man inside my vajayjay! Go away whoever you are!"

"Ahhh sorry?"

Knowing that they won't go away and now I wont find my peak I let myself flop backwards, Tyson rolling onto his back beside me. I whine, my body in a fog of unorgasmed lust, my core on fire and clenching for something that I can't have. I want to beat my fists on the bed, but that isn't a very grown woman thing to do, so instead I pout.

Tyson lets out a rough growl and then jackknifes up distract-ing me from my thoughts because who can even do that from lying flat? Not me, that's for sure.

"Sorry baby, I know you are hurting for me, but duty calls," He presses a rough kiss to my lips and gets to his feet, pulling on his shirt and cut, shoving his rainbow covered toes into his boots.

I huff out a sigh and pull on a top, whispering an apology to my girls. They're sad they're not out in the open having fun with Tyson anymore.

"Tank! We got trouble!"

We share a look and then both run out the door, down the hall into chaos.

Chapter 16

Tank

The common room is controlled chaos. Switch is yelling orders, steamrolling past Mira and I at the mouth of the hall and heading toward his clinic. Grabbing Mira I pull her further into the room as Fox and Nitro carry Jimmy down the hall, Dex holding his balled up shirt to the prospect's abdomen.

Mira gasps, her hands flying to her mouth. I pull her tight into me, burying her face into my shoulder as I stand back and take in the scene. No one needs me wading in and asking what the fuck is happening, taking the attention away from the people who know and are formulating a plan. I'll know all the details sooner or later.

"Wire! I need footage of what the fuck just happened here!" Marx bellows, gripping the back of a dining chair in his big fists, his knuckles white.

Chewy flicks on the projector, her and Remy at the main table, laptops open, eyes scanning for everything and anything.

"What are they looking for?" Mira asks, eyes wide watching

the scene. The girls and Wire madly tapping away, the brothers all vibrating with anger, the Tombs checking all security systems.

"Got him!" He watches for a moment, flicking between screens, "That fucker Big D chased the prospect down," he growls, jaw clenching.

"Anyone with him?" Rhodie asks.

"Three of those bullshit Japanese Fast and Furious cars." Wire clicks his mouse and casts his laptop to the big screen, grim look on his face.

"The kid hardly stood a fucking chance," Savage says in a low voice.

"By the looks of it, they never caught up to him until he reached Rose Grove's outer limits. He seems like he's keeping them at bay here," Wire freezes the screen for a moment to brothers muttering "good kid." "Then we hit a blind spot. By the time he hits CCTV again he's slumped over and then it's only two minutes before he wipes out in the compound."

Marx lets out a feral growl, picking up the chair he's been white knuckling and tossing it against the wall. "I want everything on this Big D motherfucker. I want his address, his bank accounts, everything. I. Want. It. All."

Wire nods, looking at his team who all agree.

Marx takes a breath and lets it out slowly. "Are all the women and children accounted for?"

I take a quick head count, noting all the Ol Ladies are here, safe and sound. "Ol Ladies accounted for," I inform Marx.

"The kids are all accounted for as well, they're in the safe room with Mama Debs," Remy adds, flicking to the safe room/movie room camera. The Bigs and Littles being watched over by Takoda.

"What's going to happen?" Mira whispers into my neck.

"Not sure yet, Doll," I murmur, dropping a kiss to her head. Having her in my arms is keeping me calm, and I have a feeling it's doing the same for her.

"Rhodie, Rider, Savage, Dex and Tombs's, I want you to lock this place down. Code Black security protocol." He holds eye contact with Gus who nods then tips his head at his brothers and Pops, my MC brothers splitting off to follow Pres's orders.

"We're gonna get fuck all done with Jimmy in the back room, so I suggest everyone chills out until we have word from Switch. The outcome will determine which play we use."

"If it's not good?" Mira asks, her face damp with tears as she looks toward Marx.

"We burn them all down," Marx says quietly, turning toward his office, his slow, steady steps thumping down the hall.

"You all heard the man," Rhodie rasps, as he enters the common room having finished his task. "We chill out and wait for word. If you're the praying kind it wouldn't hurt the kid none." I tip my chin at my VP and take a seat at one of the long tables, tugging Mira down into my lap. I need her touch to keep me from raging at the world.

Jimmy is a good fucking kid and a good fucking brother. He pours his heart and soul into the DRMC and I can't stand the thought that he's not going to make it.

I bury my nose in Mira's hair and take a deep breath, letting her spicy vanilla scent invade my senses. A gentle hand lands on my shoulder and I turn to find Lovely, holding a tray loaded with hot chocolate.

"Sorry it's not something harder. I want to keep you guys sober in case you need to ride out." she says in her gentle voice, giving my shoulder a little squeeze before placing one cup on the table, then a second. "Everything will work out, you'll see."

Mira tips her head at Lovely, murmuring a soft thanks. She takes a sip and then looks at the gentle woman who looks so different in her new clothes from the woman who landed here mere months ago. "Is it your faith in God that makes you so sure everything will be OK?"

"I have faith, but it's in the men and women we're surrounded by." She smiles and moves on to the next brother, going through the same motions, a comforting touch, a kind word, leaving cups of hot chocolate in her wake.

"She's going to make the perfect Ol Lady one day," Mira says, leaning the back of her head into the crook of my neck.

"So are you baby, so are you."

Marx

Fuck. I scrub my hands down my face, trying to wipe away the fear and the fucking guilt. What the hell was I thinking letting the prospects watch the bunnies alone? Why the fuck did I pull back on their numbers? When did I get cocky and complacent? We have not one, but two fuckers coming at us and I make the move to split the prospects up. Tonight, what happened to Jimmy, it's on me and me alone.

A gentle knock at the door has my blood pressure rising. I can't take anymore fucking problems, not now. The knocking sounds out again, two gentle taps.

"Come in!" I bark, my tone cutting.

I don't even bother to look up to see who it is, I stay leaning forward, forearms on my knees, staring down at my boots.

"I brought you something to drink." Lovely's gentle voice breaks through the haze of red, but not enough to snap me out of my mood.

"I have drinks here. I don't need yours," I growl.

I hear an inhale, then a gentle breath out. "You have alcohol in here. If you need to ride out, it will be better with a clear head."

I let out a rough snort. "What do you know about it, Lovely? Hm? What could you possibly know about this lifestyle and us 'riding out'?" I look up at her sweet face, challenging her. I'm an asshole and this caring woman made the mistake of coming in here at the wrong time, becoming the target of my ire.

Her shoulders pull in a little, shrinking before my eyes and I feel like a fucking monster until my gaze wanders to her face to find her staring at me, her dark eyes shocking me with the steel I see there.

"I may not know about 'it'," she says quietly, voice steady. "I may not know all the ins and outs of your lifestyle, but I know men. I know greed and jealousy and lust. I know rage. I know guilt. And I know revenge."

Fuck. I look away, ashamed at the words I flung her way, designed to hurt.

"I know evil men and I know good men. You, Marx, are a good man. But your judgement is clouded by rage and revenge. You don't need to be clouded by whiskey as well." She nudges the sweet smelling mug of hot chocolate my way.

"I - it was my fault, Lovely." I drop the anger, guilt overcoming me as I look up at her. "I pulled Jimmy's backup. I underestimated the danger and got him hurt, maybe killed. I -

I made a bad call."

"And you'll probably make more before your time as Pres is over." She stands a little taller, shoulders back. "The question is, are you the type of Pres who can move on from a mistake, suck it up and lead your men, or are you the type of Pres who wallows in self pity, leaving your men to fend for themselves?" She turns and heads toward the door, stopping in the middle of the office, looking over her shoulder at me. "I know which man I would want at my back."

She walks through the door, closing it behind her with a soft snick. I stare at the door long after she's gone. Fuck. She's magnificent.

Mira

The common room is a vigil to Jimmy right now. There is no laughter or familial bickering. Just quiet murmuring, a vigil to a prospect everyone loves. I glance over at Tyson, he's sitting with his brothers while I'm on the couch with the Ol Ladies. I'm not sure what I should be doing, or if I should be doing anything at all. I try to wrack my brain for ideas. What would my characters do? What do the women in the books I read do in situations like this? Usually, they tend to leave the safety of the clubhouse and get themselves kidnapped, so maybe it isn't a great idea to look for inspiration there.

"I can't wait to get my hands on the men that did this. I'd make sure my Rev Room is well stocked for them," Chewy says to no one in particular.

"Speaking of, how, ah how did it go with the last guy you took in there?" I inquire. I mean, I have time to spare and the whole Rev Room thing intrigues me.

"Boring. He didn't put up much of a fight once he realized what was in his butt," Chewy grins a little scarily.

"Wait, what was in his butt?"

"A batman bobblehead from his dash," Blanche shudders.

My eyes fly to Chewy who's sitting looking bored. "How the heck did it get in there? And was it like the whole thing?"

Chewy turns to look at me with a grossed out look on her face. "Of course it wasn't the whole thing. Only the feet, you need to have a flared base otherwise it'd get lost up there." She shakes her head and pats Chomper.

"And, just so I can get this straight in my mind, how did it get up there?"

"Oh, easy. I put it there. Mira, when you want to draw information out of someone, you want them to be very uncomfortable. You should probably write that down for your novels."

"I think I'm good. And did he really need to be that uncomfortable? Like, I'm not sure what you did to him, but I'm guessing it's pretty gross." Chewy beams at me. "But, like, did you think maybe to call that Sergeant Davies guy?"

"What? He's the worst police officer in the world! He would have let him go or something. No way. I needed answers," Chewy answers, her face screwed up.

"I think you mean 'we' needed answers, babe," Rhodie says, picking Chewy up under the arms, taking her seat and plopping her onto his lap.

"Well, yeah, but I also needed to know his obsession with

Batman. It's ridiculous for grown men to like a rich bully. Makes no sense," she whines.

Heavy footsteps stomp down the hall and we turn to see Marx with a wide grin on his face, Switch beside him.

"The kid is gonna make it!" Switch roars, his loud foghorn voice drowned out by the cheers of everyone in the common room. "Bullet was a clean through and through, missed everything important. He looks like shit and it'll be a while before he's back up and running as before, but he's strong and healthy and can have visitors in the morning." He nods at everyone, the stress melting off his ruddy face. "Now someone get me a goddamn whiskey!"

The brothers all thump Switch on the back and all the tension that was hanging over the room like a cloud disappears. I'm snatched up from my place on the couch into Tyson's arms, hugging me tightly, his face pressed into the crook of my neck.

"He's gonna be fine Doll, thank fuck," he breathes as I hold his head to me.

"Heads up Pres, we got Landrys incoming," Wire calls out.

Tyson groans and I giggle. "Who are the Landrys?" I whisper into his ear.

"Blanche and Lovely's brothers. Gator men."

"Ah shit! Sorry Pres, I forgot to call them to say Blanche was back safe and sound," Tav calls out just as three men who couldn't be anything other than Blanche and Lovely's brothers walk in.

The strength of those genes is ridiculous. Three identical looking men with black hair and short cropped beards walk in, all tall and seriously built.

"Great Zeus's beard, these guys have to be shifters."

"I know right!?" Nat crows, pointing my direction, cackling.

"Fuck this, we're outta here," Tyson says, gripping my ass, forcing me to wrap my legs around his waist as he strides back to our room to the cheers of everyone in the common room.

"Tyson!" I giggle. He swats my ass and I moan, wriggling a little on the stiff pipe in his pants that is nudging my clit with every step he takes.

"Soon Doll, soon Imma make you feel so good you'll forget all about those handsome bastards out there." He smashes his lips to mine and I hear a door slam a split second before I'm sailing through the air and landing on a soft bed that smells like Tyson.

He stands at the foot of the bed, slowly peeling his cut off and hanging it on the chair behind him. He then moves to the side of his bed, toeing off his boots and kicking them into place next to the bathroom door, his colorful toes on display. Moving back to the foot of the bed he peels off his tshirt, throwing it somewhere behind him. Now, I'm not a fan of Magic Mike because the gyrating man strippers make me giggle, but this little strip tease? This is setting me on fire. The slow, steadiness of Tyson's movements remind me of the man himself. Which I prefer. I meet his gaze, the heat shocking me into action. Holding his gaze I slowly remove my layers, peeling them off the same way he did until I'm completely naked on his comforter, Tyson enjoying the show so much he's stopped stripping.

"You have too many clothes on," I point out, and holy heck, is that my voice? When was it replaced with a husky sex worker voice?

His hands drop to the button of his jeans, he flicks it and tugs the zipper roughly, tugging them down. I'm on fire, but not enough to stop the giggles that burst forth when I get an eyeful of his sausage dog boxer shorts.

A large hand wraps around my ankle and I squeal as I'm tugged to the end of the bed.

"Are you making fun of my weiner shorts?" Tyson asks, playfully nipping at my inner thigh with his teeth.

My giggles turn into moans as he nips higher, closer to the motherland. My Batcave. No, that sounds weird. Especially after what Chewy did with that Batman- a whoosh of breath leaves me as Tyson's tongue makes contact with my swollen clit and I jackknife up, curled around his head as he devours my tender flesh. Huh, it seems I do have the muscles for that type of impressive movement.

He suckles me and I flop back onto the bed, writhing in pure pleasure as I ride his face with wild abandon, like a champion rodeo rider and her bucking bronco.

He pulls back, releasing my pussy lips with a soft suck, "Doll, I love hearing all the thoughts in your mind, but a bucking bronco?" He raises a brow and I groan, covering my face with a pillow.

He chuckles, so close to my core that I feel the vibrations through me. He blows gently before lapping me from back to front, my legs tightening around his beautiful face.

"That's it, Mira, I want to feel you come on my tongue and my fingers." He slips said fingers into his mouth, laving them with his tongue before releasing them with a pop.

His moistened thick fingers slide through my folds, slicking my cream from my empty core and spreading my lips wider for his greedy mouth. The sensation of him, everywhere, licking, sucking, pressing into me causes my body to twitch and twist in his strong hands. His fingers find a place deep within and my hips buck of their own accord.

"That's right baby, ride my fingers, make yourself come, use me to feel good, Doll," I'm bucking harder and faster, grinding and whimpering, whining, trying to find my peak. "Fuck me just like that, good girl."

Tyson's deep voice crooning that I'm a good girl sets me off, which is cliche as heck but I'm beyond caring as my body tightens around his fingers, bearing down and spasming with an orgasm so mind blowing I can feel tears in my eyes as a sob escapes me and stars burst behind my eyes, my body riding the pleasure into oblivion.

"Shhh, there she is. Hi, Doll," Tyson's gentle voice pulls me out of the void, his rough hands running down my sides, over my face, his lips gently pressing soft kisses onto my eyes, my cheeks, my lips. He's nestled between my legs, chest to chest, face to face, his weight grounding me as only he can.

"Tyson." I gaze up at him, my eyes heavy lidded with pleasure as I search his blue depths, "Tyson, I want to feel you, all of you. I - I'm clean, and I'm on the pill. I want to feel you, just you."

"As you wish," He angles his hips back, his thick cock nudging my clit, sending a shiver through me. "I'm clean too, got tested the day I met you.," He twists his hips and I feel the head of him press against me, right where I want him.

I angle myself up, wanting him, needing him inside me.

"Careful, babe, I don't want to hurt you."

"You're hurting me by not getting in me, Tyson!" I whine in frustration and try once again, this time feeling him sink in an inch or so, both of us hissing.

"Fuck you feel so good, baby." Tyson presses his forehead to mine, his blue eyes on mine as he gently rocks into me, slowly, slowly pressing in until he's fully seated. "Fucking perfect."

Chapter 17

Tank

Holy fuck she's perfect. She's tight and wet and soft and the way she's looking at me has my chest tightening and my balls pulled up ready to blow. I hold myself deep inside her, marveling at how well her little pussy takes me. She whines and circles her hips, my eyes rolling back into my head over how good she feels.

Her soft hands cup my face and she squeezes, hard. "You need to move," she says through clenched teeth, "I can't take the teasing Tyson. I need you to make love to me and fill me up." I stare down at my (not so) innocent virgin. "MOVE!"

At her command my hips pull out and piston in hard, my balls slapping her ass and we both groan long and loud. "Yes! Like that, just like that! I want more!"

Her hands grip my ass, her nails digging in as she tries to force me in and out of her, her greedy hips thrusting up and down. I roll us onto my back, my baby wants to fuck me, then she can. She looks down at me with wide eyes. "Ride me babe. Fuck me, make love to me, use me to find your peak." She doesn't move so I pinch her clit, her eyelids flutter and her head rolls back on her shoulders.

Mira circles her hips, then leans forward, and back, testing the waters. Before long my blonde beauty is riding my cock like a fucking pro, her beautiful big tits bouncing, and all I can do is hold on, my hands wrapped around her soft hips, helping guide her.

"Tys, ah Tyson, I'm so close, so close," she whines and I know I need to help her find what her hips are trying hard to seek out.

I grip the back of her neck and pull her forward, smashing her large tits between us. Gripping her ass I hold her steady as I power into her from below, fucking her harder and harder as she cries into my shoulder, letting out a guttural moan before she starts shaking, her pussy milking the cum out of my body in wave after wave of absolute ecstasy.

Our harsh breathing is all that can be heard, Mira's whimpers lessening as the aftershocks from her pussy subside. She goes limp in my arms and I hold her to me as if she's the most precious thing in this world. Because she is.

* * *

"Mhpmhh, no more Doll, you're goddamned insatiable," I mumble, rolling to pull my woman into my arms to hopefully get a little more rest. After that first time we made love, we reached for each other three more times in the night, wanting to be closer.

"And you're getting old."

I spring up in bed, making sure my junk is covered. "Fuck

Judge," I look around and notice there isn't a blonde beauty in my bed.

"She's in the common room eating bacon. Pres wants everyone assembled." He nods once, then stomps out of my room.

I'm gonna spank her plump ass, sneaking out of my bed like that. For a moment there my heart dropped into my ass when I realized she wasn't there, all those old fears I had as a kid, that I wasn't enough to keep my parents around, flooded over me for a second, and then settled because I know I'm enough for Mira. I know I am because there will never be a moment in time where I don't provide her with all she needs to be healthy, happy and whole.

I have the quickest, coldest shower ever, pull on some clothes and make my way into the common room, my boots clomping down the hall from where I never tied them. The smell of bacon wafts my way and I can see how Mira was lured from my bed.

Reaching the mouth of the hall my gaze zeroes in on my woman, and if she can feel my eyes on her, she turns, beaming at me when she sees me. I beeline my way toward her, dropping a kiss onto her lips., "Mmmm, morning beautiful." I lick my lips, a little salty from her breakfast.

"Morning stud!" she grins.

"You can wipe that smile off your face, letting me wake up with Judge's ugly face in my grill."

Her eyes go huge and then she throws back her head in laughter. "Aw, I'm sorry, I just needed food, I gotta keep up my strength you know." She gives me a slow wink and she's so fucking cute I press a kiss to her temple, deciding I'll let her off the hook. This time.

Marx lets out one of his ear piercing whistles, drawing all

our attention to our Pres, looking a fuckload better than he did last night.

"Last night I behaved poorly. It's been a long time since I've lost a brother in arms, and last night Jimmy came fucking close because of a bad call on my part. We're fucking lucky that he's a tough son of a bitch, but I'm going to do my best to make sure we aren't in that position again." He looks around the room, eyes landing on every one of us. Not just my brothers, but our extended family, the Tombs, and the Landrys. "We are not a brotherhood. We are a family, each and every one of us, and we have each other's backs. I forgot that when I freaked out and left you all hanging. I'll never fucking do that again. I got a good talking to last night that gave me a swift kick in the ass to get my shit together. Lovely?" Marx searches the room until he finds Lovely, "Thank you." He takes a deep breath, slowly letting it out. "And I'm sorry."

"Wait, what the hell are you sorry for? What the fuck did you do to our little sister?" Vic growls, rising to stand.

"Vic, it's fine. Emotions were high last night." Lovely lays a hand on her brother's arm. He looks down at her and nods, moving to sit. "Thank you Marx, I accept your apology," she smiles.

Pres nods curtly and then clears his throat. "Right. Good. Landrys welcome back. Sorry we lost track of your sister yesterday."

"Bah, don't worry. She does that shit all the time." Dom, I think it is, waves a hand at Marx. His attitude as unbothered as the Tombs' when they found out Chewy was gone.

I guess if you have sisters like them you get used to their behavior.

"Regardless, we'll try to make sure it doesn't happen again,"

"Good fucking luck," Gus mutters under his breath, ignoring the look that Marx shoots him.

"Before last night turned to shit, we were in the middle of questioning the Orc guy. Chewy, what did you find? What's the connection between him and this Big D fucker?"

"Marx, I thought you'd never ask! Morc doesn't have any real type of connection to Big D other than the woman paying him went to Big D for information. On DRMC."

Cursing sounds out around the room. Everyone knowing full well that Whitney was the longest running bunny we had, she knows shit.

"Any reason why this woman wanted that info?" Savage asks.

"She found out Mira was spending time here working on her book. For some reason she didn't like that. He also said she was pissed that Mira was ignoring the gifts she had been leaving for her at her home. Not the organs, the little things."

"The gnomes," Mira whispers under her breath. "His boss is the one leaving gnomes in my yard?" she asks louder.

Chewy nods. "Apparently. I'm guessing you weren't a fan?"

"I was confused. I thought I was being gnomed." She rolls her eyes and then leans her head on my shoulder.

"Gnomed?" Rider asks with a confused look on his face.

"It's a thing," Remy answers, "Probably the least gross thing on the dark web. You can subscribe to have gnomes turn up at people's houses. For a fee, of course."

"People are so fucking weird," Dex grouses.

Marx turns his attention to Chewy again. "Got the name of his boss?"

"No sir. Got close but he up and died on me before we finished the interrogation," Chewy says with a disgusted look on his face.

"The big fuckers always tap out early. He may be able to pump all the weights in the world but all it took was Chewy to remove that Batman outta his ass and boom! Out like a light. I think he had liver damage too. Stay away from anabolic steroids kids," Pops says, taking a sip of his coffee and swallowing it down, finishing with a loud, "Ahhhhh".

A soft hand lands on my lap, drawing my attention away from Pops and his granddaughter. "I get it now."

"Get what?"

"The reason I was warned off the Tombs family. They're kinda different huh?"

I snort, "That's one way to put it."

"Well, I kinda love them," she beams at me and I can feel my ass tighten at her words.

Shit.

Mira

This whole workshopping thing the DRMC are doing, putting all the pieces together is fascinating. So fascinating in fact that it's almost taken my mind off the ache in my under-pants. A good ache, but an ache nonetheless. Last night was whoooooweee! Tyson was amazing. The way his body moved, the noises he made, the things he whispered in my ear, both dirty and sweet, it was perfect.

"Fuck," Marx growls, pulling my attention back to the ideas

being thrown around.

"So, let me get this straight as we've come in late to this. On one hand, you have an ex bunny and this Big D guy trying to frame your men and generally being annoying dipshits," one of Blanche's brothers says. I don't know which one. They all look very similar. If they were book characters they would be three triplet mountain men who are so close that they want their one true love to be a woman they all share. Oh, whoops, he's still talking. Focus Mira! This is about you! "On the other hand, you have this writer lady," I wave, "and she's being stalked by a female fan, leaving gifts which range from gnomes to body parts."

"Yup, that's about right," Rider says.

"And yesterday, those two worlds collided when the guy who delivered the livers to the florist was seen at the mall with the dipshits." Blanche's other brother finishes off.

Marx nods at their summation and when you put it like that, it sounds less confusing. But only slightly.

"Chewy, your guest say whether he had contact with Whitney or Big D prior to meeting them at the mall yesterday?"

"Nope. Whoever is paying him was their contact. Yesterday was the first day he had met them. They were gonna point out Mira's new friends and his job was to kidnap one or more of us."

The thought that this person purposely went to this criminal man, to find out about the MC and then follow me and try to kidnap my new friends makes me feel sick to my stomach. Like what the heck man? What if it wasn't Chewy and Blanche that he kidnapped? What if it was Lovely? I feel sick. These women are my friends!

"Stop, Mira. It's not your fault." Lovely's hand lands on

mine.

Chewy stares at me for a split second, scoffing, "Of course it's not your fault. It's your crazy fan's fault. And you don't have to feel guilty about the whole kidnapping thing. We got ourselves kidnapped on purpose."

"You fucking what?" Rhodie growls.

"I did it on purpose. You don't seriously believe I'd be dumb enough and feeble enough to actually be kidnapped, do you?" Chewy squints at him.

"Well, no. You're too perfect for that."

Rider rolls his eyes and pretends to gag.

"You know what I don't get? Why the hell would a woman send her favorite author gifts and then go so far as to seek information on us when she finds out that Mira is here, and THEN pay someone to kidnap our Ol Ladies? Why would anyone do that? What's their motive?" Fox says, looking around the room.

We all sit deep in thought, mulling it over.

Finally, Tyson's deep voice breaks the silence, "She's in love with you." All eyes are on him, his blue eyes astute as he thinks through his words. "She sends you gifts, like a secret admirer. She watches you, that's how she knew you were here. Then you started spending more time at the clubhouse and she needed to know who we are and what you're doing here."

"And she goes to Big D to find out," Wire says, following Tyson's train of thought.

Tyson nods. "She saw you had people around you, new girlfriends, people who took your attention away from her."

"She's jealous," I whisper.

"She wants you to herself, Doll." His hand finds mine and squeezes, grounding me, keeping me here with him and not running screaming into the streets ready to pack up all my stuff and head to an undisclosed location.

"What do I do?" I look up at him.

"What do *we* do, Mira," Flack says.

We all look to Marx, who takes a deep breath and squares his shoulders. "Wire, get me Big D's address. Seems he's the only one who knows who this woman is."

Rhodie smiles a hella creepy smile. The kind I write my villains with. "We do owe him a little visit, what with the whole Jimmy thing."

"That we do brother."

The men all look at each other, the MC men somehow using their eyeballs to communicate with the Tombs and Landrys who all nod at the same time. It's impressive AND creepy.

"Chewy, I may need your skills, if it's alright with your Ol Man." Marx eyes up his blood brother.

"Oh if you say yes we can do butt stuff when we get back," Chewy says, loudly. In front of everyone.

Rhodie's eyes light up for a moment then narrow,. "Yours or mine?"

Chewy shrugs, "Depends where the wind takes us."

Ew. That's the worst double entendre ever.

Flack lets out a guffaw and I curse my inner monologue. Or lack thereof. Rhodie gives his brother a chin lift which I guess is a manly nod.

Marx returns it, barking, "Roll out in ten."

"Doll, look at me." Tyson gently guides my face with a hand on my cheek until my eyes lock onto his. "We're gonna get to the bottom of this. We got you, OK?" I press a kiss to his lips.

"Of course you do. Also, how damn awesome were you just then? Like a big, blonde delicious detective, deducing all the stuff. That's why people shouldn't underestimate the quiet ones, they're the ones that see all the things. I'm sooooo stinking proud that my man has such a good detective brain. Add that to that jawline and whooooweee!"

"I think you only love me for my jawline."

"Nah, I love you for the Tank in your pants too." I waggle my brows and he bursts into laughter, tugging me close, wrapping his big arms around me.

"Love you, Doll. I'll be back before you know it." He drops a kiss to my head and gives me one last squeeze.

"Love ya lots like jelly tots."

Chapter 18

Tank

I mount Winnie and wait for my signal to roll out, at the backs of my brothers. Marx raises his fist and the roar of our motorcycles wakes up the night, a low rumble like thunder as we idle. My Pres raises his finger in the air and circles it. One by one we pull out, heading toward Roxburgh and the little pissant that needs to be taught a lesson. Don't fuck with the DRMC.

A little down the road we see the signs of where Jimmy was hit, the rubber of his tyres staining the road, a mirror lying broken to the side where he said he came off his bike for a moment. I'm amazed the kid had the speed and strength to get back on it and back to the safety of the clubhouse.

My brothers and I hold our fists up as we drive past, and we all speed up a little, eager to get our hands on the little scumbag that Whitney's fucking. I mull over the facts in my mind again, how coincidental it all is. If I had a brain like Chewy's I'd be able to calculate the odds of Mira's stalker and our ex-bunny crossing paths, but I don't. I only have my brain and my brain and my gut is telling me something else is going on. I turn the facts over in my mind as I ride, the vibrations of Winnie beneath me and the wind in my hair helping me on a physiological level. My shoulders lower, my breathing steady, any tension gone from my body and lulling me.

"Roman."

"What's that brother?" Judge's voice comes through over the bluetooth in my helmet.

With what happened to Jimmy, Marx insisted we wear helmets tonight. We're also strapped into some fucking fancy ballistic shirts that are lined with kevlar on the front, back and sides. Thanks to Tombs Security, we're fucking bulletproof.

"Sorry brother, just thinking some shit through," I tell Judge.

"Is Roman the answer or the problem?"

"Don't know. Maybe both."

Judge doesn't answer, but I notice him pull closer to the group, tightening up our ranks, I follow lead and in a tight unit we navigate the streets of Roxburgh until we're parked outside of Spinners, the neon sign casting the street with a pink glow. Jules parks his SUV behind us, having come with us because Chewy needed her "special things".

"I feel like I'm going to catch something in there," Rider gripes.

"What are you talking about? This place was ranked 'No. 1 Strip Club in 2004' according to the sign," Nitro points out, trying hard to hold his laughter.

The SUV door opens and Chewy's booted feet dangle for a moment before she drops down out of the vehicle into the street. She leans into the open door, messing around with something. She pulls back with her goddamn gator in her arms.

I'm used to seeing him strapped to Rhodie's chest or in the

stroller Chewy uses. He has fucked up feet so walking isn't so great for him, but I know he's been doing rehab. We all know because Rhodie and his Ol Lady won't stop updating us. He's also usually dressed in some weird ass outfit, but tonight he's in a black harness with a spiked lead that Chewy has a hold of.

"Is it me or does Chomper look a fuckton bigger than usual?" Dex murmurs.

"Nah, he definitely looks bigger," Savage replies.

"That's because this isn't Chomper. This is Gretchen," Chewy states, like we should all know that.

"Who the fuck is Gretchen?"

"The Landrys female gator," she answers like that's obvious.

Jules sighs, "The Landrys brought her with them. It's gator mating season. She's popular, being fucked too often. That answer your questions?"

"Not really," Rider says under his breath, but judging by Jules's face the conversation is over.

Without another word Marx leads the way. The security on the door stares at us as we walk past, whispering something into his sleeve, then looking panicked as Chewy in her long leather coat slowly leads Gretchen past, a huge smile on her face. No doubt with that entrance we'll be meeting Big D real soon. Stepping into the dimly lit club, I'm assaulted by non stop bass being pumped through the speakers, the neon lights bouncing off the shiny bar in the corner. The place is packed. At least three different stag nights seem to be crammed in here. The girls on stage and working the crowd all have glassy eyes, look incredibly thin, and at least four of them look young. Too young.

"What is this fucker into?" I mutter to myself.

"We'll soon find out," Jules answers, nodding toward the

behemoth making his way to Marx.

Three other men dressed in cheap suits surround our group although I note the ones near Chewy keep their distance. Flanking our sides and back they usher us through to a weirdass function room, a single table set up in the middle with Big D front and center.

"The D. R. M. C." Big D says, sounding out each letter as if he just learned to read. "You come to do business?" He takes a long drag of the joint that's been flapping around in his mouth.

He taps something in his lap, and Whitney climbs out from under the table, hair a mess, saliva and god knows what else all smeared across her face. She plops down in Big D's lap, whispering in his ear, and running her fingers through his greasy, lank hair. Marx gives her a look that would send a grown man running, but all she does is lick her pumped up lips and bat her eyelashes. Marx ignores her, walking closer to the table they're sitting at, kicking out a chair and lowering his bulk into it.

"You clearly don't know us if you think we'd ever do business with fucking scum like you," Marx answers in a bored tone.

Big D smiles. Which is a reaction I didn't expect. Usually jacked up little shitheads like Big D jump straight to anger when they feel like they're being belittled. His reaction has me shifting slightly.

"Oh, I know all about the little Devil's Rose MC." He takes another long toke, blowing the smoke in Marx's direction. "Marx Paxton, eldest son of Mad Dog Paxton. Momma was a whore who ran away and left her little boy all alone. Awww." He pokes his bottom lip out with a pout. "It wasn't til Rhodie's momma came along that you got any real type of love."

Marx gives nothing away, not outwardly, but I know my Pres

and the line of his shoulders is pulled tight, like a coiled snake.

Big D waves towards Rhodie, "What was it like sharing your momma with a kid whose own mom didn't want him?" He snorts, "Oh, and how's your little Ol Lady? I hear she's, how did you put it babe? Defective?"

Rhodie moves to step forward but Chewy's hand on his arm calms him immediately. She steps to his side, twinning her fingers with his. Jules flanks her.

"Oh! It's the blank faced twins! Don't think I don't know your secrets. Jules. I know you like to fuck with Fox and Nitro. The question is, do you *fuck* fuck them, like they do each other, or just share bitches with them?" He laughs hysterically, throwing himself forward, hands flat on the table to hold himself up.

A swift movement to the side catches my eye and Big D's laughter turns to howls. Whitney screaming bloody murder next to him as Chewy holds up the finger she just cut off. His so-called bodyguards reach to pull their weapons but me and my brothers beat them to it, our guns already trained on them.

"No one talks about my people like that," Chewy says in her flat voice. She dangles Big D's finger in the air, then drops it, straight into the waiting mouth of Gretchen who makes a snapping sound, swallowing the treat.

"You're fucking crazy! Rhodie, how can you want this crazy bit-" Whitney's cut off by Judge slapping a hand over her mouth and shoving her into an empty seat next to her boyfriend.

"Well, now that pleasantries are out of the way, why don't you tell us about the woman that came to you wanting information on us? You know, the one that sent her man to kidnap my brothers' Ol Ladies?" Marx says, his voice cold and steady.

"He died bleeding from the ass," Chewy adds, concentrating on getting the blood off her hands with a baby wipe her brother passed her.

Big D takes two deep breaths and pulls himself together as best he can. There's sweat beading on his forehead and he looks terrible. "I'm not telling you shit," he spits at Marx, rocking a little in his seat.

"OK." Marx waves at Chewy who steps forward, her knife at the ready.

Big D tries to pull his hands away but Jules has his wrist held tight to the top of the table.

"Which one do you want me to take?" Chewy asks, brows raised, waiting for Big D's decision.

"None of them, you crazy fucking bitch!" he sneers, struggling to get out of her brother's hold.

"Well, that's not an option I'm afraid. Tell you what, I'll take the ring finger, that way you can still count to three on this hand, and you won't have to skip any." She smiles gently at him, which causes him to flinch. "On three. One. Two," Her knife comes down and his finger rolls on the table.

Big D screams, his men jumping at the sound. The one my gun is trained on looks ready to fucking run out of here and never come back.

"You said three!"

She gives him a funny look. "Everyone knows you never do it on three." She holds up his finger, peering at it long enough for him to peek at his missing appendage and then start gagging. With a shrug she drops it into Gretchen's waiting mouth. "Good girl," she pets her head.

Marx folds his arms across his chest, cold gaze on Big D, who looks more like Little Sick D, and raises his brow.

"Fine! Fuck, if I tell you will you fuck off?" He's sweating and looks really fucking green, like he could pass out at any time. Fucking pussy.

"Baby! Stop! Don't tell these assholes anything!" Whitney screeches from the sidelines. "Don't say another word!"

Judge sighs deeply and clamps his hand over her mouth again.

"We're an MC of our word. You tell us what we want to know, we fuck off." Marx says. Big D looks sceptical, but he doesn't really have a lot of options seeing as his men are outnumbered and Chewy is more than happy to keep slicing parts off the man.

"Ugh, OK, OK." He takes a couple of breaths, nursing his hand against his chest in case Chewy wants to cut off another digit. "Don't know her name, blonde, really short, slicked back hair. She runs a disposal business in Ironwood."

"Svetlana," Tav says, sharing a look with Jules who nods in agreement.

"And how do you know her?" Marx grills him.

"I use her, ah, services sometimes." He swallows thickly.

"You're a piece of shit," Marx says, standing to his full height.

He holds his hand out, waiting for Big D to take the bait. All of us except for him know what's going to happen next. We don't let a slight go unpunished. He stands on wobbly legs, using the table to hold him upright. I would almost feel sorry for him, but I don't. He slips his hand into Marx's and six soft pops ring out in the room, five of Big D's men hitting the ground while red blooms across the front of Big D's slightly off white button down.

"That's for Jimmy," Marx says softly.

Whitney stops her incessant fucking screaming for a minute to glare at us all, her hands fisted by her sides. "I will fucking ruin you, you hear me?"

"Good luck with that," Chewy says, wandering up to her with Gretchen. She corners Whitney against the wall, then turns slightly to look at Marx. "Pres?"

Marx tips his chin at her, giving her the green light. Whitney whimpers, eyes like fucking saucers, whining, pleading with Marx.

Chewy tsks at Whitney, drawing her attention. "You breached your contract, Whitney. Gretchen here is going to make sure that the punitive damages DRMC is seeking are paid in full."

"She's so hot when she talks like that," Rhodie says, watching his woman with dreamy eyes as she and Gretchen advance the bunny that started this shit storm.

The ex-bunny screams, her eyes roll back and she falls to the floor.

"Didn't anyone tell her that you never play dead around a gator?" Chewy shakes her head, removing a container of something from her pocket. Whatever it is has Gretchen looking excited. I think.

Chewy tips the contents over Whitney's prone body, humming an upbeat tune. "There you are girl," she unclips the lead from Gretchen and I turn away when the gator opens her jaws wide, the snapping sounds on flesh causing a ripple down my spine.

"Pres," Switch yells, grabbing my attention as he stands over Big D. "He's still breathing."

"Leave him. He'll die, or he'll wear a colostomy bag. Either way, he'll know never to fuck with the DRMC." Marx takes one last look at the carnage in the room then leads us out of the weird ass function room and out the front doors, stopping abruptly when we see Roman and Sasha leading four women out of Spinners, coats draped over their half-naked bodies.

"What in the fuck are you doing here?" Marx growls.

"Ah Marx, fancy seeing you and the DRMC in these parts." He ushers the one nearest him into the back of his car.

"Roman, I'm only going to ask one more time, what the fuck are you doing here?" Marx's jaw clenches.

"I'm taking four trafficked young women home to their families. As you know, I. Don't. Deal. In. Flesh." He stares Marx down, and for once there is something honest in his eyes. Maybe there's more to him than we think. "Besides, I thought I'd check out the club. I've heard the last guy who ran guns and drugs here is feeling a little unwell. There may be a gap in the Roxburgh market for me," he smirks at Marx who glares at him and steps back.

He gets into his car along with Sasha, and the four scared young women who look more than happy to be getting out of here. His window rolls down, slowly showing his face. "My men will clean up the mess," he nods toward the back end of the building. "Good night Marx, I'll be seeing you soon, I'm sure." He gives a finger wave and drives off.

"I really fucking hate that guy."

Mira

The men have been gone for half an hour and I'm already getting antsy. I tried writing, but nothing is sticking at the moment. In my novel the FMC has been kidnapped after she made a series of terrible decisions where she knew better than everyone else blah blah blah. She's currently in a dank basement and her kidnapper is about to be revealed. Am I going to go with her love interest's jealous ex, or her jealous ex? Decisions, decisions.

"Mira, you're a writer, do you think you could perhaps give Jovie a little authorly advice?" Remy asks, taking a short break from whatever it is she does on her computer. I know it's super important hacker-y stuff, but that's as far as my knowledge extends.

"Sure can! How can I help you, Miss Jovie?" I ask her seriously.

Before she can answer Cove butts in, "Her teacher told her that she needs to change the ending of her story, but her teacher doesn't know anything."

"Cove!" Blanche growls.

"But she doesn't, Mommy! Jovie's story is perfect the way it is," she harrumphs.

"Well, why don't you tell me about your story and what the teacher wanted you to change?" I say, looking at Jovie.

Cove opens her mouth and Blanche slaps her hand over it, muzzling her.

"Well, it's about a man who eats way too much chocolate. He eats it every day. Then he eats so much chocolate that he gets diabetes and he has to have his foot cut off, but it doesn't stop the spread of the infection and he dies." I blink at her once, then twice, her large eyes staring back at me, waiting for feedback.

"Wow, what an imaginative story, sweetie." I exclaim, darting my eyes toward a smirking Pops. "I, um, I think if you like it and are happy with it then it's perfect just the way it is." Good work Mira, nice solid advice and age appropriate.

"It's not an imaginary story. It happens in real life," Elio says, not looking up from his game of chess.

"That's right, it does," I answer, "My nana had a friend, Patsy. Patsy took her sock off one day and her toe fell off." I tell the children. And then realize that maybe I shouldn't have said that because kids this age probably don't need to know about old folks' body parts falling off.

"What happened after that?" Cove asks, edging closer. Even the Bigs and Landrys look up from their phones or petting my traitorous fat orange cat.

"Well, they had a cup of tea and then my nana, ah, tried to sew it back on." I widen my eyes at Blanche in the hopes that she will distract the kids away from my story.

"Did it work?" Sage asks, looking incredibly interested. "I'm going to be a nurse. This is good research for me."

"Well, no, it just kinda got more infected, and then they had to amputate two more of her toes." I shudder. Patsy was a huge fan of sandals and I could never look away when her exposed two toes would come to visit.

"Happens to old folks all the time. Not me though, I like to keep myself fit. I bet you kids didn't know I power walk 5 miles every morning, huh? And I go for an evening digestion walk," Pops says to, well, everyone. "Even lift weights. Not to be some kind of gym bro, but to keep things working well. Did you know the main cause of erectile dysfunction is lack of blood flow? You know what keeps blood flowing? Exercise." He nods at his sage advice, ignoring the fact that we have kids in the room.

"Thanks for the advice Pops," Gus says drily, from his spot on the couch.

The Landry brothers are bright red and snorting, and Takoda at the bar is also trying hard not to lose it over Pops' pecker advice.

"And another thing, never skimp on moisturizing. Good skin is important. Elio, why is skin important?"

"Because it's the largest organ in the human body," he replies, Pops nodding proudly. "And it's home to 100 billion nerve endings. Which means any part of the human body can be treated in lots of different ways to bring excruciating pain to the victim making them spill information like a singing canary."

The room goes silent and we all stare at the dark-haired little boy.

"Huh, now where on earth did you learn that?" Pops says sidling over to Elio and giving him a large-eyed stare. Which would work if Elio was actually looking at Pops.

"Sidney Carver Tombs! You better-"

"Shit, I forgot to take my evening fart walk. I better do that now. Don't want to get trapped gas. I'll check the perimeter while I'm out." Pops pulls up his chino's another half inch and hot foots it out of the common room as fast as his Skechers can take him. We all stare for a beat and then burst into laughter.

Blanche cuddles her youngest child and gently explains to him that perhaps using any of the body's 100 million nerve endings would be very painful and a terrible idea and maybe we could just love the other person until we've gained enough of their trust for them to open up to us, instead of hurting them. Elio gives her a funny look and shrugs, packing up his chess set and heading down the hall, followed by the other two Littles.

"We got this Mom," Niko says, he and Sage following after their baby brother.

"I need to see this," Vic says, looking at his brothers. "That kid is going to run rings around Niko's reasoning. It's going to be the funniest thing we've seen since Pops ran away." All three brothers grin and leave, following in the younger Landrys wake.

"Well, can I Just say that was really good parenting Blanche. Very good advice," Remy says, smiling.

"And it's all bullshit. The very best way to get someone to talk is definitely torturing all 100 billion nerve endings."

Hmm, maybe my female character needs to dig deep into her inner Blanche? How great would that be? She hasn't been a total weenie, but perhaps being locked in a dark basement will be enough to bring out her inner tough gal. I look around at the women dotted around the common room, all of them are wily and tough. I have a spark of an idea and get settled, fingers on my keyboard ready to bring my idea to life.

* * *

"Remy, are you seeing what I'm seeing?" The tone of Gus's voice breaks me out of my writing fog. Flicking my gaze down to the little clock in the corner of my laptop I'm shocked when I find I've been tapping away for over an hour now, oblivious to what is happening around me.

"Yeah, I see her. What is she doing?" Remy replies, clicking all sorts of buttons. "This is earlier footage, looks like her car broke down or something."

Gus and Remy lean forward, looking at all the security footage, playing on a montage of tiny screens. Looking around the room I notice the Littles, Blanche and Mama Debs have left the room, as have Lovely, Ana and Nat. I have no idea where the Landrys have gotten to, leaving me, Gus and Remy and Takoda here alone. Even Pops is somewhere, probably with his woman.

"What do we want to do? We can't leave a woman on the side of the road at this time," Remy says, looking up at Gus from her seat.

His eyes narrow, and he nods then turns to me. "Mira, does this woman look familiar to you?"

I look over my shoulder and then point to myself. Me? Why would he be asking me for any type of input. I'm new here, and aside from knowing that the men all rode out to try to get information from this Big D dude, who, by the way, has a terrible villain name, I have no idea how I can help in this sitch.

Snorting has me looking at Remy, who has her lips pulled between her teeth, trying hard not to laugh.

"Ah nuts! Out loud again, huh?"

"Yup, babe. Out loud," Gus nods. "I'm only asking you because we know your stalker or whatever is female and most likely a mega fan. Would you be able to recognize someone who most likely goes to your signings and things?"

My lips screw up as I think. Not to toot my own horn too much, but I have a lot of fans. I can see upwards of 100 women all wanting their books to be signed at each singing. It's a long day but even so I appreciate them all and try to chat with each and every one of them. I look back to Gus and nod, feeling pretty confident that I'd recognize someone I've spoken to. I may not remember all their details, but I should be able to recognize a face.

Gus waves me over and I peer at the screens in front of Remy, taking in the tall, thin woman on the screen. She has dark hair and aside from that she looks pretty normal. Looking back to Gus I shake my head.

"Remy, do you have enough to run facial rec? For some reason she seems familiar to me but not quite. Almost like I know a sister or aunt or something," Gus mumbles.

The woman looks up at the camera on the front fence and waves. Gus's brows pinch, but I can see on his face he still can't place her.

"Fuck, we'll have to let her in, just not yet. I'll get Mama Debs, the kids, babies and their moms into the safe room."

"What about the Landry brothers?" Remy asks, eyes still on the screen.

"I'm going to post them around the clubhouse, just in case. I've been around long enough to know that shit can hit the fan at any time around here." He looks around the room. "And where the fuck is Pops?"

He mumbles to himself as he takes off down the hall to get everyone where they need to be. Seeing Gus like this, and not as Chewy's older brother or Ana's husband, you see why he's the head of his family business and friends with Marx.

This whole time Remy has been tapping away on her computer, eyes glued to the screen. She must feel me watching her because her eyes cut to mine for a moment. "She's talking to me through the gate."

"Like through a speaker? Do you have the hearing of a bat or something because I can't hear anything,"

Remy pushes the hair back on her left side, showing me some fancy device that hooks around her ear. It also does not make anything any clearer for me.

She huffs out a laugh, "It's a bone conducting headset. Leaves me able to hear everything around me. And before you ask, I'm typing my responses, the AI voice at the gate responds for me."

I try to low whistle, instead just blowing at Remy. "You know this place just keeps getting better and better," I shake my head. "I mean, you could probably do with a few more illegal activities to make things exciting, but still, I'm glad I'm here. It's going to make my book super authentic."

I gaze longingly at my laptop, but I know that this situation probably calls for my full attention span or something. Gus's heavy footsteps grow louder as he nears the common room, cutting a path straight to Remy and reading the woman's responses online.

"Takoda, do you mind heading out and meeting this woman at the gate?" Takoda nods, stepping out from behind the bar and heading out.

"We sure about this Gus?" Remy asks. It's a very good question.

"Not at all, but we can't leave her out there."

Remy nods and watches a tiny Takoda move closer and closer to the gate.

"Buzz her in Remy."

Chapter 19

Mira

The woman follows Takoda into the room, she's tall and has long dark hair although something about her doesn't seem quite right. Instead of looking around the room like I did when I first got here, she has her gaze trained on me. Weird. Although maybe she's a little intimidated and is looking to me for reassurance. Well, that I can do!

"Hi! I'm Mira. You've caught us on a bit of a slow night, none of the men who can fix your car are here right at this moment, although I'm sure Gus or Takoda could help," I wave toward the two men, trying to show her they're trustworthy and handy in equal measures.

"Oh, thank you. I have left a message with the local towing company, so hopefully they get back to me." She smiles and then takes a seat on the couch.

"Oh, this is Remy, she's on Ol Lady here, I'm just a girl-friend." I smile at her.

"Oh? You have a boyfriend?" She sort of sneers at the word "boyfriend" and I exchange a look with Remy, checking to see if she noticed it too. She nods slightly.

"Oh, um yeah, Tank. He's everything you expect in an MC man, solid, loyal, handsome," I wink at her and she frowns a little. Hard crowd.

"Oh, you should probably text your people that you're here at the clubhouse. You mentioned at the gate that you had someone coming to collect you?" Remy says in her sweet way.

I watch her expressions intently because something is a little off about her. I really want to pat myself on the back because I feel like I'm doing a great job trying to gain her trust. I feel like this is something my FMC would do after realizing that she's been kidnapped by the MC's ex-girlfriend, someone unfamiliar to her. She would wait in the basement and plan and then go all butt kicky. Although I'm not very good at kicking butt, I'm sure I could improvise if it came down to it.

"Oh yeah, I've already messaged them, they should be here soon." She looks back at me. "When is your next book out? You're that writer lady aren't you?"

"Oh yeah, I am. Um, the next book will be a little while away. It's a new series, about an MC if you can believe that," I giggle. "I came here to do research, and then I fell in love. The MC is so nice and the women, the Ol Ladies, are such cool women to spend time with."

She waves a dismissive hand at me, as if that's not important. "Yeah, but I bet they don't know the real you. I bet these 'Ol Ladies' wouldn't even know what to get you for your birthday or anything. They'd never send you gifts or leave little surprises in your yard." She looks angry at this fact and I have a sinking feeling in my stomach that we've just let my stalker into the clubhouse.

I see Gus and Takoda stiffen, obviously thinking along the

same lines as me. We have no idea how dangerous this woman is, or if she has anyone with her. She said she was alone but that could have been a ploy to tug on our heartstrings and let her in. I bet she has more orc-looking men on her payroll. She could have us surrounded. Dag nabbit!

"Oh, um, I have had some surprises left in my yard. I like cute gnomes and I've found a few new additions."

Her face lights up. "Oh really? Did you like them?"

I nod, not trusting myself to not say something to make this weird. Or weirder than it already is. I mean, I'm just Mira, I write books, how the heck did I end up with a crazy fan?

Staring at her I'm trying to remember if I've ever seen her before. There isn't anything remarkable about her face, if I were to describe her in one of my novels I'd call her sharp, severe. Her hair has a stiff, almost unnatural look to it and I'm starting to think that perhaps she's wearing a wig. Dang, this lady is good! Right Mira, think. What would your FMC's do? Or better yet, what would Chewy or Blanche or Nat or Remy or Ana or Lovely do?

"Oh yes, they were lovely, they fit right in with the others. Like a little family. Obviously, the old grumpy fisherman would be the grandpa. Oh, and the chubby bottomed lady with the daisies would be the grandmother." Good work Mira, play it cool.

Crazy lady nods her head, eyes sparkling as she scoots closer to the edge of the couch. "What about, the, other things?" she whispers.

I'm guessing she's meaning the you know what's so I swallow and nod. She grins wide and jumps up, dancing around in front of a bewildered Remy and me. Gus edges ever closer, as does Takoda, but as he reaches for her she spins, hitting him in the head with something in her hand. I watch in slow motion as Takoda begins to buckle, Gus lunging for her and freezing as she points a gun at him.

"WHY DID HE DO THAT!? This is my time with my best friend, don't interrupt me!" she screams, waving the gun in Gus's face.

Kudos to him that he isn't freaking out. Neither is Remy who is kneeling next to Takoda checking on him.

"MOVE! All of you! You can't be trusted to butt out so you're going to have to learn the hard way." She keeps the gun trained on us and yanks three chairs out from under the table, kicking them into a line and making us sit.

She hits Remy in the back of the head with the butt of her gun and I let out a yelp when my friend slumps down in her chair.

"Um, look, we can spend time together, please, I can ask my friends to leave us alone,"

"THEY ARE NOT YOUR FRIENDS! I AM!" she screams in my face, making my ears ring.

Her eyes are crazed and then she takes a breath, straightening and pulling herself together, smiling pleasantly at me. Gus has been sitting perfectly still, eyes on her every move. She starts rummaging around behind us and I glance over to see she's cuffing Gus to the chair one handed, gun on me. With that type of dexterity, she's clearly done this type of thing before.

"Don't do anything Mira. If one of us tries to overpower her she'll go trigger happy. We just need to wait for backup." His eyes flick to the hall where a tiny movement catches my eye. That's right! The Landrys!

I want to do a happy dance but instead I sit still as a statue.

"Thank you so much for my gifts, I know that Mrs. McKenzie

really enjoyed the livers."

"I knew she would," she says with a grin. "I know all about you and what you like and don't like. I love that you leave little hints for me in your books, like the foot. No one else would have read that scene and know that you have a foot fetish, but I did."

Sorry Nana, but what the actual fuck? How the fucking hell did she get foot fetish from that scene? My face must be saying what I'm thinking because Gus pulls his lips between his teeth to stop himself from laughing. I'm about to lean over and tell him to shut up when there's some banging in the hall. My gaze shoots to Gus who seems to be completely unbothered.

"What was that?" crazy lady asks, walking to stand in front of Gus, the barrel of her gun pressed into his forehead.

"I have no idea, lady. We're the only one's here."

Her gaze narrows and she pulls out her phone. I really need to know where she got her outfit from because it seems to have unlimited pockets. Before I can ask, she starts speaking incredibly fast, in some other language, maybe Russian? She sneers at Gus then yells something at her phone, hanging up.

She opens her mouth, but whatever she is planning to say gets cut off by the beautiful sound of motorcycle pipes pulling up outside of the clubhouse.

"Don't. Move." To ram that point home she knocks both Gus and me on the top of the head with her weapon. Not hard enough to knock us out, but a good enough warning to not do anything stupid.

Not that I have to. No way, not with my viking coming through the clubhouse door like a warrior ready to avenge his love. His bright blue eyes find mine, boring into me, allowing me to see the love and fear and rage.

Oh, it's on like Donkey Kong!

Tank

After we watch Roman drive off we mount our bikes waiting for Pres's orders. The excitement of riding out and killing two birds with one stone, avenging Jimmy and finding out who's stalking my girl, has me anxious to get home and see my Ol Lady. Waiting on our orders to roll out behind Pres, I notice him check his phone and stiffen slightly as he reads his screen. Butterflies hit my gut and I can't shake the feeling that shit is about to hit the fan. Marx taps a few things then brings his phone to his ear, his murmuring too low for me to eavesdrop.I guess he'll tell us all if it's something bad.

Just when I'm starting to relax a little, Jules stiffens next to me, looking at his screen too. He whispers something to Chewy and they both do a weird sibling communication thing where they stare at each other a beat, then both nod.

"What do you think that was about?" Judge asks, his voice low next to me.

"No idea, but it can't be good," I reply as I watch Chewy efficiently place Gretchen in the SUV and pull herself into the passenger seat. Jules catches Marx's eye, giving some type of hand signal then pulling out, heading back toward Rose Grove.

"Listen up! We got a woman on the road outside the clubhouse. Her car broke down along the road. Facial rec hasn't thrown up any red flags and Mira doesn't recognize her as a fan. Gus has the women and kids in the safe room and placed the Landrys at different points around the clubhouse. Jules and Chewy will be taking the back roads and running lookout. It may be nothing," he leaves the rest hanging, because we all know this could turn out to be something. "Let's roll out."

We leave Roxburgh as if we have all the time in the world, not wanting to draw any attention to ourselves, but once we're on the main road we open up, Winnie roaring beneath me, eating up the distance between me and my Ol Lady.

Even thinking of Mira wearing my cut and my name has my cock thickening. I've waited a long time for a woman to call my own, and now that I've got her, every luscious, creative, crazy inch of her, I'm never letting her go. I'll need to order her a cut. She'll be over the moon, and so will the other Ol Ladies. They've already adopted her into the girl gang, which does worry me a little because Mira is enough trouble on her own, but I can't think of a better group of women for her to have her back. From what I've learned, she has had very few "real life" friends and even less family. Well shit, now she has more friends and family than she can count.

Pulling into the outskirts of Rose Grove I clock what must be the car the woman who needed help was driving. I signal to Marx that I'm pulling over to check it out, and in true Pres fashion he signals we all pull over. Even though Big D has been taken care of, this whole Jimmy thing illustrated that we're not as bulletproof as we once thought.

Throwing my leg over my bike I wander around the car, taking in the tires, none seem flat or damaged. The bonnet is slightly open from where someone must have checked inside and not closed it properly. Peering in I notice the spark plugs are missing.

"Aw fuck," Judge says under his breath, then gripping my shoulder hard, the pain bringing me back to myself, snapping me out of the downward spiral I was doing.

It's a fucking setup.

"Tank?" Pres asks, brow raised.

"Spark plugs have been removed," I answer, my voice tight.

"Fuck."

We run back to our bikes and I speed out, not even waiting for my brothers. I know that Gus has taken all the precautions, but I can't help but think that somehow he missed something. Somehow it'll all go wrong, and I can't let that happen. Not when I've found my Ol Lady.

The gate is open where Gus or someone else left it, letting us roll in without slowing, parking our bikes as efficiently as we can. I dismount and head straight through the doors, coming to an abrupt stop when I see my woman sitting in a chair in the middle of the room, Gus on one side, Remy on the other, Takoda lying on the floor, dried blood at his temple. If Pres lost his shit when Jimmy was shot, I can't imagine how he's going to take another hurt prospect.

"Remy!" Wire yells, rushing to his Ol Lady and then stopping in his tracks when the dark-haired woman turns her gun on Remy rather than him. Wire holds his hands up, backing up slowly, the tension in his body palpable.

My eyes dart to my woman, her wide green eyes staring back at me, but instead of fear I see, fuck, is that excitement? She beams at me and I hang my head.

"Any of you move, she dies," the woman behind her says, gun trained at Mira's head.

"Can I just point out that if I die there won't be anymore books," Mira says conversationally.

The woman behind her takes a swift intake of breath at this knowledge, turning to point the gun at Gus instead.

"Listen, Svetlana, we know who you are. Your best bet for getting out of here is putting the gun down," Marx says in a measured tone.

Mira frowns, then turns to look over her shoulder. "Lana?"

Svetlana grins at Mira, reaching to the top of her head and pulling off the dark wig, revealing slicked back blonde hair. "I knew you'd recognize me! It's fate, Mira, we're meant to be together! You don't have to be here any more, with these filthy pigs," she spits. "I know what they're like, that woman, Whitney, she told me all about them. That's why I'm here now, I'm trying to save you! Whitney said that they were going to hurt her and her boyfriend and I knew I couldn't leave you here, in a place with dangerous men," she says quickly, not even taking a breath.

"Oh, we did hurt her little boyfriend," Fox smirks.

"See Mira! They're bad men, you need to come with me now, we can run away and live happily ever after. I have my own business, I can support you, I love you!"

Mira's eyes grow wider and wider until Lana gets to the end of her pleading and then Mira's face softens. "Oh Lana, you are a great person, I'm sure of it, but I'm afraid I can't go with you. I can't live with you and I can't love you because I love Tyson." Her eyes flick to mine, "And, if Pres allows it, I have a home here, and friends here."

Lana deflates for a moment and then straightens, rage distorting her sharp features, making her seem even more unhinged. "But I LOVE YOU!" she screeches, bringing the gun up, pointing it directly into Mira's face.

I feel my body moving before my mind tells me to, but I know that if Svetlana pulls that trigger I'll be too late. I lunge toward my love and out of the corner of my eye I catch a glimpse of a Skechers sneaker, swinging in an arc and kicking the gun out of Svetlana's hand in a technically perfect roundhouse kick. A bang sounds out and then a grunt, but all I can focus on is my woman.

"Mira, Doll, look at me, look at me baby," I push her blonde curls out of her face to be met with a wide grin.

"Sorry Nana, but that was fucking awesome! Did you see what Pops did?"

Looking behind Mira, Svetlana is on the ground, Tav standing over her pointing his weapon, Gus and Pops staring down at her.

"Mr. Tombs?" She says, looking at Pops in confusion.

"Oh yeah, surprise! I can walk." Pops waves his hands and then walks behind the bar, pouring himself a drink. "Chewy and Jules have three guys they found out back, the Landrys have one a piece. What do you want us to do with them Pres? Please say Rev Room, please say Rev Room?" he pleads, mumbling something about not seeing action for a while even though they dealt with the orc guy yesterday.

Marx's answer is drowned out by Rider's whine, "She shot me in the ass! Switch, I need help!" he demands.

Switch rolls his eyes as he checks over Remy, "It's a fucking graze. And what the hell were you doing to be shot in the ass? Were you running away?"

"No! That old man had the gun doing fucking somersaults in the air and it got me!"

"You can wait." Switch turns to look at us. "Brothers, I need Takoda and Remy in my clinic. I checked their stats, both are fine but will have killer headaches tomorrow."

Wire scoops his Ol Lady into his arms and carries her down the hall, followed by Fox and Nitro with Takoda.

Switch grabs Rider by the scruff of his neck and starts to drag his big ass down the hall toward his clinic. Mira's tinkling laughter has me grinning.

Marx runs a big hand down his face. "Fuck, what are we gonna do with her?"

"May I offer a suggestion?" A collective groan has us turning toward Roman, standing in the doorway with his large blonde husband at his back. Marx glares silently at him, so he continues. "Do what you want with the men, but I will take Svetlana."

At the sound of Roman's voice Svetlana looks toward him, then drops her head, "I'm sorry Pakhan, I didn't mean for this to happen."

"I understand, Lana. Your father said you were having troubles again. How about we send you somewhere nice, and you can have a little rest?"

"At the same hospital as last time?" She looks up, eyes full of hope looking more like a lost little girl than a crazed, obsessed gun woman.

"Would you like that, *sladkya?*"

"Yes, Pakhan, they were nice to me. Is Katarina still there?" She moves toward Roman then stops abruptly, flicking her eyes at Marx who gives her a nod.

"Yes, I believe she is," Roman says in a gentle voice, showing yet another side of him. The man is full of contradictions. Just when I think I have him figured out he does something else to change my perception. I don't think I'll ever be able to figure him out.

My woman has been watching the scene, and as Svetlana

moves to pass her on her way to Roman, Mira stops her with a hand on her arm. "Lana, thank you for my gifts and for liking my books." She smiles at her gently then pulls the other woman into her arms. "Thank you for not killing me or my friends."

Lana beams at her and stares until Roman gently takes her arm. He looks toward Marx, "President?"

Marx nods, "You take care of her Roman, and we'll take care of the others." Roman raises a brow at him, "If we find out they're innocent and they didn't hurt my people, they'll be free to go. If not, then I'll leave them in Pops' and Chewy's hands." Pops fist pumps in the background, a wide grin splitting his face.

"Hopefully they're all innocent then, I'll need people to run the funeral home. What a busy night for acquisitions it's been for the Bartashevs" he smirks and gently leads Svetlana toward the door, the woman still smiling goofily at Mira.

The door shuts behind them and we all look at each other.

"Sorry Nana but how goddamn fucking cool was that!? The hostage situation and Gus being all covert and then the Landrys off sneaking around and then she went *unhinged* and THEN you all came in and things got tense and then Pops Chuck Norrised the gun outta her hand AND got Rider shot in the butt - "

Chewy, Jules and the three Landrys interrupt her roll, dragging six unconscious men onto the floor.

Mira doesn't say a word. No, she just points. "Weeeeeee! And that! Ohmygod I need to write this down."

"Well, good to see that she hasn't been left traumatized by the situation," Marx says dryly.

Judge snorts, slapping me on the back. "Good luck with that one, brother."

"No luck needed."

Epilogue

Mira

"You know, I still can't believe we had all that serious shit go down and we only got to kill one measly person. One. AND he basically killed himself with his terrible lifestyle," Pops grumbles.

"You know we're not a 1 percent club, right? We're actually just good guys trying to do good things and stay on the right side of the law. It's you lot-" Jimmy waves his arm at the Tombs family, "That apparently do all the dirty work around here."

"Damn straight kid," Pops boasts, delivering Jimmy a cold drink to his position on the couch.

His recovery has been long, what with being shot in the gut, and he's been spending a lot of time in the common room which has been nice. It turned out that no one really knew that much about Jimmy as he always liked to be posted at the gates, but after spending time with him it's clear to see how much he loves being part of the club and how good the club has been for him. Apart from the shooting. Mustn't forget that.

"So, Mira, have you managed to finish your book?" Lovely asks, bouncing baby Bee on her knee.

"Yes I have! I typed the last words two days ago and it's with my editor. Early reviews from her are that this one will be a huge hit!"

All my ladies, my girl gang let out whoops and Blanche puts her fingers in her mouth and lets out a long, loud whistle.

"We should celebrate! Pops, you know what to do!" Chewy says, giving her grandfather finger guns. He looks excited, almost too excited, so I know this is going to be epic.

He does something on his phone, then something else, then he looks up, all giddy, "The party starts in ten minutes! Ladies, you might wanna go freshen up, put on something a little dressy. Trust me, you'll thank me later."

How intriguing! I rush to Tyson's room, to the right side of his closet where he cleared out a space for my belongings. It's been a month since the whole crazy Lana thing and I've pretty much moved in. Tyson is happier to stay at the clubhouse, close to his family rather than at Nana's. It's fine with me, I'm just happy being wherever he is.

I throw on a cute dress covered in cartoon cowboys and horses, my purple cowgirl boots and fluff my curls up. Not only does my larger body feel great in this outfit, but I know that Tyson loves it. The last time I wore it we never even made it to our date, instead he took me to some remote lookout and made me ride him like a cowgirl on the back of his bike. I sigh a little, then pat my boobs, looking for my notebook. I'll be adding that scene to my next MC book methinks.

"Mira! It's party time!" Mama Debs calls down the halls so I head back out, only to come to a complete stop at the mouth of the hall.

"Surprise!" Pops and Chewy yell.

There, standing in the common room, are seven men dressed like my book characters. There's even a Guardian of Galaxis there, a huge, ripped guy painted blue. "Holy cheese and rice," I whisper.

Remy comes rushing over, linking her arm in mine, "Guess what? They're strippers too!" She squeals then tugs me closer to the action.

Lovely looks like she's having a nice conversation with my Motorcycle Club character, Grimm, and Nat is busy shaking a wad of bills at my ex-military man turned vigilante investigator John Preacher, asking him to investigate her boobs.

It's almost surreal seeing men I made up in my brain, in real life. I mean, I know they aren't the real thing, but holy moly does Pops have an eye for detail.

"Hit the music, Niko!" Pops yells out and Ginuwine's Pony starts blasting over the speakers, the bass rushing through my body.

The men move away from the Ol Ladies and start gyrating to the music, some of them removing items of clothing, others, like my alien who is already mostly naked, just move obscenely to the beat.

Jimmy's face is beet red as he's stuck on the couch watching the whole thing play out. Poor kid even lets out a little meep as John Preacher starts thrusting in his direction.

We're all so mesmerized that we don't seem to notice our men filing out of church until I hear "What the fuck is going on here?" bellowed by Marx, looking like thunder in the doorway.

"Busted."

Tank

I settle into my seat and listen to my Pres update us.

"Well, looks like Big D survived, but he's confined to a chair and shits in a bag, so I doubt he'll be causing us problems anytime soon."

"Yeah, and with Roman running shit in Roxburgh now the only option Big D has is selling dime bags on street corners," Savage smirks.

"Spinners has also been cleaned up, no underaged women, and Roman has somehow gotten them all clean. Routine drug tests the lot, unfortunately for our ex-bunnies, they failed the test and have since lost their jobs. Not too sure where they're at and don't much care after the shit they pulled accusing my men." Marx looks at me and then Nitro, giving us a head nod. "As for the other businesses Roman took over, they all seem to be flourishing. And because of our 'help'," he scoffs, "he has offered us the funeral home to use whenever we need it."

"I'll let Chewy know. Her and Pops will love that. So will the rest of the Tombs, I'm sure they're sick of cleaning up after my woman," Rhodie says.

"Are we ever gonna address the fact that your Ol Lady is our Enforcer? She needs a title on her cut." Flack points out. It's not a bad point either. Since Chewy came on board she's taken over Rhodie's position and I think it's for the best. I know that the enforcer role was weighing on my brother's soul.

"That's a good fucking point, Pres," Rider agrees, fiddling with his friendship bracelet that Chewy gifted him after he was shot in the ass. Actually, it was more when everyone noticed the huge dent in his ass cheek and started calling him the "One-

Cheeked Wonder" that she gifted it to him.

Marx nods in thought. "I agree with you. I think we organize a patch party. Our three prospects have more than proved themselves to us so I'm calling you to vote. In the case of Tav Tombs, do we vote him in as full brother?"

A roar goes around the room. "Ayes" all round, raising the Church roof. The same echoes out for Jimmy and Takoda.

"Right, votes on road names?" Marx looks around the room.

"Tav's name already sounds like a road name. I vote he keeps it as is," Sniper speaks up, unusual for him but everyone nods in agreement.

Switch waves a hand, drawing our attention, "I vote Jimmy be called 'TumTum' after taking one to the gut."

We all laugh, even though the name is slightly comical we all appreciate the seriousness of what he went through. He himself would never want a name based on his bravery or hard assedness, so Switch's suggestion fits the kid. We all agree then we ponder Takoda's road name. It's Judge who speaks up first.

"I really want to call him Barry White."

I nod, following his thinking, "Because of that fucking smooth voice of his?" Judge chin tips me.

"I refuse to have a brother named Barry White," Nitro says with a scoff.

"What about 'Chef'? After that character on South Park? Same voice, and Takoda spends a lot of time in the kitchen with Mama Debs?" Wire offers, looking around the table.

We all slowly start nodding, the name growing on me the more I think about it.

"Good, that's settled. Tank, while you're ordering in your Property patch," Pres winks, "order in three new cuts for Tav,

TumTum and Chef. I want a patch made up for Chewy but not the enforcer patch." Marx raises his hand when it looks like there's going to be a protest. "The Enforcer role enforces the rules in our charter, Chewy doesn't do that. What she does is important and demands more respect. Tank, order an Icer patch to be made."

I grin and bang my fist on the table, as do the rest of my brothers, Rhodie looking proud as fucking punch.

"What about prospects? We'll have none to do all our dirty work," Nitro asks worriedly. Only because without prospects he and Fox end up with the shitty jobs because they're always late to Church.

"Niko has asked to prospect. I've checked with his mom and she's fine with it as it's his choice."

"Fuck, the kid will be good too," Judge agrees. He thinks for a moment, "I'll sponsor him." all heads snap toward him in shock, Judge isn't the sort to want that sort of responsibility but it makes sense. He and the kid get on.

"Good. On to other business, this is in two parts. Blanche and Lovely have approached me with an idea. As we all know those two are fucking loaded, but they're not about to live it up like sugar mommas. They want to invest in the MC."

"How so?" Savage asks, sitting forward.

"We find businesses we like the look of and have capacity to run. They purchase them."

"What do they get out of that?"

"That's where the second part comes in. They want to open a place where people can go for help to get back on their feet. It might be to find housing, finish their high school diploma, learn some new shit to help them get a job. They're looking at women out of abusive relationships, people like Lovely out in the world with few skills, fuck, they even mentioned vets," Marx's gaze looks around the table, all of us feeling the weight of our brothers who weren't lucky enough to land on their feet like us. "They want the MC businesses to offer work experience, references, shit like that. Hence the investment."

Looking around the table I can see everyone is on the same page. "I'm in," Rider states, the rest of the brothers all knocking their fists in agreement.

"Good. I'll let the girls know. One last thing, Tank and Judge, I know Devil's Big Tow is snowed under. How would you feel having Lovely on reception? She wants to be our first success story, coming from nowhere and gaining employment skills at an MC business. What do you think?"

Me and Judge look at each other and share a grin. "She'd be fucking amazing. We got no problem with her bringing little Bee if need be, we can set up a nursery and shit."

"Good. I'll let her know. Fuck, what a month. I'm looking forward to shit getting back on track and quietening down. No one else get a fucking Ol Lady for a while, every time one of you fuckers falls we end up facing some shit. Just, fucking stay away from women, please." Marx eyeballs us all, then slams down the gavel. "Let's go get a drink and enjoy not having a fucking crisis. Peace and quiet, brothers."

We all stand, ready to file out. As soon as the doors open we're assaulted by Ginuwine and his Pony, and there, in the middle of the common room is a bunch of fucking strippers gyrating.

"Is that fucker blue?" Rider asks, face screwed up in confusion.

"What the fuck is going on in here?" Marx bellows, everyone freezing, including one guy who is stuck in a plank position over the coffee table.

"Busted," Pops whispers and that seems to snap us out of our daze.

Brothers start collecting up discarded clothing, tossing it out the door, half-naked men chasing after their belongings as the Tombs family walks in, watching in avid fascination.

"Why was that man blue?" Gus asks while his wife shoves past him, "You bitches! You started the party without me!"

"Yeah soz, serves you right for getting here late. What took you so long anyway?" Nat asks. Her question is answered when all eyes turn to Jules. "Wait, whose baby is that?"

There's uproar in the clubhouse as Fox, Nitro and Jules all argue over who impregnated some girl from one of their orgies and I watch as Marx hangs his head and lets out a sigh.

"Quarter for your thoughts?" Mira sidles up to me, wrapping her arms around my waist and gazing at me with her wide green eyes.

"Just that Pres can never catch a break."

Mira looks over her shoulder at the chaos, then giggles, burying her face in my chest. Wrapping my arms around her I realize I don't care about the chaos and the danger and whatever else gets thrown our way because I have Mira, my Doll, who makes everything in this world better.

She looks up at me, her eyes sparkling. "I love you Biker Man."

"And I love you, Writer Lady."

Chess

Fifteen years later

"Chess, you good?" Pres stares at me before my gaze moves over his shoulder. "Elio! Are you sure you want to do this?"

"Yes Pres, I'm sure." I take a deep breath and check my instruments, laying everything out just so.

"Son, you don't have to. Your aunt is still our Icer, I can call her in."

I turn back to look at Marx, older than he was when I first arrived here as a kid, but no less intimidating. Or caring. A quality that has made him soften over the years, and I'm not the only one who sees it. If the DRMC wants to keep our place at the top of the food chain I need to put into play what I've learned from my aunt and my Pops.

"I'm ready." I take up my favorite scalpel, the weight familiar in my hand. "Niko, my music please."

The Dead South's jaunty whistle sounds out in the Rev Room as I get to work, using techniques I've learned over the years and some of my own ideas.

When we landed here at the DRMC all those years ago, I was a kid who lived in a world not built for someone like me. In the DRMC family I found people who understood me. I found my place.

But here, in the Rev Room? With my brothers at my back, "In hell I'll be in good company" playing over the speakers, and the sounds of a man screaming for mercy, here is where I find my home.

Thank You!

Thank you so much for reading! I hope you enjoyed Tank's book, and don't worry, I won't leave you hanging. Jules' book is on its way!

If you want to know more about me, what I'm up to or whose book is next be sure to follow me

Follow me at my author page on Facebook

Friend me on Facebook

Join my group Cleo Browne's Babes

Follow me on Instagram

Cleo Browne's Books

Rhodie – Devil's Rose MC Book One

August – A Tombs Security + Devil's Rose MC Crossover

Wire – Devil's Rose MC Book Two

Tav – Devil's Rose MC Book Three

Devil's Rose MC Christmas Novella

Tank – Devil's Rose MC Book Four

Jules – Tombs Security + Devil's Rose MC Crossover
Coming next

Acknowledgements

First off, I'd like to thank all the wonderful readers who continue to keep taking chances on a kooky little woman from New Zealand. Without you all reading my books and loving my characters, I would have just faded away into obscurity, never to be seen or heard from again. So, thank you. I appreciate you all.

Second, I'd like to thank my author besties and all round good biartchs Shaye Torrel and Courtney Clark Michaels. Thank you so much for talking me off the cliff when I would freak out that I didn't know what I was doing. I still don't, but at least I'm not freaking out about it. I wouldn't be here without you!

Thanks to the lovely Gabi Brockelsby and her eagle eyes to make sure you get a typo free book.

Thanks to the wonderful Sally Howells who gives the BEST chapter breakdowns, and makes me snort laugh with her feedback.

Thanks to my betas and my ARC readers, you are all amazing and so very much appreciated.

Thanks to my partner PN. Without his constant words of encouragement, "I really didn't think MC books were a thing," I would never have finished this book. Thanks also go to my boys. Ronnie, for being completely disinterested, and Louis for your two hour long phone calls that would eat into my writing time. Love you guys.

About the Author

Cleo Browne is the pen name of a neurospicy geeky girl from Aotearoa New Zealand. As a child, she realized very early on that she wasn't a people person, so she would spend all her time reading and writing her own stories. These stories usually ended with the line "and then they died." As an adult, she has gotten slightly more people-y (not much) and better at not killing all her characters off when she writes.

Cleo loves to write about women who don't need a man to do their dirty work and the hot alpha men who turn to mush when they watch their women handling business.

When she's not writing romance novels about strong, curvy women and the men who adore them, she hangs out at home with her hubby, her boys, and her ancient greyhound who likes to creepily watch her write.